OBLIGATION

TELL ME BOOK 1 AND 2

CHARLOTTE BYRD

BYRD BOOKS, LLC

Proofreaders:

Renee Waring, Guardian Proofreading Services, https://www.facebook.com/GuardianProofreadingServices

Julie Deaton, Deaton Author Services, https://www.facebook.com/jdproofs/

Cover Design: Charlotte Byrd

Visit my website at www.charlotte-byrd.com

Identifiers

• Obligation (Hardcover): 978-1-63225-068-1

• Obligation (Paperback): 978-1-63225-067-4

• Obligation (eBook): 978-1-63225-066-7

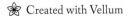 Created with Vellum

I owe him a debt I can't pay back with money.

He wants something else: **me, for one year.**

But I don't even know how he is...

365 days and nights doing everything he wants, except *that*.

"I'm not going to sleep with you," I say categorically.

He laughs.

"I'm going to make you a promise," his eyes challenge mine. **"Before our time is up, you'll beg me for it."**

Now, I want him more than ever.

Especially when I run my fingers over his chiseled body and he teases me with his tongue.

I want him so much I am going to scream. I want him so much I might even beg....

PRAISE FOR CHARLOTTE BYRD

"Extremely captivating, sexy, steamy, intriguing, and intense!" ★★★★★

"Addictive and impossible to put down." ★★★★★

"I can't get enough of the turmoil, lust, love, drama, and secrets!" ★★★★★

"Fast-paced romantic suspense filled with twists and turns, danger, betrayal, and so much more."
★★★★★

"Decadent, delicious, & dangerously addictive!" - Amazon Review ★★★★★

"Titillation so masterfully woven, no reader can resist its pull. A MUST-BUY!" - Bobbi Koe, Amazon Review
★★★★★

"Captivating!" - Crystal Jones, Amazon Review
★★★★★

"Sexy, secretive, pulsating chemistry..." - Mrs. K, Amazon Reviewer ★★★★★

"Charlotte Byrd is a brilliant writer. I've read loads and

I've laughed and cried. She writes a balanced book with brilliant characters. Well done!" -Amazon Review
★★★★★

"Hot, steamy, and a great storyline." - Christine Reese
★★★★★

"My oh my....Charlotte has made me a fan for life." - JJ, Amazon Reviewer ★★★★★

"Wow. Just wow. Charlotte Byrd leaves me speechless and humble... It definitely kept me on the edge of my seat. Once you pick it up, you won't put it down." - Amazon Review ★★★★★

" Intrigue, lust, and great characters...what more could you ask for?!" - Dragonfly Lady ★★★★★

ABOUT CHARLOTTE BYRD

Charlotte Byrd is the bestselling author of many contemporary romance novels. She lives in Southern California with her husband, son, and a crazy toy Australian Shepherd. She loves books, hot weather and crystal blue waters.

Write her here:

charlotte@charlotte-byrd.com

Check out her books here:

www.charlotte-byrd.com

Connect with her here:

www.facebook.com/charlottebyrdbooks

Instagram: @charlottebyrdbooks

Twitter: @ByrdAuthor

Facebook Group: Charlotte Byrd's Reader Club

Newsletter

DON'T MISS OUT!

Want to be the first to know about my upcoming sales, new releases and exclusive giveaways?

Sign up for my Newsletter and join my Reader Club!

Bonus Points: Follow me on BookBub and Goodreads!

ALSO BY CHARLOTTE BYRD

All books are available at ALL major retailers! If you can't find it, please email me at charlotte@charlotte-byrd.com

Tell me Series
Tell Me to Stop
Tell Me to Go
Tell Me to Stay
Tell Me to Run
Tell Me to Fight
Tell Me to Lie

Tangled Series
Tangled up in Ice
Tangled up in Pain
Tangled up in Lace
Tangled up in Hate
Tangled up in Love

Black Series

Black Edge

Black Rules

Black Bounds

Black Contract

Black Limit

Lavish Trilogy

Lavish Lies

Lavish Betrayal

Lavish Obsession

Standalone Novels

Debt

Offer

Unknown

Dressing Mr. Dalton

1

WHEN THE CHECK ARRIVES...

"WHAT ARE you doing with that thing?" my roommate, Sydney, asks, walking by my room.

I'm sitting on my bed with my hand wrapped around my knees staring at the envelope that came in the mail a few days ago. My name and address are handwritten in careful capital script and it doesn't have a return address.

I showed it to her when it first arrived and she made fun of me for wanting to actually deposit that *ridiculous* check, her words not mine.

"I was thinking that this person must've dropped it off in our mailbox directly because there's not even a stamp from the post office on this thing," I point out.

Sydney shakes her head and walks out of my sightline for a moment to change into her sweats. When I walk out into our living room, I see her boots neatly put away right next to mine in the foyer. The rain droplets skid off her coat and onto the floor where they make a little puddle, which she quickly cleans up.

I met Sydney Catalano at Wellesley College, but we didn't get really close until our second semester of senior year. She was a double major in biology and chemistry and we met in a required anthropology class that we both put off until we couldn't put it off anymore.

I don't know if it's the case with all biology majors, but Sydney is a very neat and meticulous person who always cleans up after herself, and often after me as well. Though I'm not much of a housekeeper, I take out the garbage and kill spiders to try to be a good roommate.

I pull out last night's Vietnamese takeout from the fridge and warm it up on the stove. We each pile as much as we want onto the plates, leaving the rest on the skillet, before sitting down to eat together around the kitchen island.

"So...what are you going to do?" she asks, tying up her silky black hair in a loose bun while inhaling her food.

My eyes meander over to the envelope, lying flat in between our two plates. Sydney reaches over her food and pulls out the check.

"Olive, this is a joke, okay? This isn't real," she says with a full mouth.

I stare at the numbers in the square box. They are

written in the same block script as my address on the envelope.

$167,699.

The amount is written out right under my name and signed with an illegible signature. There is no identifying information anywhere else on the check to give me a glimpse into who it might be from.

"But what if it is?" I ask.

"Why would someone send you a check for this amount and not say who it is or why they're giving you this money?" she asks.

I shrug my shoulders. Of course, I don't have an answer.

"The thing is... I looked up the total amount of my student loans today at work," I say, taking a sip of my water.

"Okay." Sydney nods.

I put down my fork and turn my body toward her.

"What?" She rolls her eyes. "C'mon, the suspense is killing me."

I shake my head. "No, never mind. It doesn't matter," I say, getting up.

She pleads for me to go on and explain but I just take my plate to the sink and wash it. If she thinks that this whole thing is a joke then I don't have to tell her a thing.

"Olive, I'm sorry." Sydney puts her hand on my shoulder. "I don't mean to *not* be supportive. I just don't want you to get hurt. Or in trouble."

I hold up the check to her face.

"You see this number?" I ask, pointing to the amount. She nods. "This is the exact amount that I owe. Down to the penny."

The words surprise her. She exhales slowly and takes a step away from me.

"Really?" she whispers under her breath, taking the check and looking at it more closely.

I nod.

"I had to make a payment today so I looked up the amount, just for the hell of it. Just to make myself feel a little worse about everything," I joke. "But then, the total looked familiar. I realized that I'd seen these numbers somewhere before. I just wasn't sure where. Then when I got home, I saw the envelope on my desk and…there it was. The *exact* amount that I owe in student loans."

Sydney sits back down, stunned by my revelation. I've had about an hour to process this but I'm no less astonished.

"The check arrived a few days ago. So, after you make this payment, you'll owe a little less, right?"

I nod, not sure as to where she is going with this.

"Most of it is going to interest, but yeah, I guess it will be a little less. But the check arrived before this payment was officially due. So, when it came, this is the exact amount of my debt."

We spend the evening talking about the possibilities of what I should do, which basically boil down into two camps.

One, I tear up the check and forget all about it.

Two, I deposit the money, or at least try to.

There is the very real possibility that the check is a fake or some sort of fraud, though whom it is defrauding I have no idea. Still, depositing it is definitely a risk.

"There's something else you should consider," Sydney says. "What happens if you deposit the check and it is real?"

2

WHEN I MAKE A DECISION...

I STARE at her for a moment trying to figure out what exactly would be the problem with that situation.

"Why would someone do this? Why would they just give you this gift out of the blue?" she asks.

"I have no idea. I'm still convinced that it's a fake," I say nonchalantly.

"And that's why you want to deposit it?" she asks, calling my bluff.

"Okay, I have no idea. If it's real and it's a gift...I have no idea who has this kind of money or why they would rain it on me."

"We are operating from the position that if this is real, it must be a gift," Sydney says, narrowing her eyes. "But what if it's not a present at all?"

"What do you mean?"

"What if it's just replacing one debt with another? What if this person wants something from you? Wants you to do something for them?"

I take a deep breath. I try to think of all the possibilities of what someone could want from me. The only thing that comes to mind is my job.

"You're a content specialist at a big company," Sydney says, always staying a few steps ahead of me. "What if this is some sort of corporate sabotage?"

I consider that for a moment, but quickly dismiss it. "I don't have any access to anything," I say. "I don't do anything with data or anything that anyone would be interested in."

"I guess," Sydney agrees. "Except that you might be the perfect person to do favors for them from the inside."

Now, it's my turn to roll my eyes. Sydney is someone who spends sixty hours a day cooped in a lab running tissue samples and the rest of the time watching way too many crime and investigation shows.

A few days ago, I applied for a raise and that application required me to submit an updated resume. As a result, I updated my resume and job responsibilities to include '*determining item selection and design for interim formative assessments; writing, reviewing, and revising items aligned to standards including traditional and innovative item types; developing analysis and scoring guides for schools;*

researching and analyzing items released by the assessment consortia.'

But what does this all really mean?

"I write math test questions for an educational company," I say. "This check has nothing to do with my job."

"Okay, fine," Sydney concedes, but not really. She just shrugs her shoulders and gives up, leaving behind a seedling of doubt.

What if she's right?

Why would someone send me this check?

What if this does have something to do with my job? And if so, what?

"I'm not agreeing to anything by depositing this check. There's nothing in the memo line. They can't make me do anything illegal," I say.

"Yes, technically, they can't," Sydney agrees. "But people who have this much money to send to strangers...they may not be the most upstanding of citizens."

"So, what do I do?" I ask, staring at the check. "What would you do?"

"I don't know, but then again, I don't owe as much as you do."

"You don't owe anything," I correct her.

Sydney's mother is from a wealthy Chinese family and they had no issues paying fifty thousand dollars a year for her tuition and room and board. I, on the other hand, wasn't as lucky. Despite majoring in mathematics, the best job I could find was this content specialist position that pays fifty-four thousand dollars a year.

Given that Boston is not the cheapest place in the world to live and that our rent is twenty-five hundred a month plus utilities, I will probably be in my fifties before I pay off all of my student debt.

I stare at the amount on the check: one hundred sixty-seven thousand six hundred ninety-nine dollars.

What would paying off this amount mean to my life going forward? Besides having an extra twelve hundred dollars a month as spending money, it would also mean freedom.

My job isn't particularly interesting or challenging and I'd love to try myself in a data analyst position at a start-up or one of the new innovative companies that are popping up around town.

But those companies pay considerably less without providing any healthcare benefits. They do offer stock options, but those stock options are a risk. Not all companies end up being successful in the end. Taking one of those positions is not a risk I could afford to take...before this check arrived.

When I catch my thoughts drifting away from me, I force myself to focus.

Olive, stop it, I say silently to myself. You can't let yourself think about all of that since you don't even know if the check is real.

"There's another possibility," I say to Sydney as she flips on the TV for some mindless distraction. "This whole thing could just be someone's idea of a joke."

"What do you mean?" she says, sitting up.

"Maybe someone is just fucking with me, Like those YouTube videos where someone sets up their friend with a fake winning lottery ticket. The friend gets really excited and then they tell them that it was just a big joke."

"Shit," Sydney says under her breath.

"Yeah...you wouldn't do that to me, would you?" I ask.

"Of course not!"

"Well, I have no idea who would."

"Someone at your office?"

My mind runs over all of the possibilities. We all work in cubicles with very little interaction throughout the day. We're not friends. I hardly know their names. I have no idea why one of them would do this to me.

"I'm going to deposit it," I say, picking up my phone.

"Now?" she gasps.

I open the mobile banking app, taking a picture of the check. I hold my breath and wait for the scan to go through.

A pop-up appears.

"What happened?" Sydney asks, looking over my shoulder.

"The mobile check deposit limit is twenty-five hundred dollars," I read the words on the screen. "I guess I'll have to go into the actual bank."

3

WHEN I GO TO THE BANK...

I HARDLY SLEEP a wink that night, tossing and turning until it is dawn. The local branch on the way to my office doesn't open until nine and I have to be at work at 8:30. I walk past their front door, knowing that I have to wait until 10:30 for my break. I'm not an hourly employee so I don't have an official break but that's usually when Marie, my direct superior, goes to the Starbucks across the street for her morning latte. It's a good time to run a short errand.

"Want me to get you anything?" she asks as we ride down the elevator together.

"No, thanks," I say. My mouth runs dry and I cough in the middle of the phrase.

I bury my face in my phone as soon as we get outside, pretending to be very busy with something very important. But what I'm really doing is waiting for her to disappear around the corner so I can head toward the bank in the other direction.

I could've easily told her where I'm heading. Depositing money is a normal errand that people run. What is *not* normal is depositing almost one hundred and sixty-eight thousand dollars in the form of a check from a total stranger.

When I walk up to the teller, my body is visibly shaking. She even comments on it but thinks it has something to do with the cold spell that just blew in from Canada.

"This has been quite a long winter, huh?" the teller asks.

She's dressed in a black business suit and her hair is pulled out of her face. There's a little hole in her nose where a piercing once lived. As she takes my identification, she moves her neck and I spot the tentacles of a large tattoo. It's hard to know what it is exactly, but she quickly adjusts her collar when she catches me staring.

"I'm sorry...it just looks like a pretty awesome tattoo," I say. Her face immediately lights up with a smile.

"It's an octopus wrapped around a large rose bush," she says under her breath. "So what can I do for you?"

My heart sinks.

Okay.

Here it is.

The moment of truth.

I pull out the envelope from my purse and take out the check. I glance at it one last time, bidding it farewell.

Is it illegal to deposit a fake check if you don't know if it's a fake check? A big knot forms in the back of my throat. Perhaps this is something I should've researched before I showed up here. What *if* it is illegal?

"Ma'am?" the teller asks, reaching her hand through the small opening and grabbing the check. When she pulls on it, I have no choice but to let it go.

I search her face for any sign of wrongdoing. Shouldn't she be impressed by the sum? Shocked even? She has access to my account and this amount is definitely not my normal deposit. But her face remains flat and completely without affect.

"Excuse me, I'll be right back," she says and walks away quickly.

Oh my God.

This is it.

She's calling the police.

I should run.

Turn around and go now!

Now!

No, I can't.

I gave her my driver's license and my bank card. What would be the point of running now? They have my address, they'll just come and arrest me there.

The teller comes back with the manager, who has a big smile plastered on his face.

He asks me if I will be taking out any money today and I say no.

At least, I think that's what I say.

I can barely hear myself think over the pounding of blood in between my ears.

"Thank you very much for your business, Olivia Kernes. Your deposit should be in your account in a few days," the manager says. "Can I help you with anything else?"

His words barely register, but I do manage to shake my head and walk away.

When I get outside, a gust of cold wind collides into me and clears my head. What the hell just happened? They took the deposit. It passed whatever preliminary checks they have.

Of course, that does not mean that I am in the clear. The funds are not released yet and they will not clear and show up in my account for a few days.

So, they can still discover that the check is fake and then...what?

Will they come and arrest me? If they don't arrest me then they'll definitely have a chat with me.

But I'll just tell them the truth. They'll have to believe me. Right?

My mind bounces from one thought to another without even a slight pause.

The rest of the day goes by in a blur. When I tell Sydney what I did, she wants to meet up on our lunch break, twenty minutes from each of our jobs, but I don't have the energy. The weight of what I have just done suddenly feels like there are two heavy anchors wrapped around my feet, pulling me down into the abyss.

I want to run back to the bank, apologize, and make amends, but these same anchors are preventing me from doing anything but sitting in my cubicle and waiting for the hours to pass.

The next two days go by just as slowly. I'm thankful that I got a lead last week on the new assessment project. Maybe this way no one will notice that during these three days, I barely manage to write twenty questions a day. It's hard to do diligent work when you're staring at a dead end for your career, and probably your life.

When I get home that evening, I am mildly shocked

that the police aren't there waiting for me. Instead, it is Sydney who greets me with a bottle of Pinot Grigio.

"Okay, don't be mad," she says with a big smile on her face. I furrow my eyebrows and brace myself for the worst.

"You remember how you needed me to log into your bank account a few months ago for that thing?" she asks.

I nod.

"Well, I still had your information saved on my laptop."

"Get to the point."

"The check cleared. You are one hundred and sixty-seven thousand dollars richer!"

4

WHEN I'M SURPRISED...

I STARE at Sydney unable to believe my ears. I ask her to repeat what she just said and again I don't believe her. Finally, she pulls out her laptop and shows me my account. I've never seen numbers go up that high before. At least, not numbers that represent money.

I let out a piercing squeal and she joins me immediately. We jump up and down as if we are tween girls at our first concert.

"So, what now?" Sydney asks after we calm down to catch our breaths.

"I don't really know." I shrug. "I guess, I'll pay off my loans."

"Just like that?"

"What else should I do? I mean, this is what the money is intended for, right?"

She nods.

"Do you think I should just do it now?" I ask. "I mean, why wait? I got the money, why not just pay it all off?"

Sydney's eyes get big. I crack my knuckles and look down at my shoes. My feet start to move on their own as I pace around the room back and forth. The euphoria that I felt only moments ago settles somewhere in the pit of my stomach, morphing into a knot.

"Well, you did want to pay them off. You could wait a week or two or you could do it now."

I nod. Or I could do something else altogether.

What if I were to take some of it, just a few thousand, and go on a trip somewhere? I haven't been on a proper vacation since spring break of my senior year and that was two years ago. Yes, there have been a few occasional weekend trips to the Jersey shore but with this money I could go somewhere exotic. Paris. Turks and Caicos. Maybe even Hawaii?!

And what's a few thousand dollars from almost one hundred and sixty-eight thousand? I could pay back it all back within a few months and be in the free and clear for life.

"What? What's that look mean?" Sydney asks as a small smile forms at the corner of my lips.

When I tell her what I'm thinking, she gives me a knowing nod.

"I'd love to go on a trip with you," she adds. "I really missed you the last time we all went to the Bahamas."

My shoulders slope down. I'm still not entirely over that. Even though I am not particularly close with Sydney's group of friends from school, she did invite me to an amazing trip that they all took a few months ago. Her job doesn't pay much more than mine does, but she's from a rich family and that means that she doesn't have to save and pinch every penny like I do. None of her friends have to either.

While she does pay rent out of her salary, her family pays for all of those other nice perks that her life has to offer: a lease on the BMW and first class airfare and lodging to exotic locations. She offered to pay for me to go with them, but I was too ashamed to accept.

Or maybe I was just too proud.

In any case, the trip was split six ways and my part would've cost me six months of rent.

Given that I have a car payment for my Toyota Prius and the student loan payments in addition to rent and utilities, there was no way I could afford anything like that.

"You totally deserve to go on an amazing trip, but maybe it's not the wisest decision," she points out.

I nod, with a deep sigh.

"What you should really do is start some sort of business."

I give her a blank stare.

"Okay, hear me out. I mean, I know that you want to do your master's degree in math and everything, and that's nice, but it's not going to make you money in the long term. You'll always have to work for someone, instead of building up something of your own."

"Is that what you would do?" I ask.

She shrugs. "Yeah, it's something I've been thinking about. I enjoy my work at the lab, but now that I've been there for a bit, it's getting to be monotonous. Every day is the same. Plus, I don't see myself ever making any real money."

"And by real money, you mean what exactly?" I ask.

"Fifty, seventy, one hundred grand... a month."

I smile.

Sydney's concept of wealth varies a lot from my own, but I guess that's understandable since she does come from significantly more money than I do.

"Can you seriously tell me that you will be happy doing this job twenty years from now?" she asks.

"I can seriously tell you that I am *not* happy doing this

job now," I say. "But businesses take money to start. And I don't have any."

"Well, you sort of do," Sydney says.

"But I don't even know what business I should start." I say. "Besides, they require work, too. And the money isn't guaranteed."

"Yeah, that's true," she says. "I'm not trying to tell you what to do—"

"Yeah, you kind of are," I point out, smiling.

"Okay, yes, maybe I am. Or maybe I'm just trying to live a little vicariously through you."

"That would be a first." I start to laugh.

Sydney's expression gets serious and she looks away from me twirling a strand of her hair.

"I guess I'm just imagining what I would do with that kind of cash," she says, staring out into space.

"What would you do?" I ask.

5

WHEN I DO IT...

SYDNEY HAS an answer for me without missing a beat.

"What would I do?" she asks. "I'd like to start a lifestyle brand. Cute clothes, accessories, bags. Everything organic, cotton, or bamboo. Eco-friendly. Something that looks good on all sizes and women could wear it at all times. Clothes to live in, you know?"

Sydney has always been somewhat of a fashion icon around campus. But recently, her personal style has really evolved to casual wear.

It might have something to do with the fact that she doesn't have to wear a suit to work or it might have something to do with her discovery of dressy leggings that feel like yoga pants. She has a number of pairs from different companies, all of which she has spent days trying to improve upon.

"If that's something you are really interested in, why not?" I ask.

"I've actually done quite a bit of research on it and it shouldn't cost me very much to start it. I'm thinking of investing about thirty-thousand dollars into the whole thing. Spending about six on developing the products and the rest on warehouse fees and shipping, website design, that kind of thing."

"That's awesome," I say. "But you can't have any of my money."

I say it in a joking manner, but I mean every bit of it.

"I don't need your money," she says with a laugh.

I know that that's one hundred percent true.

Her parents give her a modest (her word, not mine) allowance every month, so all she'll have to do is limit some of her expenses for a bit and she'll have her start-up money.

While she talks, I make a decision.

"Okay, I'm going to do it," I say, taking a deep breath.

Sydney focuses her attention on me and waits with anticipation. I grab my laptop and pull out one of the bar stools around our kitchen island.

My fingers immediately turn to ice and I can barely feel the tips hitting the keys. Once I log into the main account, I stare at the amount at the bottom.

I pull the cursor over the Pay Now button.

Once I click that, the site takes me to the page where I have to put in the amount I want to pay. The amount due is nine hundred ninety-seven dollars and forty-nine cents but the total amount on this site is twenty-three thousand five hundred eighty-nine dollars.

"I'm going to do it," I say and type in the full amount.

Once I press send, I'm taken to the confirmation page.

Thank you for paying twenty-three thousand five hundred eighty-nine dollars.

JUST LIKE THAT, I'm almost twenty-four thousand dollars poorer.

My soul is almost twenty-four thousand dollars lighter.

"I thought you owed a lot more than that," Sydney says.

"I do, that's just one of the loan servicing companies that owns my loans," I explain, clicking over to the next one. "By the way, last year some company bought my loans from another company but didn't even bother to contact me or tell me because, according to them, it's my responsibility to somehow know this information. I didn't find out until after a collection agency called me."

"Shit," Sydney says under her breath.

"Yeah, this whole thing is shit," I concur.

The second company gets a payment of seventy-six thousand two hundred seventy-six dollars.

"One more." I click over to the last account.

"This is so exciting," Sydney says, smiling. "I'm sure they'll be happy to get all these loans paid."

"I think they'll be disappointed that I won't be paying them six percent interest for thirty years. Can you imagine how much they'll lose over the lifetime of the loan?"

I pause before making the last payment.

I stare at the big Pay Now button and imagine the trip that I could take with just a small percentage of this money instead.

Or maybe I could just put some of it into savings, for a rainy day?

These would all be amazing things to do with the extra money, but there's one thing that I probably should do instead: help my mother with her medical bills.

She's had back pain for a number of years and the surgery seemed to have made things worse. She has to pay over twelve hundred dollars a month just to maintain her medical insurance and there's still a big copay for her monthly medications and doctor visits. In addition, she owes about thirty-thousand for her portion of the surgery expenses.

I don't like to think about this much, and I talk about it

even less. Sydney knows the broad strokes of my mother's medical condition but not the stress that comes with not knowing how you're going to pay for all of these expenses without losing your apartment.

Maybe I should use the money to help her? But the thing about medical expenses is that more and more of them come every month. If I were to pay off my student loans then I would be free of them forever.

I type in the numbers one by one.

6..7...8...3...4

I place the cursor over the Pay Now button and press it without another hesitation. A confirmation page appears.

Thank you for paying sixty-seven thousand eight hundred thirty-four dollars.

I let out a big sigh of relief. Sydney grabs me by my shoulders and gives me a big hug.

She wants to jump up and down but I don't have the energy.

I feel like all of the wind has been knocked out of me.

I'm in shock by what I've done.

Stunned.

It is only later that night, when I'm lying alone in my room, that tears start to flow down my face. My whole body starts to shake uncontrollably.

I wrap myself in my comforter and get into the fetal position to weather the attack.

The tears are hot and salty. My eyes burn as does the small cut that I had on the inside of my lip.

After some time, the flow slows down. Suddenly I am able to catch my breath and a few moments later, I wipe my cheeks for the last time.

It is only then that I realize that these weren't tears of sorrow, but rather tears of joy and relief. Whatever may or may not happen in the future, at least this part of my life is over. This debt that has been weighing so heavily on me, making me feel like I'm drowning, it's gone.

Vanished.

Vanquished.

Erased.

And now, I'm free.

6

WHEN I GET AN INVITATION...

THE FOLLOWING WEEK goes by in a blur. My mother has one of her pain episodes and I spend two nights at her house helping her out and making sure that she has everything she needs. Whenever her back acts up, her mind always goes to a dark ugly place and she starts to blame my father for everything that went wrong in her life. If my father hadn't gotten her pregnant at eighteen then their strict parents would've never forced them to marry. If they had never gotten married then she wouldn't have spent her life taking care of him.

"I had dreams, you know, I wasn't always this fat and ugly," she says, lying in her bed, watching television while holding her iPad in her hand.

She doesn't care what I have to say or how this makes me feel, she just needs me to be here to listen. So, that's what I do.

"But it's having you kids that made me this way. It's having your good for nothing alcoholic father that made me eat everything in sight. Do you know what it feels like to have your husband spend every paycheck at the bar, leaving me alone to take care of you brats. On what money? I had to beg the next door neighbor to lend me some so I could buy you milk."

I want to roll my eyes, but I resist the temptation. It's not that I'm not sympathetic to everything she has been through, it's just that I've heard this series of stories over and over again all of my life.

"Patrick," she says, looking wistfully at the window. "If only he had lived, then everything would've been fine."

Yeah, all of our family's troubles would be immediately solved if only my mother's favorite child was still alive.

"He would've married a nice Catholic girl and they would've given me four or five grandkids to be busy with," she continues. "Not like you...or your brother, Owen."

"You can barely take care of yourself," I mumble under my breath.

"What?!" she hisses. "What did you say?" She pulls the iPad away from her as if she's going to swat me with it.

On impulse, from a decade of memories, I cower away from her.

"I wouldn't have any of these issues if Patrick was still here!" she roars.

Usually, I just tune her out and go through what needs to be done. Today is no different. What I want to say is that she can't just blame Dad and Patrick's death on every shitty thing that happened in her life. But this would be adding fuel to her fire.

Patrick, my oldest brother, died on his eighteenth birthday in a car crash. Our father gave him a car and he crashed it into the side of a hill. The police said that they estimated his speed was well over one hundred miles per hour, but Mom doesn't believe a word of that report. She also refuses to believe that he had a high blood alcohol level because he promised her that he would never drink and drive.

She doesn't say anything for a while, letting me fold her laundry in peace. But during the commercial break, she turns to me and asks, "So, what about you?"

"What do you mean?"

"When are you going to give me some grandchildren?"

"Mom, I'm not seeing anyone."

"That hasn't stopped almost every other girl in this neighborhood from toting around a toddler on her hip."

"I don't want a child...right now," I say.

"What does that matter?" she asks, sitting up a bit in

bed. Her pain medication must've started working because she's suddenly full of energy. "If people only had children they wanted, the world would be a lot less populated."

I fold a large fitted sheet and put it in the back of the closet with the rest.

"I mean, it's not like Owen can give me any grandkids at this point," she says. "So I guess I'll have to settle for yours."

Owen is doing ten years in the state penitentiary for an armed robbery charge.

"He may get parole," I point out.

"Yeah, right!"

"I have years to have kids and so does Owen. I'm sure that you'll get some grandkids in the future," I say to make nice.

Mom sits up a bit, narrowing her eyes. Her hair is stringy and unkempt and she's dressed in her usual long puffy nightgown that she wears day and night. Her face is splotchy and looks much older than her forty-eight years.

"Are you stupid or something? Why did you waste all of that money on education if you're still as dense as you were growing up? Don't you get it? I want *you* to have kids for *me*. I want *Owen* to have kids for *me*. I want some damn grandkids *now*."

I used to think that she looked older than she was because of her hard life, her drinking, and her pain medication. But now I think she looks older because of her meanness.

Luckily, the commercial ends and her attention goes back to her program. I head into the kitchen to make lunch, but then sneak out onto the back porch for some fresh air.

The trees are only now starting to bud and the weather is still cold and unwelcoming. But the cold feels good on my face.

When I first paid off my loans, I wasn't sure if it was the right decision. My mother has a lot of medical bills and perhaps I should've used some of the money to help her. But the last two days told me that I did the right thing.

Paying off my mom's bills wouldn't have improved her situation that much and she wouldn't have even appreciated it if I had.

Zipping up my coat, I slip my hands into the pockets. Feeling the outline of the envelope that arrived yesterday sends shivers up my spine. The paper is thick and luxurious and the letter itself has gold foil around the border.

I pull it out and look at it again. I run my fingers over the insignia at the top. There are no floral leaves or lions standing on their back legs, but it is no less elegant and exquisite: a large C enclosed in a box.

Dear Ms. Olivia E. Kernes, I begin to read the words again silently, but moving my lips.

7

WHEN I READ THE LETTER...

"WHAT THE HELL are you doing here?" Mom swings open the screen door, hitting me with it in my back. When the meds are working, she doesn't need the cane and instead uses it as a weapon.

I drop the letter onto the floor and quickly scramble to get it.

"What is that?" she asks, pointing her cane at me.

"Nothing, just...bills."

Holding the door open, she waits for me to walk past her and then grabs the letter out of my hand.

"What are you doing?" I reach to get it back, but she pushes me back with her cane.

"You have always been so secretive. Even when you were just a little kid. Writing stuff in your little diary, putting a lock on it and hiding it under your bed," she says.

Unwilling to physically grab it from her, I stand and wait.

"Dear Ms. Olivia E. Kernes," she starts to read. "Thank you for accepting my gift. I know that you have used it in a meaningful way. What is *this* about?"

I shrug and shake my head.

"I know that you must have questions as to who has sent it to you and why. I would like to alleviate your curiosity and invite you to my home for an introduction. Please know that any and all expenses will be taken care of. I hope to see you there."

I have read this letter so many times since it arrived that I have the words memorized. Below that is the signature line that reads,

Sincerely, NC

Maui, Hawaii

PS. If you accept my invitation, please email me at nc@apricotway.com

"What the hell is this about?" Mom demands to know. "What gift?"

I'm not sure how to answer this question except I cannot tell her the truth.

First of all, she doesn't know the extent of the loans that I owed because she thought me wanting to get an education was my way of wanting to be better than her.

Second of all, I cannot tell her that I received a check in that amount and didn't share a penny with her.

"I got a gift in the mail. I wasn't sure who it was from, but it was nice and I kept it," I lie.

She narrows her eyes.

Unlike my brother, I'm not a very good liar and she's a very good investigator. One of the things that I did learn from Owen is that the best lies are those that are closest to the truth.

"What is it?" she asks.

I hesitate.

I can't tell her that I got any money because she'll expect me to share it with her. But I do have to tell her something.

"A small statue of an...elephant," I mumble.

A few days ago, I saw this clay elephant at my favorite thrift store and I considered buying it. But it was forty-five dollars and kind of an extravagant expense for a pretty useless object. Now, I make a mental note that I have to go back and get it, if for no other reason than to have it in my possession in case she asks to see it.

"An elephant? Why would someone send that to you?"

"I have no idea."

"And now this NC wants you to go see him?" she asks, pointing to the letter. "Go to Maui, all expenses paid?"

I shrug.

Mom comes so close to me I can smell the stale cigarette smoke on her skin. Her dark eyes look vicious. I take a step back but the hallway is so narrow that my back touches the walls. There's nowhere to go.

"What the hell are you up to, Olive? You trying to find yourself a rich man or something?"

"No, ma'am." I shake my head.

"'Cause you know that you can't. You're too ugly and fat. Why would he want you?"

Her words land as if she was actually punching me.

Tears start to well up in my eyes.

My mouth gets parched and I try to swallow the big ball forming in the back of my throat.

I've heard her say these things to me since I was a little kid so you'd think that I would be used to hearing them by now. But I guess that's the thing about mothers, you only get one and you keep giving her chances because you don't want to lose her.

She takes a step back and pours herself a cup of stale coffee. "You want any?" she asks.

"No, thank you."

"Listen, I don't mean to be hard on you but that's the kind of world we live in. You seem to live in the clouds. You are pretty enough to make someone a wife, but you're not pretty the way those Hollywood actresses are. I just don't want you to be disappointed, honey."

I nod. Her sudden shift in tone and her pretense that she is saying all of this for my benefit makes me feel even worse.

"Listen, I have to go," I say.

"You're not going to stay tonight? What if I need you?"

"You'll be fine. I set up all of your medicine next to your bed, the laundry is done. The food will be here shortly," I say, grabbing my duffel bag and my phone and charger out of the wall.

"Fine, go!" she says coldly.

"Can I have my letter please?"

"No, absolutely not," she says, shaking her head. Then she takes out a cigarette and lights my letter on fire with the lighter.

I don't bother grabbing it out of her hand. Instead, I

stand there in a trance watching it burn. The same fate came to my high school diploma the day after I graduated and my first passport when I was foolish enough to have it sent to our house.

"This is for your own good," she says.

"Okay," I say, walking out.

"You're not going to say goodbye?" she yells after me as I close the door behind me.

Tears start to stream down my face before I get inside my car. I can barely see through them as I open the Note app on my phone and type up the letter that I have committed to memory. When I'm finished, I stare at the email address that NC provided.

I don't know who sent this gift or why, but I do know two things. One, I am going to accept this invitation. Two, I am never going to see my mother again.

8

WHEN I GET READY...

"You can't go there by yourself," Sydney says, walking into my room and closing my suitcase. I go into my closet and grab a strapless dress I haven't worn since last summer.

"What do you think about this one?" I ask, pressing it to my body and extending one leg in front of the other. It's very soft and has a light floral design, hanging loosely like a tunic. The neckline is made of a twisted gold material that gives it a bit of flair.

"Olive, you're not thinking clearly. You just spent a few days at your mom's and that always makes you a little crazy."

"I'm not doing this because of her," I say.

"So, why? Why are you doing this?"

I shrug. "I want to know who sent me the money."

"This could be a really dangerous thing, Olive. You could be sex-trafficked for crying out loud."

"I doubt that."

"What makes you so sure?" Sydney asks.

"Sex traffickers don't usually send you over a hundred and fifty grand ahead of time."

"Whatever." She throws up her hands. "You know what I mean. What do you even know about this NC?"

I shrug.

"He has an email address, woohoo!" she says sarcastically. "Apricot Way. Do you know what that is?"

"No, I tried to look it up but I couldn't find anything about it."

"Well, I found out something."

I fold another pair of leggings and look up at her. "What?"

"There are like a hundred people with the acronyms N. C. In Maui."

"I don't doubt it," I say.

Sydney walks up to me and puts her hands around my shoulders.

"What did your mom say to you, Olive?" she asks.

Her lips are trembling and she looks terrified. I've never seen her this concerned about anything before.

Sydney is the one person in my life who knows the most about my mother and what she has put me through. Lately, it seems like all I do is complain to her about what's going on in my life, but she has always been there for me. I appreciate her listening more than she will ever know.

"Nothing special, just the usual shit," I say.

Thankfully, she has never asked me why I put up with all of it. She has her own issues with her parents, mainly the fact that no matter how much she succeeds she never seems to quite live up to their expectations. So, she knows exactly why I put up with all the crap that my mother delves out.

My mom's mean and angry and has never had many friends. The few that remained were driven out of her life over the last year when her pain and her hatred got worse. My father went out for a carton of milk never to return again. One of my brothers is dead and the other is serving a long prison sentence. My mother is all I have and I can't just give up on her. At least, that's what I always told myself to get through it before.

"I'm done," I say quietly.

"What do you mean?"

"I've had enough. She caught me with that letter, she read it, she mocked me, and she lit it on fire."

"I am so sorry," Sydney whispers, putting her arm around me.

"I can't keep letting her treat me like this," I say. "I know that she has a lot of pain, but I have to stop accepting that as an excuse."

"Is that why you're doing this?" she asks. I shrug.

I open my underwear drawer and pick out a few black panties and my favorite t-shirt bra. I decide to pack another significantly less comfortable lacy one as well, just in case a special occasion comes up.

"Yeah, that's partly why I'm doing this. I need to get away. I took a week off work and I figure I'll take my chance on this."

"I know that you want to go somewhere but...I'm just worried that this isn't a safe thing to do," Sydney says.

"I'll have my phone on me. As soon as I get there and I know exactly where I'm going, I'll text you. I promise."

She walks over to my closet and pulls out a red dress. Folding it up carefully, she packs it into my suitcase.

"But this is your favorite dress," I say. It's also one of my favorite ones to borrow.

"I know, but I want you to take it. For good luck." I wrap my arms around Sydney and give her a kiss on the cheek.

We say our goodbyes as I wait for the car to pick me up downstairs.

Once I wrote back to the email address provided in the letter, Amelia Dual, a concierge, wrote me back immediately with all of the arrangements.

Even though I'm not much of a phone talker, I didn't feel comfortable doing all of this online. So, we video chatted and she explained what will happen.

She will send a car to pick me up at my apartment, which will then take me to Logan International Airport. I received the flight information in my email: a First-Class ticket to Maui, Hawaii, with a brief stop in Los Angeles. Once there, another car will take me to my final destination.

I get to the airport an hour before my flight and wander around the shops, leafing through the magazines and debating what kind of junk food is the healthiest to buy for the plane. I message Amelia about the exact location of where I am going, but she refuses to provide me with any additional details.

An email trail, car service, and first class tickets definitely make me feel safer about the fact that I am probably not being kidnapped.

Still, Sydney's concerns echo my own. The thing is that I don't really know what I'm getting myself into and I'm doing it all alone.

First-class passengers board first and a flight attendant offers me a warm towel and asks for my drink order.

"She'll have a bloody Mary," a familiar voice says, grabbing the empty seat next to mine. "I'll have one, too."

"What are *you* doing here?" I ask.

9

WHEN SHE SURPRISES ME...

Sydney takes the seat next to mine with a mischievous look on her face. She takes her time and builds anticipation with first putting her carry-on luggage in the overhead bin and then unpacking her earbuds, iPad, and phone, putting them into the compartment in the back of the seat in front of her.

Finally, she turns to me and says, "I'm coming with you."

I start to laugh, shaking my head.

A wave of relief sweeps over me.

I hadn't realized until this very moment how much I was dreading doing this on my own.

Sydney is not technically invited, but I don't care. They can't expect me to go out there all alone, not knowing what I am walking into.

"So, you just...what? Booked a ticket yourself?"

"Yep," she says, tossing her shiny hair from her shoulders. "I saw the itinerary and the flight that you were on and I booked mine the same day."

"You're so sweet," I say, squeezing her hand. "It must've cost you a fortune."

"Don't worry, I told my dad that I need some girl time with my roomie and we're getting away for the week."

"You're staying the whole week?"

"I can easily change the tickets if you don't want me to. Don't worry."

THE FLIGHT IS long but uneventful.

I read a book on my phone, I stare into space, I page through the magazines I got at the gift shop back in Boston.

I eat two packets of peanut M&M's even though I promised myself that I would save them until Hawaii.

I try to sleep but my mind keeps running around in circles so I entertain myself with three movies and consume an enormous amount of pretzels and two packets of salt and vinegar potato chips.

When we arrive and get our bags, we walk up to the

man holding a sign with my name on it and follow him to his car.

He has jet black hair with a few wisps of gray, dark olive skin, and a mega-watt smile.

Dressed in a flowing Hawaiian shirt, khaki pants, and leather flip-flops, he looks exactly like what I imagined every man on this island to look like.

"Wow, interesting choice," Sydney says, looking around the new model Jeep Wrangler as Thomas, our driver, loads our bags.

I guess I was expecting a man in a black suit and a Lincoln town car or a BMW because I'm just as surprised by the greeting as she is.

On the drive out, I plaster my face to the window staring at the lush vegetation on either side of the highway.

"The first explorer to come to Maui was Admiral Jean-Francois de La Perouse in 1786," Thomas, our driver, says.

"It's so beautiful here," I say, looking at bright blue water and the pristine beaches on one side of us.

"Maui is the second largest Hawaiian island with over 120 miles of coastline and beaches. The island itself is over 727 square miles."

"It looks very wild." Sydney points out to the luscious green jungles on the other side of the road.

"It is. Not all roads around here are easily drivable but that's partly what makes it so charming. It has a lot of hidden places. One of which is where you are going."

My ears perk up.

"And where's that?"

"I am under strict instructions not to reveal a thing, I am sorry," Thomas says, quickly changing the subject. "This road, the Hana Highway, is considered one of the most scenic ones in the world."

I look down and watch the way the asphalt looks as if it's almost hugging the cliffs. Sydney, who is terrified of heights, moves closer to the middle of the car and shields her eyes.

The highway doesn't match any normal definition of a highway. There are hundreds and hundreds of breathtaking and hairpin turns that alternate between waterfalls on one side and soaring and plunging sea cliffs on the other.

We drive for nearly two hours then turn onto a poorly paved road that goes through the lush tropical rainforest, so thick that it's just a sea of green. Rain comes and goes, leaving behind a sparkling rainbow.

We drive out onto a clearing, a beautiful green pasture. There are dramatic mountains behind us and miles of a deep blue ocean in the front. The grass moves slightly in the breeze almost as if it were dancing. Were it not for the sprawling home positioned near the cliff, this place would be completely wild.

As we pull up closer to the house, I am surprised by how it looks. Instead of the brand new Mediterranean type of estate that I imagined this would be, this house is a blast from the past.

Thick plantation shutters, a ranch-style design, and a wrap-around lanai gives me a feeling of old Hawaii, the kind that I've only seen in movies. There is extensive ocean frontage with an infinity pool that looks out onto the water below.

Slightly to the back of the house, there are two cottages painted the same soothing taupe color as the main house. They also have matching thick shutters and oscillating ceiling fans on the porches.

My eyes are immediately drawn to something in the distance that is perched almost over the cliff.

"What's that?" I ask.

"That's our gazebo. It's perfect for watching turtles, whales, and other wildlife," Thomas says.

"Can I go take a look?" I ask.

"No, not just yet," he says, getting my suitcases.

"I will show you to your cottage, Ms. Kernes, and our staff will get the other one ready for you, Ms. Catalano," Thomas says.

I don't know if he's just too polite to say anything about me bringing a friend along, but now suddenly I feel very uncomfortable about Sydney's presence. I am an invited guest, maybe I had no right to invite my roommate along on this trip.

When we follow Thomas to my cottage, a beautiful woman with dark flowing hair and a flower behind her left ear walks up to us. She's dressed in a casual summer dress and wedges and gives me a warm hug.

"It's so nice to meet you, Ms. Kernes," she says. "I'm Amelia Dual."

10

WHILE WE WAIT...

AMELIA SHOWS US MY COTTAGE. It's a spacious one-bedroom with comfortable off-white furniture and a beautiful marble kitchen island. A large television hangs above the fireplace. I'm immediately drawn to the floor-to-ceiling sliding doors that span the whole side of the place, looking out onto the ocean below. Large palm trees cradle the place on either side, putting me strangely at ease at being here.

"Mr. Crawford hopes that you will be comfortable here, Ms. Kernes," Amelia says.

"Please call me Olive," I correct her. "And she's Sydney."

"Yes, of course," Amelia says. "Would you mind waiting here, Sydney, while I get someone to set up your cottage?"

"Of course, no problem." She nods.

Amelia is also too nice to say anything, but I feel like I have to.

"Sydney can stay with me, it's no problem," I say. "I'm sorry that I didn't tell you about this earlier but...I was unsure about coming here all by myself since I don't know why I was even invited here."

"You don't have to apologize. You are our guest and Mr. Crawford will understand," she says and leaves.

Sydney and I exchange looks. She doesn't have to say a word, I know exactly what she's thinking by the expression on her face. She thinks this place is amazing and is very impressed with the professionalism of the staff.

There's a plate of fruit and pastries sitting on the edge of the kitchen counter along with a collection of teas, some of which are Hawaiian. I forgo the traditional ones like Earl Grey and peppermint and steep a bag of the local mango, pineapple, and passion fruit. Sydney makes herself a cup of Royal Kona coffee and takes the tray of food out onto the lanai overlooking the sea.

"So, what do you think?" she asks, taking a sip.

My mouth salivates at the sight of the slices of bright yellow starfruit and I quickly bite into one.

"I don't know what to think," I say. "I mean, why am I here? Who brought me here?"

"Apparently, Mr. Crawford did," Sydney says, her eyes lighting up. "Do you know of any Mr. Crawford?"

I shake my head no.

"Think hard. Do you know of anyone with the last name Crawford at all?"

I think about it for a moment. But the answer is again no.

"I don't remember anyone named Crawford growing up. I don't remember even meeting a Crawford before."

We sit out on the porch enjoying the light breeze and watching the whitecaps of the ocean below collide with the pristine white beach. The flight was long and tiring, and I can't help but sit back in my rocking chair and close my eyes. I listen to the chirping of birds somewhere in the distance until I fall into a deep sleep.

"She's coming back," Sydney whispers to me, rousing me.

I don't know how much time has passed but there are three fewer croissants than there were before I fell asleep.

Amelia walks up to us and tells us that Sydney's cottage is now ready.

Sydney insists on carrying her own bags so I just follow her down a footpath to her place, which is identical to mine in every way down to the nautical decorations and throw pillows.

"Mr. Crawford is hosting a cocktail party tonight at six at the main house. He would like to invite you both there," Amelia says.

"Yes, of course," I mumble, rubbing my eyes.

"It's only three now, so if you want to take a rest or a dip in the pool, feel free," she says. "There are towels and bathing suits and anything else you may need in your cottages."

After Amelia leaves, Sydney says she's going to take a nap but I want to go on a walk to clear my head. I'm afraid that going to sleep now is just going to make me more drowsy for the party. Hey, maybe I'll even do a few laps in the pool.

I change out of my sweaty leggings and black t-shirt and into a light sleeveless beach dress. It's unfitted and airy, like a long t-shirt, and finally I enjoy the way the breeze feels wrapping around my bare legs as I make my way toward the cliff.

"There must be some way down," I say to myself, looking down at the ocean below. I'm standing at the edge of a nearly twenty-foot cliff.

I walk over to the batch of swaying palm trees to one side and examine the rugged terrain again. The overhang back toward the main house is a near straight up and down face, but there does seem to be more of a path in the direction toward the rainforest.

I head in there and then slowly start to make my way down the narrow winding trail down the rocky bluff.

This walk is no joke and I'm about halfway down before I realize that this may have been a really bad decision.

With each step, I kick up the sand and rocks and a few fall straight down below. Each time I place my feet onto the ground, I test it first to make sure that it's stable but one time I'm wrong. My foot slips and I land on my butt and start to slide all the way to the bottom.

"Are you okay?" A guy runs over to me.

Putting down his surfboard, he kneels down next to me and we both stare at my bleeding leg. I move it around to assess the damage.

"It seems to be okay," I say. "Just a few cuts and bruises."

"Did you just come down this way?" he asks, pointing to the precipice above. The trail that I thought was a path doesn't look anything like it from this direction and I'm kind of shocked that I even made it all of the way down without breaking my back.

"I wanted to touch the water," I say, getting up and straightening my dress.

"Well, if you want to go back up, make sure to go that way." He points a little further down the beach. "That's where the real trail starts."

I'm about to ask him for his name, but he dives into the water before I can get the chance.

"Thanks!" I yell after him. He raises his hand for an acknowledgment and disappears below the waves.

11

WHEN WE GET READY...

I CAN'T HELP but wade in the water and swim around a bit. I would go skinny dipping, but the surfer is still somewhere on the horizon so I go in with my dress on.

When I get to my cottage, I hang up my dress and jump straight into the shower. Fresh water feels good on my scrapes as the tingling from the salt finally goes away.

When I examine my legs closer, I see the scratches from the rocks go almost the whole way down from my thighs to my ankles. The bleeding has stopped, but after the hot shower, the scrapes look pretty bad.

Wrapped in a towel, I go through my suitcase trying to figure out what to wear to this cocktail party. I have no idea how dressy or not dressy it is and I'm always a little uncomfortable in being overdressed. Unlike Sydney, I'd rather be the girl that few people notice.

I'm ready half an hour ahead of schedule and go to see

Sydney who is probably still in the midst of her transformation. She lets me in with her hair still wet and a tornado of clothes on her bed.

"Is that what you're wearing?" she gasps.

I smile from getting the reaction that every girl dreams of when she takes the time to get a look together.

"What's wrong with this?" I ask.

"Jeans? Really?"

"They aren't jeans, they are black jean leggings and they make my butt and legs look really nice," I say.

Paired with a pair of nude wedges and a flowing, sleeveless top with a plunging neckline, I know that I look sophisticated but not overdressed.

"And what if this is some sort of black tie thing?"

"It's a cocktail party, I'm wearing cocktail attire. C'mon, you're the one who always says that a nice pair of heels dresses up any outfit."

"Yeah, I know," she says loudly over the sound of the hairdryer. "I just thought you'd wear my dress."

I shrug. I'd given that a thought as well, but I couldn't. I don't know what I'm walking into here and I need to feel as comfortable as possible. I'm not good at heels and dresses in general, and I'm only willing to sacrifice one of those tonight. Sydney knows all of this, of course, so she doesn't push me any further.

Even though it doesn't look like she would have enough time to do everything that she needs to get done for her to look presentable, Sydney is ready by exactly six o'clock. It's amazing how quickly she dries and straight irons her hair, applies her makeup, and slips on her little black dress.

"I figured that I'd go with the classic cocktail look," she says, applying one last coat of red lipstick to complete the look.

"You look beautiful," I say.

"As do you." She gives me a quick squeeze on the hand. "I'm sorry if I made you feel bad earlier, I was just joking."

"I know you were." I smile back at her.

THE SUN IS JUST STARTING to set and the wrap-around lanai is illuminated with a brilliant explosion of pinks, yellows, and reds. Waiters, dressed in black tuxes, meander among the guests who are dressed in almost casual attire with men wearing Hawaiian shirts and khakis and women floral dresses. Some are sleeveless, others are strapless, and wrap-style but all move softly in the light breeze coming off the ocean.

I don't have the skills to be able to walk up to a perfect stranger and start a conversation, but luckily Sydney does. Within a few moments, I am engrossed in a discussion about Boston with a couple of women in their thirties who have never been there.

They both grew up in Hawaii, on different islands, and now work in real estate. If it were up to me, I would just keep talking to them all night, but Sydney has an effortless way of flowing in and out of conversations and quickly we move on to new people. Within the hour, we have talked to almost half of the attendees.

There are a few commonalities among them. Most are in their thirties and forties and live on Maui. Many of the women do not work and those who do, work in real estate. The men are involved in various investment projects 'on the island,' that's what they say when referring to this place.

In every conversation, I keep meaning to ask about Mr. Crawford, but then I always get a little bit shy. I don't really want to go into the reason why I'm here and I fear that if they find out that I don't even know who he is then I will inevitably have to.

As Sydney leads us to yet another group of strangers for another round of small talk, I look around for Amelia or Thomas, the only familiar faces who know him. I spot Amelia inside, by the grand piano. The party seems to congregate outside, with barely anyone inside the main living area. I pull away from Sydney and follow a waiter through the sliding glass doors.

"Hey!" I yell to her from across the room. I'm so eager

to speak to her that I barely notice the cathedral ceilings, the minimalist furniture, and the expansive view of the water.

Amelia meets up with me by the stone fireplace.

"Are you having a good time?" she asks. "Oh, you don't have a drink!"

"No, I'm good," I say, realizing that I left mine on one of the tables outside.

Despite my protestations, she flags down one of the waiters and I take a glass of white wine off his serving tray. I'm not much of a drinker, but not having a glass in your hand at a cocktail party, even if it's just water, seems off-putting.

"I just wanted to ask you about Mr. Crawford," I say, with hesitation in my voice. "I don't know if I was supposed to meet him out there or ...not."

"No, he actually just got delayed with a business meeting so he is running quite a bit late," Amelia says. "He told me to tell you that he hopes that you are enjoying the party and your stay here and he will see you later."

I nod, as if I understand a word of what she is saying. Then I decide to just come out with it.

"Okay," I say slowly, carefully picking my words. "Can I ask you something?"

"Sure." She shrugs her shoulders in a casual nonchalant manner as if she has not a care in the world.

"Who is *he*?" I blurt out.

"Who is Mr. Crawford?" she asks, surprised.

12

WHEN I WAIT...

"Yes, who is he? What does he look like? Do I know him from somewhere?" I ask Amelia. The words burst out of my mouth, all at once.

Suddenly, Amelia's demeanor changes completely. The smile on her face vanishes and she shakes her head.

"Do you know why I'm here? I mean, do you know what he did for me?"

"I know that he sent you a gift and he was thankful that you accepted it," she says coolly. "Actually, I was the one who took care of the arrangements."

"Yes, I figured that much," I say. I wait for her to continue but she doesn't. Instead, she just stares at me like a deer in headlights.

"So...can you tell me anything about him?" I nudge her again.

"No, I'm sorry. I really can't." She shakes her head. "He gave me strict instructions to not reveal anything to you about who he is."

"Do you know why he sent me the gift?"

"That I actually do *not* know."

At a loss as to what to do next, I look back at the party on the deck.

"Does anyone there know who he is?" I ask.

She hesitates. Her eyes drift down to the floor and then cautiously back to me.

"Please tell me," I plead.

"They are just his friends and business associates, but he likes to keep his private life private."

My eyes light up.

"Olive, please." Amelia touches my hand. The expression on her face is intense and serious. "Please don't ask them. Mr. Crawford doesn't want the surprise spoiled and none of them know what he did for you. It is his wish to keep that a secret."

Her eyes meet mine and she doesn't let me go even when I take a step away from her.

"Please, promise me that you'll wait," she says.

I don't know what the right thing to do is so I nod and give her my word. If that's what he wants, then that's the least I can do in return for him giving me such an extraordinary gift.

I spend the rest of the evening avoiding all the people that I have met earlier. I figured that I have done enough socializing for one party and now that the illusive Mr. Crawford isn't making an appearance, I'd rather just enjoy this view in peace.

When the night comes to a close and the sky becomes spotted with millions of stars, Sydney runs up to me in a huff. She's so excited that it takes her a moment to catch her breath.

"I have a date!" she finally manages to say.

"Really? With who?" I ask.

"This guy I met at the party. He is tall and has this amazing luscious dark hair and a beautiful tan."

"Everyone around here has a beautiful tan," I point out.

"Whatever." She waves her hand. "He's also a doctor!"

"Oh, a doctor! Your parents will be so proud," I joke.

"No, they won't," she says proudly. "He's a pediatrician at this clinic for the poor. If he has money it doesn't come from his job."

"Oh, I see, he's a medical rebel!" I say, smiling. "So... where is he taking you?"

"To dinner and a drive," she says. "Don't wait up."

I feel the expression on my face fall. "You're leaving now?"

"Yeah, why do you care?"

I shrug.

I shouldn't.

I should be happy for her, but I'm concerned nevertheless.

"But you just met him, what if he's some...creep or something?"

"He's not! Besides, how is this any different from me meeting some doctor at a party in Boston?"

I shake my head. "Well, neither of us have ever been here before, for one. What if you get in trouble? You don't know the area at all."

"I'll have my phone with me."

"There's no reception here on that main road, remember?" My thoughts return to our two hour drive.

During daylight, it was magnificent but the fact that I couldn't get a signal at all was a little bit annoying. Now, that's it nighttime, the road seems treacherous and dangerous.

"I'll be fine," Sydney says and I let it go. I don't want to ruin her night by acting like her mother, or worse, but I still have my concerns.

"Look, it's going to be fine. Amelia knows him. It's not like he's a total stranger. Besides, you're the one you should be worried about."

"What do you mean?" I ask.

"Mr. Crawford? Wasn't he supposed to be at the party? And he's a no-show?" She laughs, tossing her hair off her shoulders.

"Maybe he was traveling here on that crazy road, fell off a cliff, and doesn't have reception to call for help," I joke, and then immediately regret it.

That seems like something that probably happens a lot around here and I feel bad for even kidding about it.

"So, what is going on with the illusive Mr. Crawford?" she asks as I follow her back to her cottage.

"I don't know. Amelia said that he got held up with something but who knows if that's true. She was being very cryptic about everything and asked me not to ask the guests about his whereabouts."

"How odd," Sydney agrees.

She walks into the bathroom and applies a fresh coat of deodorant to her underarms. Then she props up her leg on the sink to check if she needs to shave them again. The knees and the area around the ankle of her left leg don't pass inspection so she gets out her razor and shaves those hairs off.

The doorbell rings. Sydney's eyes light up in

excitement. She practically runs over, but then takes a moment to gather her thoughts prior to opening the door.

The man on the other side is indeed tall, dark, and very handsome. He gives her a brief peck on the cheek and then introduces himself to me as James Dupree.

"Please don't take this the wrong way, but can I have the name of the restaurant where you are going and your phone number and address? Just in case," I say.

I'm rarely this forward but I know that I will regret not having this information were she to spend the night with him.

He smiles and asks for my number so that he can text me all the info.

"I'm sorry but we're just not from around here and I wouldn't want anything to happen to Sydney," I say as he types his message.

"No offense taken, you're being a good friend," he says. "Just sent it."

I follow them out of her cottage and head toward my own.

"Wait, James!" I yell into the dark. I follow the path toward the two figures somewhere in the distance. "Can I ask you something?"

They're holding hands and Sydney has an annoyed expression on her face.

"I just wanted to ask you about the guy who owns that house. I don't know if Sydney told you anything about why we're here..." My words trail off.

"No, not really," James says.

I hear Amelia's request in my mind and hesitate to tell him anything else.

"So, do you know the owner?" I reiterate the question.

"Nicholas Crawford?" James nods. "Yes, of course. He's a good friend of mine. We go surfing a lot."

"So, he wasn't at the party this evening?" I ask.

"Nope." James shakes his head. "I heard that he got stuck on the other side of the island and couldn't make it. It probably has something to do with that resort."

"What resort?" Sydney asks.

"He's one of the investors in a large resort over there and they've had a lot issues getting permits and stuff like that. It has been kind of a headache."

I nod, taking it all in. From what James says he seems like a normal guy.

Maybe I don't have anything to worry about after all.

So, why does my heart still keep skipping beats?

13

WHEN SHE INTERRUPTS ME...

After Sydney leaves, I take off my clothes, wash my face, brush my hair, and climb into bed. The long flight and the two hour drive along with the excitement and built-up anticipation of the party have all taken a toll on me. I'm not sure what time it is in Boston right now or how little I slept in the last twenty-four hours and I'm too tired to figure it all out. I turn off the lights and close my eyes.

That's when the thoughts start running through my mind. I run over every person I have known in my life, trying to remember if there's anyone by the name of Nicholas Crawford.

Nick? Do I even know any Nicks?

No, I can't say that I do. I mean, there were probably Nicks who I went to high school with, it is somewhat of a common name, but I wasn't friends with any of them.

Realizing that the fatigue of the day has somehow made my mind wired, I reach for my iPad and open a reading app. I love the feeling of a real book in my hands, but I hate having the light on and physically holding the book and turning the pages, especially when I am tired.

EBooks make everything so much easier. I can store thousands of them in my device's library and read whichever one I'm in the mood for that night.

Of course, like many women, I can't really resist the ones that are a little bit explicit. Most movies and TV shows fade to black as soon as the characters start to kiss, but in books, their stories continue. In bed... that's the best part of it, isn't it?

After all of the drama that they endure, after all of the ups and downs of life, when they finally get together... that's bliss!

I bookmark my favorite parts of my favorite novels and re-read them again. Sometimes, I like a short and dirty scene, but other times I like it when the details go on for pages and pages. And it's not all sex, it's more than that. There's the pillow talk, their laughter, their arguments. A lot of things can happen in between the sheets.

I turn to my favorite scene in a novel set in the West. They have loved each other since they were children and they sleep together for the first time in a field right next to the rushing Colorado River. The details are so exquisite that I can't help but close my eyes and smell the dry swaying grass and feel the spray of the cool water on their bodies.

My fingers slowly make their way down my own body, as I feel the contours of my thighs.

The skin is soft and inviting and I run my fingers down to my belly button. It moves up and down with each breath, quickening in tempo as my breathing speeds up.

Whatever bad thoughts I typically have about my body all seem to disappear, or fade into the distance.

Now, I relish in it. A familiar tingling sensation starts to build up within me, starting at the tip of my toes. I flex my feet and the sensation runs up my thighs.

I'm dressed in a blush pink, soft pajama set that I bought for the trip.

Both the t-shirt and the shorts are incredibly soft and the t-shirt has delicate ruffled sleeves.

I pull the bottoms off, along with my underwear, and toss them onto the bed next to me. I prop up the iPad so that I can keep reading the words on the screen while having the use of both of my hands.

My fingers run up my shirt and touch the outline of my breasts.

I feel my nipples get hard and I arch my back from pleasure. Keeping one hand there, my other travels back down my body and my legs open wide.

They tease me by first running up the inside of my thighs, before touching the warm, wet center of my body.

I tilt my head back as my fingers start to move in familiar circles and plunge deep inside. When I get closer and closer, my fingers speed up and my hips start to move up and down.

A knock on the door startles me. It breaks through my concentration, immediately taking me out of the moment.

For a moment, I keep my fingers where they are and just listen. Maybe it's nothing. Maybe it's just a critter walking outside. But they knock again. This time it's louder.

"Olive?" Amelia asks. "Olive! I'm sorry to bother you but I have to speak with you."

"Just a second!" I yell, hoping that she won't just let herself in. "I was sleeping."

My jaw clenches with irritation as I search around in the dark for my shorts and underwear.

I search the floor next to the bed before realizing that I had buried them under the sheets next to me.

"Yes?" I say in a very dismissive manner, opening the door.

I should be nice, but she shouldn't be bothering me at this hour.

"I'm really sorry for coming here now, but Mr. Crawford would like to see you," she says, shuffling her feet and looking down at the floor. I stare at her in disbelief. Did she really just say this to me?

"He just got back and he requested to see you," she repeats herself.

"Now? Are you serious?" I ask.

I look her up and down. She's dressed in the same thing she was wearing at the party, but she looks different. Her hair is a bit of a mess and she's no longer wearing makeup. She was clearly roused out of bed as well.

"Yes, I'm afraid so," she says.

I consider doing it for a moment, but then I get a hold of my better senses.

Yes, he did give me a big gift.

But I traveled all of the way here to meet with him and he stood me up at the party. And now, he wants to meet me at this hour?

"No, absolutely not," I say definitively without leaving any room for negotiation.

"Please, you can't say no to him."

"Why not?"

"Very few people do," she says.

"Well, I don't work for him. He invited me here and I

showed up. I was at the party, he didn't come. I will see him tomorrow but for now I need to get some sleep."

I close the door as her mouth drops open and wonder if I have made a terrible mistake.

14

WHEN I MEET HIM...

My words come out strong and powerful and self-assured but inside I feel like I'm dying. The look of concern on Amelia's face scares me.

Did I make a mistake?

Was coming here some sort of mistake in general?

Even so, there is no way that I'm going to meet him in this state.

I'm not ready.

Earlier this evening, I looked pretty and presentable.

But now?

Naked face, bed hair, no planned outfit. My mom always taught me that first impressions are everything, and even though she has probably been wrong about everything else she ever told me, I'm certain that she was right about this.

I pick up my iPad and try to focus my mind on something else. But the book that hit the spot so perfectly only a few moments ago fails to grab my attention.

I look through my library trying to find something else to read. Eventually, I turn to another one of my favorites.

It's by Charlotte Byrd, one of my favorite writers, and it's a lot darker in tone. Ellie goes to an exclusive yacht party and decides to participate in an auction where she has to spend the night with one of the eligible bachelors.

The men are young, rich, and incredibly good looking and the money is astronomical.

Why not, right? You only live once. I turn to my favorite part where she is lying on the bed with a blindfold over her eyes waiting for the man who bought her to come in.

My mind starts to clear and my breaths start to quicken. My fingers quickly make their way down my body and underneath my shorts. I don't bother taking them off this time. This isn't going to take long. My legs open up and my butt starts to move and up and down. My anticipation builds as my fingers move in neat concentric circles around my core before making their way inside. I point my toes as a warm soothing sensation amplifies and spreads throughout my body, slowly at first and then all at once.

My breath gets caught in my throat and my heart skips a few beats before pounding so loudly that I can't hear another thing. When the moment passes, I flex my feet over and over again to get the last bit of pleasure out of my body.

It takes a few minutes for my breathing to get back to normal. I summon the little strength that I have to get up and use the bathroom before falling back into the bed.

There's another knock on the door.

What now?

I'm not going to talk to him now, no matter what she says.

Doesn't she get that?

"Amelia, I already told you, I'm not going," I say, opening the door, and the motion sensor on the porch comes on.

Instead of standing further back, he leans on the door frame, propping himself up with his left arm. His head is tilted down allowing his dark straight hair to fall into his wide sparkling eyes.

"I heard that you didn't want to see me," he says confidently.

His words catch me by surprise but I don't let that phase me. "I was at the party," I say, straightening my back. "I thought you were going to be there."

"I got held up," he explains without providing an explanation of anything.

"So...do you want to see me?" he asks. His thick pale pink lips curl at the corners, revealing little indentations in the middle of his cheeks. Those dimples make my knees weak.

"I'm here, aren't I?" I manage to say as I watch him run his fingers along his square jaw.

If this were daylight and I'd had the proper sleep, I would've apologized for not coming to see him at night. But something infuses me with extra strength and I refuse to do that.

"Yes, you are," he says slowly, tossing his hair. It's razor straight and falls perfectly from one side to another.

I meet his eyes and force myself to not look away first. He seems to find this charming and gives a little chuckle in response.

"Well, I just wanted to introduce myself. My name is Nicholas Crawford." He extends his hand. I wipe the sweat off my palm on the back of my shorts before shaking his.

"It's nice to meet you," I say. "I'm Olive Kernes."

"Well, I'll let you get some rest now," he says.

A light breeze picks up and sways his light V-neck t-shirt, pressing it hard against his torso.

My tongue hits the roof of my mouth as I count six clearly defined abdominal muscles. Even though he is wearing a pair of loose-fitting board shorts, they fit snugly around his tight apple butt, leaving little to the imagination. I watch him disappear into the darkness.

Suddenly, something occurs to me.

"Wait!" I yell after him. "Didn't we meet before?"

He walks back into the light and smiles at me.

"At the beach, earlier today?" I ask. The sun was right behind him, blinding me, and I was too focused on my injuries to get a good look at him, but now I'm certain of it.

"Yes," he admits.

"Why didn't you say anything then?" I ask.

He takes a step back and moves his jaw from side to side.

"I thought it would be better if we met at the party but then I got called off on business."

I nod. Yet another answer without much of an explanation.

"I want you to meet me tomorrow at seven, at the gazebo overlooking the cliffs," Nicholas says, his eyes meeting mine and refusing to let mine go. "I have something to discuss with you."

15

WHEN I SEE HER...

THE FOLLOWING MORNING, I knock on Sydney's door right before nine and it's the latest that I can possibly wait. She yells for me to come in, but the door is locked. Begrudgingly, she gets out of bed and stomps over to let me in.

"What time is it?" she asks.

"I don't know," I lie.

She shakes her head.

Her long straight hair falls in all directions but will only require a brief run of the brush to bring it back to its usual luster. She heads straight to the kitchen counter and starts a pot of coffee.

Her robe falls off her shoulder. She's not wearing anything underneath yet she's not too quick about pulling it shut. One of the things that I admire most about Sydney is that she doesn't have the body of a model and yet she acts and feels like she does. Her confidence is contagious. She has big breasts, a narrow waist, and a large booty and she loves every single one of her curves.

Sydney struggled with her weight and body image immensely as a teenager, going through a series of crash diets and binge eating marathons. It didn't help matters that her mother's family are all Asian with naturally thin frames and tiny bones.

Neither of our mothers made us feel anything but shitty about the bodies that we live in, blaming us for whatever extra weight we carried as some sort of deficiency in the quality of us as human beings.

Yet, somehow, about a year ago, Sydney emerged with this completely different attitude. Instead of waiting to live her life until she lost those extra fifty pounds, she just embraced who she is right now, in this moment, appreciating the body that she wakes up in every day. That's when she started sleeping naked and walking around our apartment in nothing but a silk robe in the mornings.

I am about her size, and I try to follow suit. I know that it's wrong to hate the extra fat around my hips and the fact that my thighs don't touch. I know that I shouldn't complain about the folds that my stomach makes when I sit down. Yet, it's all I can think about.

Especially here.

At least, back in Boston, I could hide behind a heavy coat and sweaters for nine months of the year.

But in Maui? The sun and the humidity and the tropical weather makes it impossible to hide the body that I have.

What happens when I have to wear a swimsuit?

"So...how was your date?" I ask. I'm eager to tell her about Nicholas but I'm equally eager to hear about James.

She takes a sip of her coffee and flashes a mischievous smile out of the corner of her mouth.

"All I'm going to say is," she teases me. "He's great in bed."

I put my mug down onto the counter.

"No, no, no. I need details!" I demand to know, feeling my eyes lighting up. There's nothing better than hearing a juicy story of last night's escapades.

Not that this is a normal thing for Sydney, far from it.

In fact, it was me who'd had a few one-night stands over the last two years, never to return the guys' calls again.

Sydney, on the other hand, has dated the same guy all throughout college and one year into us living together.

Their parents were already making wedding plans when he got drunk one night and confessed to her that he was gay. He comes from a strict traditional family where being gay is out of the question. In fact, he said that he still wanted to marry her and was willing to come to an arrangement where both of them would keep their lovers discreet.

Sydney told him that this was 2019, not 1879, and she would not be marrying anyone who was not one hundred percent in love with and sexually attracted to her. Given that her mother was best friends with his mother since they were young girls, her mother did not understand and even refused to accept the fact that her friend's son could be, in her words, *one of those.*

"Are you going to tell me everything or what?" I ask as Sydney takes one tiny sip of her coffee at a time.

"He took me to this beautiful cove where we walked on the beach and talked about everything from school, our work, our parents, the moon, and the stars," she says, her eyes twinkling.

"The moon and the stars?" I ask.

"Astronomy is a hobby of his. James just got this big telescope that he uses to look at everything up there," she says, pointing up. "I don't know anything about it since I got that one C in Bevler's Intro to Astronomy. But the way he talked about it, it made it sound, I don't know, interesting somehow."

"Yeah, a hot guy walking with you on the beach under the moonlight would make just about anything sound interesting," I joke.

"Oh, c'mon now, that makes me sound like a total creep," James says, walking out of the bedroom and startling me. I jump a whole foot away from her, spilling my lukewarm coffee all over myself.

Sydney starts laughing.

"You weren't going to tell me he was here the whole time?" I ask.

"Eh, I was waiting for him to scare you." She smiles.

As I clean myself off, James walks over to Sydney, puts his hand around her shoulder, and pulls her cheek close to his for a kiss.

"Hey there, beautiful," he whispers into her ear quietly so that I won't hear it.

I hang out in the kitchen with them for a while, watching them swoon all over each other. You'd think it would be annoying, or gross even, but I'm really happy for her.

She spent a long time dating someone who never made her feel good enough and then more time alone thinking that she would never feel like anyone liked her again. So, watching her now with him makes me utterly happy for her, from the inside out.

I still want to tell her all about Nicholas, but for now that will have to wait.

16

WHEN WE SPEND THE DAY TOGETHER...

WHEN JAMES GOES TO WORK, Sydney and I decide to spend the day together. We look up some stuff today and ask Amelia if we can borrow a car. She offers for Thomas to drive us but we decline.

On the drive over to the nearest hiking trail, I tell her about Nicholas and what happened the night before. I gloss over the intimate details and just focus on the fact that he first asked me to come see him through Amelia and then showed up directly at my door in the middle of the night.

"I don't get it, he just showed up?" she asks, tying her sneakers in the passenger seat. I lost the coin toss and got the dubious honor of driving down the winding Hana Highway first.

"Yeah, and with this attitude, too. Like I owe him something."

"Well, you sort of do," she points out. I roll my eyes and turn up the music. "So, what did he look like?"

"Really, really attractive. He looked a bit like Tom Cruise in Jerry McGuire actually."

"I like him better in Mission Impossible," Sydney says.

"How can you tell the difference? He hasn't aged in decades," I joke. She laughs.

"But Nicholas is taller, over six foot two, I think. With broad shoulders. Really nice abs."

"You saw his abs?"

"He was wearing this really tight t-shirt and the breeze pushed it against his torso. Once I saw it, I couldn't look away."

Out of the corner of my eye, while trying to focus on the sharp turn around a cliffside, I see Sydney lick her lips. She has never been this exuberant or lusty. I don't know if it's the tropical heat or the physical heat between her and James but she's different here. More alive somehow.

"But I didn't tell you the whole story," I continue.

"Okay…" She braces herself by holding onto the side of the car, turning her body toward mine.

"He asked me to meet him tonight at seven at the gazebo," I say the words slowly and deliberately. I wait for them to sink in before adding the last part. "He said that he has something to discuss with me."

"What the *hell* does that mean?" she squeals in an excited, high-pitched manner.

I shrug my shoulders. "I have no idea."

I park near a small turnout, near the beginning of a hiking trail. I grab my backpack, which is stuffed with a water bottle, granola bars, and other goodies as well as an external charger for my phone, a small tripod in case we want to take any stylistic photos for Instagram, and a paper map of the area that Amelia insisted that I take. Sydney puts on her own backpack and we follow the sign leading down a small path into the tropical rainforest.

The leaves are wide, thick, and incredibly green. Only a few steps into the forest and I can barely hear the traffic outside or see the road. The leaves all around us are covered in droplets of water, as if it had just rained. A few rays of sunshine stream in, creating a kaleidoscope of light.

We walk for some time, filling the space around us with voices and laughter, and then we reach the waterfall. It comes from somewhere high above our heads, dropping the water into a small pool right at our feet. It's about the size of a small pond, but it never grows any bigger and I wonder how that is physically possible.

"Here, let me take a picture of you here," Sydney says. I groan silently to myself, thinking that she won't notice.

"C'mon. This place is beautiful. You're beautiful. Don't let this moment pass you by without a picture," she says as I take a few steps toward the waterfall and position myself into the pose that I have practiced a million times in the mirror.

I square my shoulders with her and turn my torso to the side, bending the leg that's closest to the camera. I place my hand on my waist to create the angles that all the models on social media are always photographed with.

I've always hated myself in pictures, but after I watched some YouTube videos and practiced a lot in the mirror, I memorized the position that my body should be in and now the pictures all turn out pretty well. Occasionally, I stick my head out too far back instead of elongating my neck or slouch a bit too much. But this one turns out perfect.

"There!" Sydney announces, looking back at it on her phone. "See, it's perfect!"

Yeah, I say to myself, letting out my stomach that I have sucked in until it couldn't be sucked in anymore. The pose is God-awful uncomfortable, but it also makes me look incredibly slim and photogenic. It's a small price to pay.

"So, what do you think he wants to talk to you about tonight?" Sydney asks as she strips down to her bikini and poses in front of the waterfall like a model with years of experience in front of the camera: she extends her arms to the sky, pops her back, and sticks out her butt. Her smile is effortless and relaxed and the photo comes out magical.

"I have no idea," I say, letting out a sigh.

17

WHEN I MEET HIM AT THE GAZEBO...

WE GET BACK from hiking wet and sweaty and I immediately jump into the shower. I have an hour to get ready and I have no idea what that even means. What exactly am I getting ready for? What does he want to discuss with me?

Sydney sits on the couch waiting for me to finish before taking her shower. She can just as easily go to her cottage, but we have been roomies for so long that old habits die hard.

"What are you going to wear?" she yells over the rushing water. That's the million dollar question.

"I have no idea!" I yell back.

"Did you get the vibe that he's into you?" she asks when I come out with a towel wrapped around my chest. The water from my hair drips onto the floor, making a little puddle.

"Why don't you ever wrap it up in another towel?" Sydney asks, exasperated, throwing her hands up.

We've had this discussion before, more than once. The thing is that I don't like the feel of a towel piled on top of my head. It's heavy and cumbersome, and it makes me feel like I'm about to fall over. Instead, I pick up the other towel off the counter and dry the ends.

"The hair on your head is still wet," she points out. "Unless you dry all of it and wrap it up."

I shrug my shoulders. "Can we *not* discuss this now? I have enough on my mind."

She smiles and comes over, squeezing my shoulders a little.

"C'mon," she whispers into my ear. "I'm just trying to distract you a little. I know that you're a ball of nerves."

I nod and give her a little smile. I take a moment to collect my thoughts after she undresses and gets into my shower.

What should I wear?

It's getting dark, but the weather is just as humid and warm as it was earlier this afternoon. I don't know what I'm walking into so whatever I wear, I have to be comfortable. Nothing that pinches me or digs in anywhere. At the same time, it should be flattering.

The shoes are the easiest decision. I only brought three pairs: beige wedges, flip-flops, and sneakers. I wore the wedges to the party last night, and while they are agreeable enough, they make me feel a little bit too fancy. I know that Sydney will protest, but I'm going go with the flip-flops.

I turn my attention to my clothes. I could go with the leggings again, but they left me quite sweaty at the party. No, I need something that will let some of the breeze through. Luckily, I brought a short dark blue dress with cap sleeves. It looks nice for a dinner out, but paired with the flip-flops, it has an easy going, casual feel to it.

"You look beautiful," Sydney says, coming out of the bathroom. I smile and mouth thank you. I am glad that she does not make me second-guess my outfit more than I already am.

My hair is still damp by the time it's almost seven, but I don't blow dry it. The strands around my face make loose, beachy waves that are actually quite pretty. I do take a moment to reapply my eyebrow tint, a fresh coat of eyeshadow, another swatch of the eye liner, and the mascara. I finish my look off with a peach-colored lipstick that glistens in poor light.

"Good luck," Sydney whispers. "I'll be waiting on pins and needles to hear what happens."

She takes my hand in hers and gives me a little squeeze. My stomach makes a loud rumbling sound and I cover it to try to calm my nerves.

"It's going to be fine," she adds. "Trust me."

We promised each other that we would stop making promises that we can't keep a while ago, but I'm glad that she breaks it.

I walk down the path away from my cottage with trepidation.

I see the gazebo in the distance, in front of the house. There are lights strung up around it, and I try to remember if they were there last night.

As I get closer, I see the outline of a man leaning on the railing. As I get closer, the path turns from dirt to large flat stones. My flip-flops make a loud smacking sound with each step and Nicholas hears me approach.

"I am glad you came," he says, extending his hand toward mine and helping me up the step into the gazebo.

"Thank you," I say breathlessly, mainly as a result of my nerves.

I feel his eyes moving slowly up and down my body. There's an intensity to them, the kind that is difficult to describe. It's almost as if he were looking straight through me, through my clothes, through every armor that I put up, and into my very core.

I look at him in return.

Dressed in a black slim fitted suit, his legs look long and

toned. The collar of his white shirt is starched and his tie has a tiny asymmetrical design to it.

The jacket is buttoned in the front. His shoulders are broad and his hands are back in his pockets.

The man I met at the beach, the surfer, and the man who came to my door last night seemed to have vanished completely. But then he runs his fingers along his jaw just like he did last night and I see a glimpse of him.

When a strand of hair that has been slicked back breaks free and falls into his eyes, I see another.

"I wanted to thank you again for accepting my gift," he begins.

His words are confident, strong, sharp.

"Of course, I wanted to thank you for being so generous. I mean, that's a lot of money."

"Not for me," he says without a trace of hesitation in his voice. "I wanted you to have it."

I give him a slight nod.

"Now, let us discuss what you can do to repay your debt," he says.

18

WHEN HE ASKS ME...

I TAKE a step away from him. The floorboard creaks under my left foot. The chirping of insects gets louder along with the heartbeat pounding near my temples.

"What do you mean?" I ask.

My whole body starts to tremble so I lean back on the railing for support.

"I did you a favor and now I would like you to do something for me," he says. His eyes meet mine. Suddenly, there's a coldness in them. A darkness even, one that I have never seen before.

Of course. How could I be so stupid?

No one does anything for anyone without wanting anything in return.

He didn't just find me sitting next to a gas station and

give me a buck out of his pocket. He sought me out. He did research on exactly how much I needed.

"I thought you said that the check was a gift," I remind him.

"It is." Nicholas' eyes narrow, looking into the distance over the ink-black water.

I pull my eyes away from his and look out into the abyss before us. The moon illuminates the crescents of the waves with its cool light, but only a little bit.

Suddenly, I see a fin. One followed by another. The dolphins dive in and out of the water making a high-pitched giddy sound that makes me smile.

"I've never seen dolphins before," I admit.

"You should come out here to this spot in the mornings. You'll see dolphins, whales, birds..." he says, letting his words trail off at the end.

When he turns his body toward mine, I know that the sightseeing portion of the evening is over.

"If something is a gift then it doesn't have any strings attached," I say.

"You don't even know what I am going to ask you to do," he challenges.

His tie gets bunched up a bit, so he unbuttons the two buttons of his jacket and straightens it.

"I don't want to even hear about it if it's something illegal," I say.

"It's not."

I clench my jaw. I feel my reasons for saying no starting to disappear.

"Why did you send me this money? How did you even know that I needed it? Did you hire a private investigator to study me?"

"Which one of those questions do you want answered first?" he asks smugly. I cross my arms around my chest and wait.

"You'd be amazed what you can find out about someone with a good private investigator, but I didn't need that. All I had to do was run your credit score. They showed all of your debt. A lot debt."

I catch myself slouching, so I straighten my back out in defiance.

"Yes, I know that I had a lot of debt. I wanted to get a good education. So what?" I ask.

"You didn't have to accept my gift," he says, leaning back on the railing.

He has me there.

Now, I wish I hadn't.

I'm about to say something else, but he puts up his arm to stop me.

"Okay, do you want to hear what I have to say or do you want to argue with me?" he asks.

I give him a brief nod.

"I paid off your debt, every last penny," he starts. "Now, I want you to do something for me."

I wait.

"I want you to spend 365 days and nights with me," he says slowly and deliberately. "Live with me. Go everywhere I go. Business trips. Dinners with clients. You will act charming and happy to be there. The people I deal with will have to like you. A lot. Some will have to want you."

I hear all of the words that he says but my mind focuses on only one of them: nights.

"What do you mean by I have to spend 365 *nights* with you?" I ask.

"Exactly that."

"I won't have sex with you," I say categorically.

"You don't have to," Nicholas says, his eyes challenging mine. "But I promise you one thing. You will be begging me to do it before our time is up."

The words send shivers through my body, the good kind.

My tongue touches the roof of my mouth and it takes actual effort to not let it lick my lips.

I hate to admit it, but one of the reasons I even came here tonight is because of how incredibly sexy I find him.

If he were a lot older or not so attractive, I'd probably find this proposal absurd and degrading.

But with him, I feel this chemical pull toward him.

"I don't understand why you need me to do this," I say after a moment. "I mean, couldn't you hire someone to be your girlfriend instead?"

"Isn't that exactly what I'm doing?" He tosses his hair out of his eyes, flashing a crooked smile.

"But why me?"

I ask. "Why fly a total stranger across six thousand miles to ask her to do this?"

He opens his mouth just a little bit, pressing his tongue on his lower lip. That's when it occurs to me. We are not strangers at all. He has to know me.

"How do you know me?" I ask.

Now, it's his turn to look down at the floor. Now, it's his turn to hesitate.

"You have to tell me or I won't even entertain this offer," I threaten even though I don't think that I'm really in the position to *not* consider it.

Nicholas looks up at me.

His irises grow big and dark.

He straightens his broad shoulders and folds one of his hands into a fist.

I don't know how but I sense that I'm in no danger from being with him, he's just trying to keep the anger building up in him at bay.

"You owe me a debt, Olive," he says slowly. "I don't have to explain anything to you beyond stating the terms of how you can repay it."

"I know," I concede. "I just want to know why me."

A moment passes without him saying a word. Then another. The first feels like a decade while the second feels like a century.

"If I tell you, you have to promise to not tell anyone about this," Nicholas finally says. "Not Sydney, not anyone."

I think about it and then say, "I promise."

19

WHEN I REMEMBER...

THERE's a bench that goes around the perimeter of the gazebo and Nicholas takes a seat. He points to a place next to him and I sit down as well.

"When we used to know each other, my name was Nicky Reed," he says. "That's my biological father's last name."

I search my memory for anyone with that last name, but nothing comes to mind.

"Do you remember a girl named Ashley Price?" he asks.

Thin, scrawny, with long red hair that she used to wear in braids like Laura Ingalls from *Little House on the Prairie*. The kids in my middle school used to tease her mercilessly for her crooked teeth and her freckled face.

I stood up for her when I could, but if you take

someone's side too much in middle school the powers that rule, the popular seventh grade girls, can quickly turn against you as well. I devised another plan: we would pretend that we had work to do at the library and hide out there during lunch. Technically, eating wasn't allowed in the library but we could eat our sandwiches if we were really quiet.

"Ashley moved away when we were fifteen in the middle of the year," I say. "We were really close but she never told me that she was leaving. I was shocked when I heard that from one of the teachers."

"Our mom made her go live with our distant cousins in Mississippi because she got pregnant," Nicholas says.

Something that sounds like a helicopter taking off makes my head pound. My thoughts ping-pong back and forth between two revelations. One is that my childhood friend, Ashley, is related to this man standing before me. Two, Ashley got pregnant. I'm not sure which one to start asking about first, but my mouth has a mind of its own.

"We knew everything about each other," I say. "Ashley wasn't dating anyone. I would be the first person to know if she had a boyfriend. She wasn't even into boys. She thought she liked this girl in our math class."

I remember the exact moment when Ashley told me about having a crush on Christy. Her face turned two shades paler than usual and her whole body was shaking. She cracked her knuckles over and over again and said that she had to tell me something but she was afraid of losing me as a friend. I had no idea what she could tell me but I promised to be there for her no matter what. And I was.

"You only knew what Ashley wanted you to know," Nicholas says. "Our mother's husband, our stepfather, had been molesting her for months. And then he raped her. She was terrified of telling our mom because she knew she would blame her for seducing him."

My mouth drops open. Why didn't she tell me? She could've come to live with me. I could've protected her.

As if he can read my mind, Nicholas answers, "She didn't tell anyone until...later. She found out she was pregnant and she was terrified of both our stepfather and our mother. I tried to be there for her, but I spent most of my youth on the streets trying to get myself out of that house. Plus, she kept everything in this vault around her. She never told me anything until..."

The words are difficult for him to say.

I wait for him to gather his strength to continue. But he doesn't. Instead, he just looks away into the distance.

"What happened?" I whisper under my breath.

"Mom kicked her out of the house and sent her to Mississippi to live with not very nice people. She wanted to get an abortion, but she didn't know anyone there, didn't have a car, or money. She was all alone and scared to death."

"Why didn't she reach out to me?" I ask, tears are starting to build up in the back of my eyes. I don't know what happened yet but I can sense that it was something terrible.

"If I had known any of this before...I would have helped her. She was my sister but she kept it all from me. I didn't even know about the pregnancy. Mom just said that she was going to Mississippi to visit Mom's cousins," he says. "I should've asked why. I should've demanded some answers, but I was never really home. I hung around a bad group of guys and did anything I could to survive."

I nod.

"But it's no excuse. And not a day goes by that I don't think about..."

There is something he is not saying. It's the reason why I haven't heard from Ashley in all of these years. The lump in the back of my throat gets bigger.

I slide a few inches closer to him and take his hand in mine. I don't know if I'm doing it to comfort him or to comfort myself.

"Tell me," I say, giving him a squeeze.

Nicholas looks down at the floor.

His hair falls over his eyes.

Without letting my hand go, he says, "Ashley killed herself two days after she arrived in Mississippi. She hung herself in a closet while everyone else was watching TV in the living room of that trailer."

The ground starts to shift under my feet. I focus my eyes, but they get cloudy with tears.

"What do you mean?" I whisper even though he couldn't be any clearer.

"She sent me a long email explaining everything that had happened. Everything that she never told me," Nicholas says, looking up at me. "Our stepfather coming into her room at night when she was eleven. Mom getting drunk and then waking her up in the middle of the night and punching her to make herself feel better. The rape. The pregnancy. Mom finding out and calling her a slut for sleeping with her husband. Mom calling her a murderer for not wanting to keep her baby. Mom sending her away to live with strangers. The cousin's husband making sexual jokes about her body after her being there for less than an hour. Being horrified of being forced to give birth."

"Oh my God," I say under my breath, covering my mouth with my hand.

"Her email was like a long confession of everything that she had been keeping bottled up. At the end she wrote, *I hope this explains why I'm going to do this*. And then she hung herself."

I shake my head in disbelief.

"I was partying that night," Nicholas says. "I was drunk and high like I was every night back then, trying to deal with my own shitty upbringing in the only way I knew how. So, I didn't find out what she'd done until the next day. But by then, it was too late."

20

WHEN I TRY TO FORGET...

NICHOLAS and I sit there for some time, each trying to process our own grief. I bury my head in my hands and try to keep my tears at bay but they just keep coming. After a few moments, I give up trying. Ashley was my best friend and one day she just stopped going to school. I called her phone, I called her house, I talked to her mom. Her mom said that she thought I knew because they'd all moved away, but that was a lie. Whenever we spent time together, we either went out to a local fast food restaurant, the library or, on occasion, to my house. I was always embarrassed to invite her to my place, but she said that there was no way we could go to hers.

After her mom told me that they had moved away, I should've gone to her house. But I didn't even know where she lived.

Still, I should've tried to look her up.

I should've done some research.

Someone must have known something.

But I didn't.

I was devastated and I missed her and I was a kid.

The thing about going through shit is that it makes you a very self-centered person. We were friends but we never really confided in each other the way we should have.

I could've been there for her, had she just opened up to me a little bit. And given what she had been through, I now know that she could've been there for me as well.

Instead, we just orbited each other.

Never really letting one another in.

"What happened after that?" I ask, my tears still wet on my cheeks.

"My mother said she got what she deserved," Nicholas says, moving his jaw around from one side to another. "She refused to pay for her body to be transported back to Massachusetts. She said that our family didn't believe in suicide."

His words ring in my ears.

Didn't believe in suicide?

What is there to believe in? It happens. People do it all the time.

Is it an option for some people? Unfortunately, yes.

Could it have been prevented had Ashley had a different mother? A different stepfather? A better best friend. Most definitely.

"How do you know me?" I ask Nicholas.

"We met once, in passing. I gave you two a ride back from school," he says.

That doesn't seem like enough of a reason to do any of this. I wait for more.

"She wrote about you in my email," he says. "She told me not to blame myself for anything that she did. She said that there was nothing I could do to help her, but if I still wanted to help someone, I should help you."

My heart begins to pound and then to swell.

"After that I got clean. I got on my feet and I've been checking up on you over the last couple of years," Nicholas says. "You are actually doing really well."

"Thank you," I mumble, through the tears running down my cheeks.

My friend's dying wish was for her brother to help me. The clarity that she must've had at that moment is difficult for me to imagine, even now.

I'm no longer a teenager and I don't have anywhere near that kind of understanding.

Yet, she still decided to end her life. Why? Didn't she know that things would get better?

Teenagers don't have the experience of years to know that it's possible to go through a lot and still live a happy life. Life is long. Full of many ups and downs. Things get worse and then they get better.

"I didn't know how I could help you, but then I saw the loans that you had. I was in the position to help and I'd made a promise to my dead sister. So I did."

"But now you say that I owe you a debt," I say, challenging his interpretation of his charity.

The expression on his face changes. The pain that existed only a few seconds ago gets buried somewhere deep inside.

A coldness appears.

His gaze turns to ice.

"I was in the position to help you and now you are in the position to help me," he says.

"Three hundred and sixty-five days is a long time," I say. "I have a job."

"You will be compensated handsomely."

I wait for him to say a number, but he doesn't. I feel myself drawn to him. Yes, my heart beats a little faster in his company. Yes, my palms get a little sweatier. But it's more than on just a physical level. There's something more to this. My thoughts return to Ashley.

"Why do you need me to come with you on your trips?" I ask, realizing that I don't even really know what he does for a living.

"That's my business," he says.

"Where will we go?"

"Not sure yet, but you will need your passport."

I've never been abroad. I don't even know how to apply for one. But I've always dreamed of traveling.

Am I actually entertaining this offer?

Why?

Ashley.

She brought us together. She forged this connection between us. It's not just Nicholas that I owe this debt to. I owe it to her, too. I should've been there for her and I wasn't. Perhaps, now I can do this to make some sort of amends.

Nicholas gets up and looks at the moon above.

This is a crazy thing to do: spend a year with a man I hardly know.

And for what?

What would be the point?

I stand up and lean on the railing next to him.

Our shoulders are so close they are almost touching. I look at the way the collar of his shirt makes an almost perfectly parallel line to his razor sharp jaw.

"What do you mean that I will be handsomely compensated?" I ask.

"Did you think that the almost one hundred and sixty-eight thousand was a generous amount?" Nicholas asks.

"Of course."

"Do you have any reason to believe that I would not be equally generous if you were to do this for me?" he asks.

I shrug.

This conversation is going in loops and is giving me a headache.

"I don't know what you mean," I say. "I didn't even know that there was any money in this deal."

"There is," he says cryptically.

"Look." I turn to face him. "I can't just give up my life for a year if I don't know what I'm getting into. I can't just give up my job, my apartment, my whole existence. ... for what exactly?"

"You owe me this," Nicholas says without any affection in his voice.

"You gave me a gift," I remind him.

"Then you owe Ashley."

Anger rises up deep within me. It bursts up to the surface and I taste bile on the back of my throat.

"Fuck you!" I yell at him.

A droplet of spit leaves my mouth and lands on his cheek.

I don't wait for a response.

I turn around and walk away.

There is nothing for me to consider.

There is no way I'm going to do anything he asks. Or demands.

Who the hell does he think he is?

He made a promise to Ashley to help me and he did.

I accepted his help.

From the looks of this place, the money he sent me did not put him into the poorhouse. I doubt that it even made a dent in his bank account.

"I will pay you a million dollars," Nicholas says.

21

WHEN WE LEAVE...

WHEN I GET to my cottage, I immediately start to pack my bag. I should not have ever come here. I need to get off this property as quickly as possible. I pick up my phone to call a ride share, or a cab, but the reception is terrible and I can barely get online.

My heart beats loudly, drowning out the thoughts spinning in my head. Nicholas wants to pay me a million dollars to spend a year with him.

A million dollars.

Is he insane, or am I?

Who the hell would pay someone that much and for what exactly? And how the hell is that a way for him to repay his debt to his dead sister?

Ashley.

The last time I saw her, she was spinning around with

her arms up to the sky as rain fell on top of her. We were both laughing, the kind of infectious laugh that is both contagious and consuming. I don't remember what was so funny, but I do remember the peculiar way that the asphalt smelled as late afternoon steam rose off it.

How could that girl kill herself? She was so happy.

I shouldn't have ever taken a week off from work. I should have never unpacked my bags or hung my clothes in the closet. I should have never planned to stay here for such a long time.

What was I thinking?

It's obvious, of course. I've never been to Maui. This was the opportunity of a lifetime to see the world outside of eastern Massachusetts.

As I toss Sydney's dress into my suitcase, folding it in the middle and then rolling it into a baguette, another *shouldn't have* thought crystalizes.

I *shouldn't* have ever taken his money.

I owed a debt to the government, or rather three private companies that were servicing my debt on the government's behalf. I would pay thousands in interest over the lifetime of the loans, and if I couldn't make the payments, I would go into default.

My credit score would drop. I would have to pay a much higher interest rate for a car, were I to ever want to buy another one again. I would probably never be able to get a mortgage and buy a house.

People who spent a hundred thousand or more at casinos and financed their addictions by putting it all on their credit cards could declare bankruptcy. It would ruin their credit for only seven years, after that everything went back to normal. All debt was forgiven and it was like nothing ever happened.

But when it came to student loans, the government took another position. Congress made sure that no such opportunity existed. They wrote it into the law. You go bankrupt with any type of debt except student loans.

Still, I should not have taken his money.

It's a gift but not really. I have no idea what kind of business Nicholas is involved in, but I've seen enough movies. On this trip he asked me to spend the year with him. *But is it really a request?*

When I said no, he offered to pay me a million dollars.

Again, I said no.

What about next time?

When is he going to stop asking?

My heart jumps into my throat. No, I'm not going to wait around and find out.

I throw my bag across my body, grab my suitcase, and walk over to Sydney's cottage.

"I was waiting for you..." She opens the door, the excited expression on her face vanishing.

"We have to go," I say.

"What happened?" Sydney asks, shaking her head.

"Pack your things, we have to get out of here."

"Tell me what happened," she insists, sitting down on her bed.

I walk past her to the bathroom and start throwing all of her makeup and beauty products into the large bag sitting on the counter.

"What are you doing?" She runs up to stop me.

"We can't stay here. Pack your shit and I'll tell you on the way."

Finally, something seems to get through.

Without another word of protest, she packs all of her things. The reception is better in her cottage and our ride share arrives right when she finishes.

The mobile app says that it's going to cost $149 to get us to the airport, but I'm just thankful that there's even a driver available in the proximity to drive us all the way back there.

When we climb into the car, Sydney asks if I had checked the flights. "Are there even any flights going out tonight?"

I bite the inside of my cheek.

No, I did not.

I look down at my phone: no service. I probably won't have any cell reception for another hour if not more.

"We'll figure something out," I say. "We can even stay at a hotel by the airport if necessary."

Sydney exhales slowly.

"Are you going to tell me what happened?"

I pick at the plastic cover on my cell phone. My nails feel soft and limp from the tropical humidity. I find a weak spot on one and peel off the dry polish.

I've bitten my nails since I was a kid and only recently figured out a way to cope with that. I pull out Nail Growth Miracle, the thick clear nail polish that makes my nails thick. I quickly apply a few coats to the nail on the ring finger that I just scratched off. Something about its thick texture curbs my need to bite and pick during stressful situations, at least temporarily.

"Olive? What the hell did he do?" Sydney whispers. "Did he hurt you?"

I shake my head.

"Should we go to the police?"

"No," I say.

"So, what the hell are we doing?"

I glance in the direction of the driver. "I can't tell you *now*. I'll explain everything when we get there."

But Sydney is not satisfied with waiting. She points to her phone and mouths, text me.

I focus on the keys, trying to figure out where to start. The texts won't go through but that's probably a good thing. She'll just read them and then I'll delete them.

He asked me to stay here with him for a year. 365 days and nights.

I turn the phone toward her for her to read.

22

WHEN SHE REFUSES...

SHE STARES at the words for a long time, reading them over and over again.

Sex? Sydney types.

No. I shake my head, trying to remember exactly how he had phrased it.

He said I wouldn't have to do anything I wouldn't want to, but he promised me that I will be begging him to do it before our time is up.

Sydney's mouth drops open.

"What the fuck?" she asks.

Why does he want you to do this? She types.

He said I owe him a debt. For him paying off my loans.

But that was a gift. Sydney types.

I shrug. I debate whether I should tell her about

Ashley, but that seems like an impossible thing to get into over text.

What about your job?

He offered me $1 million to do this.

"What?" Sydney gasps.

I nod.

Why?

"I don't know," I say. It's not exactly a lie.

I don't know why he wants me to do this. He already paid his debt to Ashley by helping me. What exactly is this going to accomplish?

What does he want you to do? Sydney types.

Accompany him on his business trips. Maybe flirt with potential clients. He said I will need a passport.

Like an escort?

I guess, but no sex, I remind her.

Maybe he's really into you?

I shrug and type, *We just met.*

This doesn't make sense.

I know.

"So, why are we leaving?" Sydney asks after a moment.

Did he do something to scare you? She adds in a text.

I shrug and type, *Yeah, kind of. I refused his offer. He then offered me money. I got the feeling that it wasn't really an offer I should refuse. I didn't know what was going to happen next. I needed to leave.*

She nods.

You don't agree? I ask.

Doesn't seem like a bad offer to me, she types, adding a smiling emoji.

I roll my eyes. She wasn't there. She doesn't know how it felt. Besides, she doesn't know the whole story.

FINALLY, we arrive at the airport. I pay the driver the fare and the tip through the app and he puts our bags on the curb.

We don't have tickets and I wasn't sure which terminal to instruct him to go to, so I asked him to drop us off at the same airline which we used to fly here. There isn't a soul outside, and there is only one ticket agent at the far left corner.

As we walk over, Sydney buries her face in her phone.

"There are no more flights tonight," she says. "I really wish I had checked before you dragged me to the no service zone."

"I'm sorry but I really needed to get out of there," I say. "Let me just ask the ticket agent."

Sydney grabs my arm. Her irises are dilated and her eyes look cold.

"I followed you here because I thought that something bad had happened. I thought you were hurt."

"I was scared."

"So, he made you this offer. So what? You can say no."

"I didn't want to stay there tonight."

"Did you think that something would happen?" She challenges me.

I want to lie to put her mind at ease but I can't bring myself to do it.

"No, but the conversation we had...it wasn't...normal."

"Tell me everything," she says.

Still holding on to the handle of my suitcase with my crossover bag resting on my thighs, I tell her everything.

I tell her how he knows me.

I tell her about Ashley.

I tell her about her suicide and his promise to her.

Her death is still raw inside of me and I glance up at the unforgiving bright lights above to keep my tears at bay.

Sydney puts her bag down and places her purse on top of it. I know what she's about to ask me so I jump ahead.

"At some point, I got this feeling in the back of my neck that made my hair stand up. You know? There isn't any logical reason for it but it's your body telling you that something is wrong. That you're in danger. That's when I decided to leave."

"Just like that?" Sydney asks.

I narrow my eyes and focus in on hers. Her face is expressionless and impossible to read.

"I didn't want to be one of those women who is found lying in a ditch somewhere because she didn't listen to her intuition," I say, walking away from her.

A lump in the back of my throat grows bigger and bigger and I begin to sob. I'm angry and disappointed that she doesn't believe me, but I know myself well enough to realize that the tears are also a result of exhaustion. I haven't slept well the whole time we were here and anytime I am not well-rested I am more susceptible to emotional waterfalls.

"Olive, I'm sorry." Sydney catches up to me before I can get to the ticket agent. "I didn't mean to make you feel bad. I'm just...disappointed."

I nod.

I know how much she has been enjoying this trip and James, in particular.

She must be torn between wanting to be my friend, and to listen to my crazy intuition, and staying here a little bit longer for her.

"Are you crying?" she asks, putting her arm around me.

"It's nothing. I'm just really tired and exhausted."

"Yeah, you need some sleep," she says.

"I'll get some sleep on the plane," I say. "We both will."

She doesn't say anything in response. I look up at her. When our eyes meet, I know.

I shake my head. No, no, no. There must be something I can do to make her come.

"Please," I whisper.

Sydney tosses her hair out of her face.

"What are you going to do?" I ask.

"I'm going to get a hotel room and stay here until my return flight later this week," she says. "I'd like to see more of Maui and...James."

I nod.

"Stay with me," she pleads. "We can get an Airbnb together. He won't even have to know."

WEEKS LATER...

23

WHEN I WAIT...

I WATCH him start to undress me. The ground moves my feet, but it's my knees that are shaking. The temperature in the room goes up a few degrees. My breathing quickens.

I watch his fingers pick at my tank top. Nicholas slides one hand underneath. He runs his fingers over my torso, presses them against my stomach. They move up and down with each one of my breaths.

"Tell me to stop," he says.

My eyes look up to his. There's a fleck of gold in his irises that I never noticed before.

I don't want him to stop. I've waited too long for this. My mouth doesn't cooperate. The words don't form.

A strand of hair falls into my eyes. I try to blow it away, but it comes back again and again. Nicholas reaches over and tucks it in with the rest of my hair between my head and pillow.

He runs his fingers up my left arm, tickling me slightly. He checks on the silk tie holding my wrist in place. It's still tight.

"Tell me to stop," Nicholas said earlier when he led me here.

"Tell me to stop," he said when he fastened my arms to the headboard.

"Tell me to stop," he says now when he lifts up my shirt. He waits for my answer. Again, I say nothing and let him pull it up to my collarbone.

He unties my left wrist and slides the shirt over my head and onto the other side.

Now, I lay topless before him. My breathing speeds up. My heart pounds so loudly inside my head I feel like I'm going to go deaf.

Nicholas presses his lips onto my skin and slowly makes his way toward my nipples. When he takes one into his mouth, my skin gets covered in goosebumps. A fire starts to build in the core of my body. My legs open on their own.

"Not yet," he says, pushing them closed again.

But my hips don't listen. They move up and down to their own rhythm.

"Tell me to stop," Nicholas whispers, taking my nipple in between his teeth, and biting on it ever so lightly.

I flex my toes to keep the explosion at bay. I've waited so long for this. I can't let it consume me before he's inside of me.

"You are so beautiful," he whispers, looking at my body.

Whatever insecurities I felt about it a few moments ago disappear and I suddenly see myself through his eyes.

My curves are round and voluptuous.

My stomach is soft, but strong. My breasts are round and voluminous.

I watch him admire my body and I can't help but admire his. But he's not naked yet. I want to run my fingers down his hard abs, but he's still wearing a t-shirt and my hands are tied.

I reach my head out to kiss him. He flinches away for a moment, and then presses his lips onto mine. They are soft and powerful. He takes my mouth with his. His tongue quickly finds mine and the tingling sensation in between my legs makes my back arch.

"Take off your clothes," I say through his kiss. "I want to see you."

He smiles, pulling away from me. The trance that existed only a few moments before is broken, along with the kiss.

Nicholas furrows his brow and gives me one shake of his head. No.

Sitting up on the bed, he touches the top button of my jeans.

"Tell me to stop," he says.

"No, no, no," I whisper, tilting my head back.

After unzipping my jeans, he pulls them off in one swift motion. I want my panties to come off, too. I open my legs to help him along but instead of pulling them off, he nestles his body in between and pulls my underwear to one side.

I stop breathing and wait. For his tongue. For his fingers. For his dick. For anything to touch me.

"Tell me to stop," he says.

"No," I exhale.

Nicholas runs his fingers over my thighs, toying with me. Teasing me. He's getting off on this.

Before I agreed to spend a year with him, I thought I would spend the year pushing him away.

I thought he would make his moves and I would stay strong. I never knew that I would want him this much. I never knew that he would be stronger than I am.

My hips move up and down with each invisible concentric circle that he draws on the inside of my thighs. My body is begging for him. Pleading. Now, my mouth has to do the same.

"C'mon," I say.

"What?" Nicholas smiles. "What did you say?"

I kiss him again. He squeezes my nipple and I open my legs. He presses his lips onto the outside of my breast. I flex my toes and hold my breath.

"I need you inside of me," I whisper.

"You have to beg me," he whispers back. "Remember?"

I lift my head off the pillow and look at him.

"I made you a promise. I intend on keeping it," he says, smiling out of the corner of his lips.

"What do you mean?"

"Unless you plead, and I mean, really beg, it's not going to happen."

"I don't believe you," I say, challenging him. He shrugs, continuing to run his fingers up my thighs just close enough before pulling away.

He wants me as much as I want him. There's no way he could say no to me. I lean over to him and start to kiss him again. But he pulls away.

"I'm sorry," he says. "It's not going to happen tonight."

My mouth drops open.

"Are you going to beg?" he asks. His eyes twinkle as he speaks, making me even more aroused.

"No," I say firmly.

"I'm sorry to hear that," he says, reaching over to the headboard and untying my wrists.

TODAY...

24

WHEN I SEE HER AGAIN...

THE ONLY TICKET that I can afford, and that's using the word liberally, is five hours later in coach with two stops. My seat is narrow and cramped and everything including a glass of water comes at an additional charge. Since the ticket is so last minute, it costs close to $1300. I put it on my credit card, knowing that I will have to pay this horrible flight off for the next year.

Despite the tiny seat, the three dollar bottle of water, the passengers next to me who take up both of my arm rests, I fall into a peaceful and deep sleep. I only wake up when the wheels touch the ground in Los Angeles. I get to my next flight in a daze, take another brief nap during my two hour layover and then fall into another trance on the next flight to Chicago.

My layover there is five hours and I spend the time reading standing in the airport bookstore before grabbing a croissant and a tall black coffee from Starbucks. It is only on my final leg over to Logan

International that I begin to feel somewhat normal again. Everything that happened in Hawaii seems like a bad dream. Maybe it all happened to someone else. Perhaps, it's even something that happened in a Netflix binge.

When I drop my bags on the floor of my apartment, Sydney's not here. I realize that Maui was not a dream. I head straight to my bedroom, take off my jacket and boots, and climb into bed. I sleep for the next twelve hours and when I wake up Sydney is still not here.

I TOOK a week off work for this trip and there are still a number of days left. I stay in bed until I can't stay here anymore and then I force myself to go outside. Walking along Boston Commons, I watch a duck making a zigzag pattern across the water. She darts back and forth before floating up to the edge where a little girl throws crumbs into the water.

Maybe I've been too hasty.

Maybe I shouldn't have made my decision on so little sleep.

Maybe I should've just got a hotel room by the airport with Sydney and enjoyed the rest of my vacation.

When will I ever be in Maui again? Probably never.

The girl makes a sudden move and the duck quickly

swims away. No matter how much she wants the bread, she can't risk getting hurt.

Just like the girl, Nicholas didn't make any threats.

But when he said he would pay me the million dollars, I had to leave. It felt too dangerous to stay and my intuition is all I had.

Don't second-guess yourself, I say silently. You wouldn't have enjoyed the trip if you would've stayed the rest of the week. You would've been looking over your shoulder the whole time. That's no way to take a vacation.

My phone vibrates.

I look at the screen hoping that it's a text from Sydney telling me what a big mistake I made leaving. Maybe it's even a selfie of the happy couple smiling on top of a volcano. But I'm wrong.

I'm in trouble.

It's my mother. She has been blowing up my phone ever since I left. I wrote her back once saying that I am no longer coming back to see her, and I've resisted the urge to reply each time she texts.

I NEED YOUR HELP.

HER OTHER MESSAGES were pleas and exaggerations.

Most filled up almost the entire screen. All told me how much she missed me while at the same time telling me how terrible of a daughter I am. But these two catch my attention.

This doesn't sound like her. Of course, she could be using another angle to get to me. I could be falling for it all over again.

I put the phone down on the bench next to me.

I try to ignore it.

She's not my problem anymore. She's mean and full of hatred. She just wants to control me. She has money coming in from her social security and it's enough to live on. She can get around by herself and if I'm not there to abuse, then she'll just have to be nicer to the nurses that will come by (also paid by the government) and not drive them out by screaming profanities.

I pick up the phone again and click on the News app. I scroll through the headlines mindlessly as if reading the news has ever made anyone feel any better about anything.

I need to talk to you. I owe a lot of money.

My mother's texts come in as a notification on top of the screen. I read it before I can stop myself.

Despite my better judgement, I grab the keys and drive to her house. I arrive there without texting her back. She

lives in a peeling row house in Charlestown, the oldest
area of Boston. The Irish Mob used to run this place in
the sixties and seventies but now parts of it are a desirable
neighborhood with many hip city moms pushing their
strollers around to yoga studios and coffee shops.

Charlestown is a lot less gentrified than other parts of
the city, still making it relatively affordable. Of course,
it still has dilapidated apartment buildings where the
landlords don't keep up with repairs because the
renters have no better options. Mom lives in one of
these buildings. My brothers and I grew up in countless
of these apartments, all in Charlestown and all shitty in
their own ways.

Different layouts, same scenery.

Different streets. Same heating and plumbing
problems.

Different neighbors. Same school district with metal
detectors in the front.

When I walk into her narrow living room, I look
around at the piles of cardboard boxes and trash that
she's generated since the last time I was here. The place
stinks of old pizza and rotting food. I fight the urge to
clean. That's *not* what I'm here for.

"Ma, it's me!" I yell.

Ever since high school, I have fought hard to get rid of
my nasal Boston drawl, but being here in her presence,

her name comes out as a mush without any final sounds.

I brace myself for a slew of hurtful remarks and name calling but instead her whole face lights up when she sees me.

"Thank you for coming," she says, putting down the glass she had been using to water the plants on the windowsill.

25

WHEN I FIND OUT...

I'VE NEVER SEEN my mom like this before.

I have seen her passed out on the floor covered in her own vomit after a night of drinking and partying. I have seen her writhing around in pain after her doctor cut off her opioid prescription and before I could get her a few pills from a dealer at the corner. I have seen her consumed with tears and pain, wailing and banging on Patrick's casket before it went into the ground.

The look she has today is one of total detachment. Her eyes are glassy and stare somewhere into the distance behind me. While they are usually quick to meet mine and make me cower, this time they barely make eye contact.

"What's going on?" I put my arm around her. "Ma?"

"I thought that this time I would win for sure," she finally says. "I was certain of it."

"What? What do you mean?"

She picks up the cup of coffee off the windowsill and picks at the W in *World's Best Mom*. Patrick made her this cup when he was in elementary school and it's her most precious possession.

"What are you talking about, Mom?" I ask.

She nods toward the iPad. I turn it on. I already know what she did, just not the extent of it.

Her favorite online poker room turns on. A pop-up urges me to put up more credit to play another hand.

"How much money did you lose?" I ask, holding my breath. I have to inhale before she answers.

"Thirty-thousand," she says slowly, chewing the words in her mouth as if they were one of her cigarette butts.

"Thirty-thousand dollars?" I gasp. "Oh, Ma. No."

"Yesterday," she says quietly.

I don't know if I heard her correctly.

"What are you talking about?"

"I heard from this forum that this one game was a sure thing. It was supposed to be rigged. It was a secret forum and only a few people knew about it. We all play together. We all share the profits."

I stare at her in disbelief.

I knew that my mom enjoyed gambling, going down to Atlantic City.

I knew she dreamed of going to Vegas someday, but I always thought that she just played the slots. Poker?

"We were going to make eighty each. But only if we all put in thirty. I didn't have the money," she says, looking out of the window. "My credit cards are all maxed out."

"What did you do?" I ask.

She shrugs. Rummaging through the pocket of her bathrobe, she pulls out a lighter and throws a cigarette in her mouth.

I wait for her to take a long drag.

"I had to ask Marlo for the money," she says, exhaling slowly.

She uses the word had as if there was no other choice. As if the sentence is as natural as *I need oxygen to breathe*.

A lump forms in the pit of my stomach.

"You didn't have to," I say.

"I did. This was a sure thing. We were all going to make money and I would be able to pay off all of my debts, including my medical bills."

The only problem is that whenever someone says something is a sure thing, it's not.

"What happened?"

"It worked. At first. But then the poker website found out about it," she says. Imagine that. "They closed our accounts. They didn't explain anything, they just sent me this form letter saying that my account is closed as a result of an irregularity."

That's one way to put it.

"Someone must've tipped them off. Maybe someone who lost money."

I look down at her hands. They are balled up in fists, with the whites of her knuckles showing.

"This shouldn't have happened," she insists. "We've done it before and it worked."

My mouth drops open.

"What do you mean?" I ask.

"We did it a week earlier. We each put in seven thousand. We each won twenty."

I don't know how the details of this particular scam work but I have a feeling it goes something like a normal pool hall hustle. A hustler comes in, loses a round, makes everyone around the table feel comfortable with the fact that they suck, and asks for another chance to win their money back. A false sense of security makes it impossible for the others to resist taking the sucker's money again. Only this time, the hustler wins. Big.

"Why Marlo?" I ask.

"I can't get any more credit. I haven't paid my minimal payments in months. You should see all of my past due bills," she says, defensively.

"Why didn't you make your payments?" I ask.

"I don't have any fucking money, Olivia!" Mom snaps.

I knew that she had medical bills but I didn't realize that her credit cards were maxed out. I didn't know things were this bad.

"You could've told me," I say quietly.

"I know everything that you have done for me. You've done enough," she says, shaking her head.

It's words like this that make me forgive her for every goddamn awful shitty thing that she has ever done or said to me. She buries her head in her hands. I wrap my arms around her.

"Why Marlo?" I repeat my question.

"Who else is there?" Mom shrugs, her shoulders slope down as she slides onto a rocking chair.

She's right. Around these parts, there is no one else.

Marlo is the Alpha and the Omega.

The First and the Last.

She's the Beginning and the End.

There used to a number of different bookies and organized crime bosses but as Marlo consolidated power, the others were either swept under her wing or taken out completely.

"So you borrowed thirty-thousand from her?" I confirm.

"I borrowed more."

I take a deep breath and ask the question that has been sitting on the tip of my tongue the whole time I've been here.

"How much do you owe her?"

Mom looks down at the floor. Her stringy hair covers her face.

"Mom?" I prod.

"Fifty-thousand dollars," she says quietly.

26

WHEN I TRY TO FIGURE OUT
SOMETHING...

I've never seen Marlo before, but I've lived in this neighborhood long enough to know which rumors to believe and which to ignore.

She is charming and effervescent and likable and cruel and unforgiving. She has a long memory and likes to hold a grudge. The people who pay their debts, get a smile and a pat on the back, and an offer of another debt. The others?

Some are lucky to get away with a broken ankle or knee. After, they still pay the principle and the interest. Others, who can't pay at all, are never heard from again.

Mom never told me this, but Owen did. It was the night before he went to prison. He hung out with me that night, which was unusual, and drank too much, which wasn't. We sat and talked for a long time. After a while, he told me the truth about Dad.

I always thought that he just walked out on us one day. Got sick of fighting with Mom. Got sick of her yelling at him for spending his whole paycheck at the bar. But, according to Owen, Dad owed Marlo fifteen thousand dollars. He liked to bet on the ponies and, just like Mom, he heard that one was going to be a sure thing. The race would be fixed that day and this one horse was going to win.

Well, something happened, either he had the wrong intel or they lied to get him to bet big. He lost all of the money that he'd borrowed from Marlo. He couldn't pay her one week. He couldn't pay her another. On the third week, he went out for a carton of milk and never came back.

We called the police.

We filed a missing person's report.

His picture was on the 10 o'clock news that night.

But nothing came of any of that.

Mom told me that he just left and I believed her. Then Owen told me that Marlo had him killed. Either way he never came back again.

"Why do you owe her fifty instead of thirty?" I ask, trying to get the full grasp of what has happened.

"I already borrowed another twenty-thousand two days prior and lost it. I had no way to pay that off without going in on this," Mom says. "I thought I would be able to pay off the whole fifty when I won and still have thirty left over for my own bills."

"When do you have to pay?" I ask.

"Thursday."

"In two days?" I gasp.

She nods.

"I don't know what to do, Mom. I don't have this kind of money."

"I know you don't, but what about credit? You must have some credit."

I'd run over the credit card limits of my five cards. Two are maxed out and the other three only have a limit of three thousand each.

"I don't have anywhere near that amount."

"I don't know what to do, darling," she says.

I can't remember the last she called me that.

"Maybe you can...disappear? Go somewhere and lay low for a while. Until, this whole thing blows over," I say, thinking out loud.

"Where can I go? I don't have any money."

"It will take a lot less money for you to start your life somewhere else under another identity than to pay Marlo back," I say, with an idea starting to brew in my head.

"You always wanted to go out west. Texas. New Mexico. Arizona. Wherever. You can stay in cheap motels on your way out and then get a weekly rate somewhere far away. I can get some money together for a studio apartment for you. I can rent it under another name."

Yes, this is possible.

This isn't the end of the world. Or the end of her life.

Maybe that's what Dad should've done. Marlo has a big name and a lot of power around Boston, but that doesn't mean that she has enough connections or people to find someone hiding out in a dusty one-horse desert town near Tucson.

"It will take me a week or so but I can send you a fake driver's license, maybe even a passport. I will send you some money," I add.

Mom considers this. I take it as a good sign that she's even thinking about it because she has never been further away than New Jersey. She knows how to drive but hasn't had a car in years. And now she's actually contemplating driving alone across the country.

"What about my prescriptions? I have to go to my doctors every month to get them filled."

If there's something she can buy at those truck stops along the way it's opioids, but Mom has never made a drug deal in her life. She always left that kind of dirty work to her kids. Her diabetes medication gives me pause. That's going to be harder to find.

"I'll get you new identification," I say. "I know a guy who does really good work. You'll just have to tell them that you don't have insurance and pay for them out of pocket."

"What if the doctor discovers that I have a fake ID? What if the pharmacy does? Then they'll call the cops and the whole thing will be up."

Well, not exactly because the cops aren't exactly Marlo, but it's not going to make things easier.

"It's the only way I see around it, Mom. It's the only thing you can do."

It's a lie and I hope that my face doesn't betray that. It's not the only thing I can do. I can also call Nicholas. His offer will probably still be on the table. I can make this whole thing go away with one phone call.

But I'm tired of making sacrifices so that my mother can sit on her butt and do nothing. If she's really afraid of Marlo, I need to see it.

"I will get you more pills tonight. They will tide you over for a week or two," I say. "It will take you a few days of driving to get out there. I'll get you a new phone and you can call me and tell me where you are. I'll find you an apartment. Where do you want to go? Arizona? You've always wanted to see the Grand Canyon."

"No, there must be another way," she says, shaking her head.

"If you have one, I'm all ears," I say.

Mom looks up at me with her pleading doe eyes.

"What if you just go work for her?" she says. "She asked about you again."

27

WHEN SHE PUSHES ME...

I BITE MY TONGUE, trying to keep the anger boiling up inside of me from exploding to the surface. My hands ball into fists.

"Don't look at me like that," Mom says, raising her eyebrows. "You're not that innocent."

Beads of sweat soak into the shirt underneath my arms. How does she know?

"I don't want to embarrass you, honey," Mom says sweetly. I can almost taste the saccharine in her voice. "But, c'mon, would it be such a big deal? You are a pretty woman. New girls in the neighborhood always fetch good prices. You could have this worked off in two months tops."

My index finger runs over the knuckles of my other hand, feeling the smoothness of the taught skin over the cartilage.

I don't know the extent of what my mother knows about what happened back then.

Ashley had just left and an older girl from school befriended me. I never had money for anything, not like her. She didn't have rich parents, but she had the right shoes, the right jacket, the right jewelry. The only right thing I had was a leather jacket that I tried on in the store and walked out with, without paying.

Beyond all the material things, this girl also had Tyler, the right boyfriend, at least that's what I thought at the time. He drove a red BMW convertible with the roof down, even in the middle of a Boston winter. He smacked her on her butt and said funny things to her friends.

"I don't know why I have to tell you this, Mother, but I am not going to prostitute myself so that you can pay off your gambling debt," I say sternly.

"I came to you for help, Olive. I need your help."

"And I'm here for you."

"No, no, you're not," Mom says, shaking her head. "I can't just run away. I can't drive away from here and start my life somewhere else. My life is here."

"There are people who live elsewhere. You'll make new friends. This is what you have to do when you fuck up," I say. "You can't just have Owen and me clean up your shit all of your life. At some point, you'll have to grow up."

Mom looks frail sitting in her rocking chair.

When I was a child, I didn't think she was scared of anything. I thought that she was fearless because she was so mean. But now I know that what made her so mean was that she was afraid of her own shadow.

"Leaving the state will be good for you," I say. "You'll finally get to see the real world out there."

"You're talking to me as if you've ever been anywhere yourself," Mom says.

I shrug. "I'd like to."

"So, why don't you fucking go?"

"Because I have to babysit you. I have to be here cleaning up your vomit and your literal and metaphorical shit, Mom. Without getting anything so much as a thank you in return."

"You want a *thank you*, you ungrateful little bitch?" she asks. "For what exactly? I raised you for eighteen goddamn years. I changed your diapers. I wiped your snot. I rocked you to sleep. And I never even wanted you in the first place. Your *father* made me keep you. Your *father* was the one who wanted a girl. I never wanted you. I never wanted anyone but Patrick."

Her words are like slices of razor blades against my heart.

"Yes, we know that." I roll my eyes trying to keep my tears away.

Don't break down in front of her.

Don't do it, Olive.

Mom gets off her rocking chair and walks up to me. She stands so close to me I can hear her wheeze as she breathes.

"Listen to me," she says. "I am not going anywhere. This is my home. This is where I live. But *you*, you're going to do something for me."

I start to inhale, but she grabs me by my shirt and my body shuts down just like it used to when I was a kid.

"Your friend, Samantha, has moved up in the world. She's got a spot in Beacon Hill now, servicing senators, congressmen, and hedge fund managers. It's all discreet and you are the type of girl who is right up her alley. Educated. Without a trace of that accent that everyone tries to get away from. She gives her cut to Marlo but she pays her girls well. Real well. More than you get paid at that stupid job of yours."

After letting me go, Mom straightens my shirt with her hand.

"How do you know all of this?" I ask.

"People in this neighborhood like to talk. Especially her mom."

You'd think that nothing would surprise me now, but my mom's knowledge of Sam's business practices sends a shock wave through me.

My mouth drops open.

In high school, Sam met up with men in motel rooms and Tyler stayed out front making sure that she didn't get hurt. Even back then she had her sights on something bigger. I was the first girl she tried to recruit. She would take half of my fee in exchange for setting the whole thing up.

The one and only time I went to that seedy motel room on the outskirts of town was when we got evicted and I came home to find all of our belongings on the curb.

Mom never bothered to tell me that she hadn't paid the rent in months.

Instead, she just said to pack a bag and go stay with a friend. I called five of them, but the only one who took me in was Sam.

I was hungry, I had no money, and my college applications were due in a week.

A snowstorm was supposed to blanket all of New England with feet of snow in the coming days and the weekly rent at the motel was $250.

If I wanted a roof over my head so that I could finish my essays and get the applications in on time, I needed to take Sam up on her offer. She promised me $300 for a night's work.

"C'mon now, Olive. You never know, maybe you'll even make a connection with one of them. You are pretty easy on the eyes when you try even if you could stand to lose forty pounds. But some men like that kind of thing."

Mom's words come in one ear and go out another. I hear her but my mind is somewhere else.

I remember how much my body shook that time I walked up to the door.

My boots made a loud clinking sound on the pavement and the bracelets Sam made me wear jingled when I knocked.

My face was smothered in so much makeup that I could practically feel it caked on my skin. My lips tasted of chemical cherry lip gloss.

"You can work the appointments around your schedule," Mom says, taking my silence as acquiescence.

The guy who opened the door was a few years older than I was. He was a senior when I was a freshman, but I didn't know him well.

Even then I knew that Sam was just trying to break me in softly.

"Look, this isn't going to be that bad," she said. "He's not old or gross or a total stranger."

It worked for a moment and I walked inside. But then he came closer to me. All he had to do was touch my hair and I turned around and fled.

Luckily, the snowstorm caused power outages around the Northeast forcing the city to create additional shelters to provide temporary housing for everyone who lost heat. I got a cot and spent my week going to school and working on my essays, doing anything to take my mind off the path that I'd almost gone down.

I walk out of the room without saying a word.

"Where are you going?" Mom hollers after me.

"I'm not an escort. I'm not a prostitute, and I'm not a streetwalker. And if I were to ever have sex for money, I surely would never do it on your account."

She stares at me, dumbfounded. Grabbing my bag and walking out of the door, I add, "I told you what you can do to get out of this mess that you got yourself into. I told you how I would help you."

28

WHEN I SEE HIM AGAIN...

I SPEND the next two days trying not to think about what my mom had asked me to do for her. It would be a lie to not admit that there are moments when I waiver in my decision.

She may have asked me to prostitute myself, but she only did that because she is desperate.

Marlo is not someone you fuck around with.

She's not someone you *don't* pay your debts to.

Her request was insulting, but she only asked because she thinks I don't have any other options.

She doesn't know about Nicholas.

She doesn't know about his offer.

My thoughts return to Maui. The soft breeze coming off the ocean. The luscious peach colored flowers growing out of every bush. The way the palm trees remain constantly in motion.

If I had stayed there for just a little bit longer, then I wouldn't be dealing with this shit right now.

If I had stayed there for a little bit longer, I could've found out more about Nicholas.

Who is he, really?

Sydney stays in almost constant contact with me, putting my mind at ease for leaving her.

She sends texts, pictures, and videos doing everything that I've dreamed of doing in Hawaii: snorkeling with brightly colored fish, swimming in clear blue waters, laying out on the white sand. James is there with her in all of the pictures and, in the latest one, so is Nicholas.

Nicholas and James are tossing a frisbee around in the background of Sydney's selfie. They are on the sand and he's wearing only a pair of board shorts.

They hang low on his long defined torso, revealing the protruding muscles in the form of a V going down into his pelvic region.

My mouth waters a little bit as I zoom in on him and look at the way the light wraps around each one of his abs.

Wish you were here, Sydney texts.

What are you doing with him?

James invited him for lunch to his house. I'm making salad!

Her texts are both informative and without substance.

Why are you spending time with him?

Why is he there?

Didn't you read a word I wrote?

I call her, but the call goes to voice mail.

Instead, she sends a canned response: *Sorry, can't talk now.*

My heart skips a beat. Something's wrong.

Are you okay? I text.

Of course! Just about to sit down for lunch. Call you later.

I go over everything that happened that night.

Could I have been completely wrong about him? Yes, he did scare me a bit. His request was unusual and out of line.

But was I actually ever really frightened? Did I ever think that he would actually hurt me?

I didn't get much sleep.

There's a good chance that my intuition was driven by insomnia and its radar was off.

Or maybe this is just a ploy.

Nicholas and James are friends. He knows that Sydney is my friend.

Maybe he's just using her as a way to get closer to me.

But why? Why me? Why is he so interested in *me*?

There's a knock on the door.

It startles me. I'm not expecting anyone and I immediately think that it must be my mother. But she has never even stepped foot in here. I'm not even sure if she knows my address.

"Who is it?" I ask, looking through the peephole. He's in his forties with short dark hair and dressed in a casual jacket and slacks.

"I'm one of the managers of the building. We've been having some issues with the boiler and I'd like to ask you a few questions."

As soon as I open the lock, he pushes the door in my face and closes it behind him.

"What the hell are you doing?" I ask.

He shoves a revolver in my face.

My eyes stare down the barrel of the gun.

Everything else becomes a blur.

"Your mother said that I'd find you here," the stranger growls.

"What do you want?" I ask, moving my head away from him.

He presses the gun to my cheek again.

A sweet smell of iron and sweat permeate through my nostrils.

"She owes Marlo a big debt."

"So what?" I ask, brazenly.

"She can't pay it."

"That's not my problem," I say.

That's partly true.

The other part is that I don't want him to know that I care about my mother at all.

In his business, feelings are leverage. He's got plenty without me giving him anymore.

"Well, neither can she, so I thought I'd make it your problem," he says.

I cross my arms and pop my hip out to give myself as much attitude as possible.

"My mother and I are not on good terms. So, I don't know what exactly your game plan is here but I don't owe anyone any debt."

He stares at me for a moment, and then exhales and lowers his gun. He reaches into his front pocket, pulling out a card.

"We are holding your mother in an undisclosed location," he says. "You have five days to come up with fifty-thousand dollars. If you don't come up with it, they'll never find her body for you to bury."

29

WHEN I ASK FOR HELP...

HE HANDS me a card with the name Shephard Sudler and a phone number on it.

"That's my cell, call me anytime you get the money together. Your mother will only be safe for the next five days. No extensions."

"What do you expect me to do to come up with this?" I ask, shaking my head.

"You're a smart girl, figure it out."

He turns around and walks toward the door.

"How am I supposed to get it to you?" I ask.

"I accept only cash. But I will drive anywhere in the tristate area to pick it up, if necessary," he says and closes the door behind him.

I drop Shephard's card on the table and melt into the couch.

What a clusterfuck!

I should feel angry instead I feel nothing.

I stare into the distance at some point in the corner of the room.

I can't even bring myself to feel scared for her.

She has been a disappointment all of my life and yet I keep going back and helping her. When I walked out of her apartment, I was so certain that I'd cut off ties. I was so certain that she would go on the run and maybe escape her crappy little life once and for all. Now, I know that was nothing but a dream. A fantasy.

My mother is never leaving Boston.

My mother is not one to think outside the box to solve a problem.

She's not one to take a chance.

She gambled and drank and did drugs her whole life thinking that was the only way to make her life better. But you can't keep doing the same thing over and over again and expect different results. That is the definition of insanity.

But what now?

I can do nothing and just let things take care of themselves.

Let Marlo do to her what she probably did to my father.

Perhaps that would serve her well. Perhaps that is what I should do, just cut my ties with her once and for all. But there's a child inside of me that just can't let the adult in me do that.

I can't give myself permission to let her perish. Especially since I do have another way.

Sydney.

Sydney's family on her mother's side is incredibly wealthy and generous. She has been saving up her allowance to start her business but she might lend it to me if I were to explain what's happening.

Later that evening, she returns my call. We connect over video chat and she turns the camera away from her to show me the beautiful aquamarine water, her toes buried in the white sandy beach, and the enormous margarita in her hand.

It's not lost on me that if I had stayed then it wouldn't be up to me to save my mother from Marlo's henchmen.

"I'm so jealous," I say.

"I'm having an amazing time!" Sydney squeals.

"Where are you?"

"I stayed at a hotel that first night but I've been at James's house since then. He invited me over and I never left."

Her skin is a few shades tanner making her teeth even more pearly white than usual. She's wearing her hair in two braids. She doesn't have an ounce of makeup on and she has never looked more beautiful.

"So what's going on with him? Are you two dating?"

"Yes, more than that. We're talking about moving in together."

"What?" I gasp. My mouth drops open.

"I mean, I have no idea how that's even possible but we both want to. I mean, he asked me to stay."

She doesn't say anything more, just smiles from ear to ear.

"And?" I prod her.

"I don't know. If it weren't for my job, then yes, I'd stay," she says, shrugging.

I clear my throat to remind her of another obligation.

"You, of course, you!" Sydney laughs. "But you're my best friend, nothing is ever going to change that." She sends me an air kiss.

"You moving six thousand miles away across six time zones might put a damper on our evening Netflix marathons," I say.

She nods, trying not to smile. But she can't.

I laugh.

"I'm really happy for you, Syd," I say.

I ask her to tell me more about James and she tells me about his job at the hospital and the pediatric clinic that he volunteers at in his spare time to help out the poor families on the island who can't afford medical care.

"He just really loves his job," Sydney says. "I haven't met anyone like him before."

"What about your job?" I ask.

She might not like the particular lab or the people who work there but she believes in what she does and I can't imagine her giving it all up to live on an island in the middle of the Pacific.

On the other hand, recently, everyone (including me) has been doing things that are difficult to imagine.

I try to find a gap in the conversation in which I can bring up my particular predicament but when it doesn't come, I just blurt it out.

"Sydney, I need your help."

"What's going on?" she asks, sitting back in her chair. The rain starts to fall behind her and I hear it splatter against the roof.

I don't know where to start so I begin with the guy who shoved a gun in my face. I go into detail over my mother's debt and save the request for last.

"I have five days to get Shephard fifty-thousand dollars. Otherwise they're going to kill her."

Sydney rubs her temple and stares vacantly into the screen.

"I'm telling you this," I continue, "because I was wondering if you could lend me the money."

30

WHEN I WAIT...

SYDNEY LOOKS AT ME. The distance that separates us no longer exists. It's just her and me, talking, sitting curled up on the couch together.

"That's a lot of money, Olive," she says as a matter of fact. There isn't a tinge of attitude in her statement.

"I know." I nod. "I wouldn't be asking if I had any other way. I tried to apply for a bigger credit limit but I can't get anything more than another two grand. I don't know what to do."

I stare into her almond shaped greenish-black eyes.

Anyone else would ask why I'm doing this.

Anyone else would say that this is your mother's problem and after everything that she has put you through you should just let her deal with it.

Well, I did.

And this is what it has come to.

I open my mouth and words just spill out.

I tell Sydney about my plan for her to drive away. Go out west. Live in a string of cheap motels under a new name.

This plan would've worked.

This plan was the one that I should have insisted on her taking.

I don't know who picked her up, whether it was Shephard Sudler or some other man who works for Marlo.

What I am certain of is that they didn't have to go far to find her. They probably found her at home or buying cigarettes at the corner store.

Since she doesn't like to drive, those are the only two places she would've been.

Since she doesn't like to drive, she didn't want to go on the run.

She didn't want to take a chance and help herself. That has been my mom's modus operandi her whole life.

She never had a steady job, relying instead on my father and complaining when he'd spend the little money that he did bring in. After he left, she did work at a few places, mainly retail and as a housekeeper, but those positions never lasted long.

The day that I started college, I took the train to Wellesley alone. Putting my suitcases on the floor of my dorm, an overwhelming sigh of relief swept over me.

Tears started to roll down my face and my new roommate's mom wrapped her manicured fingers around my shoulders and told me that homesickness was a very normal thing and that I could call her anytime I needed a mom to talk to.

She thought I was crying for the same reason everyone else was, but the truth was I was crying because I was finally away from *her*.

My mother's lack of inertia is contagious.

Why do anything when nothing is ever going to work out?

Why take a risk?

Why even do the bare minimum when you could just wait and maybe someone else will do it for you?

When I was in elementary school, she would hit me for getting a C on a test. When I got to high school, she would mock me for studying too hard.

Most of the time, someone did show up to help her out of the messes that she'd made. At first, it was my dad. Then Patrick. Then Owen. And then me.

And now?

The one time that I actually walked away from her, everything became much worse.

If I had forced her into the car, if I had even driven her out of town myself, set her up in some studio apartment somewhere in Texas, then Shephard Sudler wouldn't be handing me his card.

But because I walked away once, her death will be on my hands.

Sydney doesn't ask why I'm asking her for this money because Sydney knows the guilt that I feel. Instead she says she'll call me back after she sees how much money she has in her account.

The rain stopped, leaving beads of water on the outside of my window. One droplet begins to roll down in a zigzag, colliding with another one and building up steam. Now traveling with great mass they bulldoze their way down the glass consuming unsuspecting droplets along their path.

A few hours later, my phone rings. I take a deep breath as I press the Accept button.

"I don't have enough," Sydney says. "I only have seventeen thousand I can get on my credit cards as an advance and my mom refused to even entertain giving me a loan. I have another six that I saved up for my business but that's it."

With my three thousand that's still twenty-four short. I can perhaps use this money to buy more time, but what's that going to get me? Another few days is not going to make all of this money magically appear in my account.

"You know what you have to do," Sydney says.

I nod. I don't want to even think about it.

"I don't even know if his offer still stands." I shrug.

"You have to ask."

I move my jaw around and bite the inside of my lip.

"What's he like?" I ask. "You had lunch with him, right?"

"He's actually really great. Fun. James is really close friends with him."

I nod.

"Charming. Has lots of interesting stories to tell. Plus, he's quite easy on the eyes."

"I know that part," I say, smiling out of the corner of my lips.

"This isn't such a terrible option, Olive. I know that things didn't go well between you two back there but why not give it a chance?"

"Wait a second." Something occurs to me. "You're not just saying that because you want me to come to Hawaii with you, are you?"

Sydney's eyes light up.

"It could be fun. I mean, think about it. When was the last time we did anything reckless?" she asks. "We've both worked really hard to get into this super prestigious college and then majored in really hard subjects while everyone else seemed to just party. Then we started working right away...maybe we're due for a break. Just some time off with some hot guys in the most beautiful place in the world?"

"You make it sound so...carefree." I laugh.

"I'm just trying to put a positive spin on a pretty shitty situation," she admits.

"I know." I nod. "I appreciate it."

"Are you going to do it?" Sydney asks after a long pause.

31

WHEN I MAKE THE CALL...

Sydney gets Nicholas' number from James and I jot down the digits on a piece of scrap paper. After we hang up, I stare it for a while, running my fingers on the rugged edges, trying to decide what to do.

It feels like I have a choice, but I really don't.

He is the only one who is in the position to give me this money.

Can I do it?

Can I take him up on his offer?

Can I do it for *her*?

No matter how I would like to spin it in my own mind, no matter how much I would like to pretend, calling Nicholas would be doing it for her.

The stakes may be higher. I am not coming over and

helping her with the laundry while listening to her criticize me.

I'm not just paying her share of the rent.

I am saving her life.

And as much as I want to be done with her, to kick her out of my life for good, I am not willing to let her die, especially if there's something I can do to prevent it.

I dial Nicholas' number slowly and add him to my contact list.

Then I press the big green button and wait.

"Nicholas Crawford," he says, answering on the third ring.

I can't believe he is actually one of those obnoxious people who answers a call by saying his name.

"Um...this is...Olive Kernes," I say, keenly aware of just how many pauses I took to get this sentence out.

"How are you?" he asks without missing a beat. I'm surprised by how unsurprised he seems to hear from me.

I want to hang up immediately.

I look away at the screen and contemplate pushing the red button.

Hang up.

Hang up.

It's not worth it.

"Olive?" I hear him on the other side. "Don't hang up."

"I don't know why I'm calling."

"Yes, you do."

"Do you?" I ask.

"I may have an inkling of an idea."

I put him on speaker phone and crack my knuckles.

"I enjoyed spending time with your friend Sydney."

My body tenses up.

I can't quite pinpoint it but he has some sort of effect on me.

His voice energizes every cell in my body and there's nothing I can do to calm them back down.

"She said she had fun, too," I say slowly.

"James is a really good friend of mine," Nicholas adds.

I know what he's doing.

He's trying to put me at ease.

If Sydney likes him, if her boyfriend is close friends with him, that means I can trust him. That means nothing bad can happen.

But is that enough?

"Do you know what happened to my mother?" I ask.

I didn't tell Sydney to keep this quiet, but I wouldn't be surprised if James already knew and then told Nicholas.

"No, is she okay?" he asks, his voice is marked with concern.

I inhale deeply.

"She's in a lot of trouble. She borrowed money from the wrong person and now she can't pay any of it back." I bite my lower lip and pause.

Nicholas waits for me to continue.

"They're holding her hostage until I pay her debt," I finally come right out with all of it. "They are going to kill her if I don't come up with the fifty-thousand."

"What's your bank account number?" he asks without waiting for me to ask.

"Um..."

"Look it up," he instructs.

I click on the banking app on my phone, sign in and read off the number.

A moment later, my phone beeps.

A notification appears.

He has deposited fifty-thousand dollars into my bank account.

Another notification: the money is already in the account.

Apparently, he wired it from such an account that the bank doesn't need the normal three days to process it and make sure that there's money there.

"Wait...I didn't even...I'm...thank you," I finally say. "Thank you so much."

"You're welcome."

I don't know what else to say. I wish that we were on video chat so that I could at least look at his face and thank him in person.

"Nicholas, are you still there?" I ask after a moment even though I can hear his quiet deep breaths on the other side of the phone.

"Yes," he says.

He's waiting for me to take the initiative.

But I am too taken aback by what he has just done to put together a coherent sentence.

"Thank you so much." My words come out hesitantly, but I'm thankful they come out at all.

"You're welcome," he repeats himself.

"Why...why did you do that?"

"You needed help."

"But what about...your offer?"

"That has nothing to do with this."

My shoulders slope down.

I slouch in my seat.

My mind doesn't understand what he means.

"You don't want me to spend the year with you?" I ask.

"That's not what I said," he says. His voice is even and without much affection.

"What does that mean?" I ask. "I don't understand."

"I want you to spend the year with me. But that has nothing to do with this money. Your mother's life is in danger. I can help her with a swipe of a few buttons. That's what I did."

"Thank you," I say. "You're so...generous."

"Anyone in my position would do the exact same thing."

"No." I shake my head. "No, they wouldn't. I just wish there was something I could do to repay you for your kindness."

"If you insist, there is something you could do."

I wait for him to explain.

"I'd like to have dinner with you tomorrow night. There's a beautiful restaurant in downtown Maui that I think you'd adore."

My heart skips a beat.

"Will you have dinner with me, Olive?"

32

WHEN I HAND OVER THE MONEY...

Now THAT I have the money, I am not entirely sure how to make the exchange. I glance over at the five envelopes of cash that I retrieved from the bank earlier today.

I can give Shephard Sudler the money, but how does that guarantee my mother's safety?

I don't know anything about him except that I can't trust him. This is a lot of money and I need assurances that my mother will be released.

I message a few people on Facebook and then call the number that one of them gives me.

"Samantha?"

"Yes, how may I help you?" Her voice sounds peppy and upbeat as if she were a customer service representative at a five-star hotel.

She doesn't have a trace of her old New England accent and each word comes out crisp as if she were a polished, wealthy woman. I guess that's exactly what she is now.

"This is Olive Kernes, I need to speak with you."

Sam and I meet at a Starbucks in Harvard Square. We hug, tell each other how wonderful we look, and then both order lattes.

Samantha has long caramel hair, a trim yoga body, and flawless skin. Dressed in leggings, boots, a figure-hugging jacket, she looks like a regular suburban mom stopping in for an afternoon pick me up. Little does anyone around here know that she is the most connected madam in the Northeast.

At least that's what my research told me. Once my mother made her suggestion, I couldn't resist finding out more about my old friend.

"It's nice to see you again," she says as we make small talk about our lives after high school. But when the conversation hits a lull, I don't waste any more time.

"I know that you work for, or with, Marlo," I say.

She doesn't respond, giving me neither a confirmation nor a denial. There's no point in being indirect. She won't help unless I tell her the truth.

"My mother owes her a debt, which I'm going to pay on her behalf," I start. "Someone who claims to work for

Marlo wants me to pay him directly, but I don't know if he actually works for Marlo. I need to get in contact with her directly."

Sam sits back in her seat, folding her arms across her chest.

"What do you want from me?" she asks.

"Can you help me?" I ask.

"Maybe."

She narrows her eyes and takes another sip of her latte. Then she gets up and walks away.

"Follow me," she instructs, leading me to the bathroom.

After locking the door, she turns to me and says, "I am going to check if you're wired."

"I'm not," I promise.

"You'll have to excuse me if I don't just take your word for it."

I don't fight it. I'm not wired and I have no intentions of getting the police involved.

First, she goes through my bag, carefully emptying it of its contents and then examining every part of the lining. I don't know anything about bugging devices but they must be quite small if she is so meticulous in her search.

After checking everything that she has dumped into the

sink, she turns to me. She begins with my hair, asking me to first take off my scrunchie and then moves down my back and around my torso. She pats practically every part of me including in between my legs, and then asks me to remove my shoes. After checking my ankles, feet, and even the inside of my sneakers, she finally looks up with satisfaction.

"I'm not working with the police. I'm just trying to help my mom," I insist.

"You can never be careful enough in my line of work."

I nod, wishing that she hadn't even mentioned that. The less I know about what it is that she does, the better.

"What do you want to know?" Sam asks.

"How can I get in touch with Marlo?"

"Something easier," she says.

"Do you know people who work for her?"

She shrugs. I take that as a yes.

"Do you know of someone named Shephard Sudler?"

She shrugs again. This time I don't know how to interpret her body language.

"Okay...what can you do for me?" I ask.

Sam takes a deep breath. "Marlo has a lot of people

working for her doing a variety of things. I am not aware of everything that she has going on."

"I...I just need to pay her my mom's debt and that's it. Shephard said that her life is in danger. They're holding her hostage. But I don't want to pay this money to the wrong person."

Sam blinks. I'm not getting through.

"You're the only person I know who actually knows her. I don't know who to trust," I say.

"One word of advice," she says, pointing her finger in my face. "Trust no one."

I nod, looking down at the floor.

"I just don't know what to do. He said they would kill her..." My words trail off.

It wasn't until this moment, standing in this clean sanitized public bathroom that I realize just how much I actually do want to save her life.

When I think of my mother, the memories that flood in aren't of our fights or all the mean names she has ever called me. It's the other ones.

It's waking up to the smell of freshly baked cupcakes one Sunday morning when I was six.

It's her kneeling down next to my bed with me so that we could pray together for my brother, Patrick, when he was in the hospital.

It's her running a comb through my hair and then braiding it in a French braid.

"Your mother has been a loyal customer of Marlo's for a long time now," Sam says. My eyebrows rise.

"I had no idea," I say.

"She likes to gamble. And she has won quite a bit. When she's lost, she has always paid her debts."

"Do you know where I can find Marlo?" I try again.

"I can't tell you that," Sam says.

"What can you do?" I ask.

"I can reach out to Marlo and see what she says."

She pulls out her phone.

"Now?" I ask before I can stop myself.

"I can wait if you'd like."

"No, no, no. Of course not," I quickly correct myself.

"Wait for me outside." Sam ushers me out of the bathroom.

Two hours after Sam and I part ways, I pace around my living room waiting.

Sam makes the arrangements.

Someone is supposed to come to my house and make the exchange.

I am not entirely clear if my mother is being brought here and suddenly, I have a horrible feeling in the pit of my stomach.

What if I made a mistake?

What if I should've believed her when she told me that I shouldn't trust anyone?

What if she's just sending someone here to take my money?

My door buzzes. They're here.

33

WHEN THEY COME...

Looking through the peephole, I'm unable to believe my eyes. She's here. She's really here. A sigh of relief washes over me.

I open the door and shake Marlo's hand. I've never been introduced to her but given how well known she is in the neighborhood I know what she looks like. I've never seen her without her entourage, but she's here alone.

"I've heard about your predicament," she says. "I'm here to confirm that yes, your mother does owe me fifty-thousand dollars."

Marlo walks around my living room as if she's my mother-in-law, checking on the quality of my living arrangements. Her stilettos make a loud clinking sound on the parquet floors and she wipes her index finger across the bookshelf in the corner, turning up dust.

"Not much for housekeeping, are you?" she asks.

I shrug.

"Don't worry, I'm not either. Still, it's important to know your strengths and weaknesses and to account for them accordingly. That's why I have a housekeeper come by twice a week."

I don't know what to do with this unsolicited piece of advice, so I just smile politely and nod.

She runs her fingers through her ash-blonde hair and then down her neck and over her voluptuous bust. She is one of those people who would exude sexuality even if she were dressed in a potato sack. But dressed in a tailored blazer, dress pants, and a bright pink blouse, Marlo is impossible to dismiss.

"Let's get right to the point, shall we?" she suggests as if I'm standing here making conversation about the weather. "Your mother, Eleanor Kernes, owes me fifty grand."

I nod.

"Will you be paying her debt?"

"Yes," I say. She smiles. "So, where is she?"

Marlo's face contorts into a question mark.

"You are...holding her somewhere," I say.

"What are you talking about?" Marlo asks, crossing her arms.

I furrow my brow, trying to figure out if she is just being cautious in case there's a recording device anywhere in my house, or if she actually doesn't know what I'm talking about.

"Shephard Sudler, the guy who works for you," I elaborate. "He came in here and pointed a gun at my face on your behalf."

"Excuse me?" She takes a step back from me, surprised.

"He said that he's keeping my mom hostage somewhere, *on your behalf,* and I had until tonight to pay him."

Marlo shakes her head, slowly running her tongue over her bright red lips.

"What else did he say?"

"He said he would kill her if I didn't pay him what she owed."

"You mean, if you didn't pay me?" she clarifies.

I shrug. "Yes, I guess."

Marlo shifts her weight from one foot to another.

"So, why did you seek me out?"

"Because I know that she owes you the money. But I had no idea who Shephard Sudler is. And I wanted to make sure that you were paid so that you would let her go."

Marlo taps her French-manicured nails on the countertop. Her bracelets jingle with each tap.

"You've got yourself a problem," she says after a moment.

"What do you mean?"

"I have no idea who Shephard Sudler is, but he does not work for me. I also did not authorize anyone to kidnap anyone on my behalf."

I stare at her, trying to figure out if she's telling the truth or lying to not incriminate herself.

"Do you have a balcony?" she asks.

"No," I mumble.

"Rooftop?"

"What?" I ask.

"Does this building have a rooftop? Somewhere private where we can talk?"

I nod.

We take the elevator in silence and she holds the door to the roof open for me.

I follow her to the edge and touch the railing.

Instead of looking out into the distance, she walks up to me and starts to pat me down.

"I need to make sure that what we are about to say stays

just between us."

I lift up my hands and spread my legs and wait for her to finish. I'm a total stranger and I want her to be as candid with me as possible.

"Why did you take her?" I ask. My voice is despondent and tired.

"I didn't."

My body perks up.

"What do you mean?" I ask.

"What I told you earlier is the truth. I do not know who Shephard Sudler is and I did not authorize anyone to take your mother. She owes me a debt, it's not due back for another week. Plus, she has been a good customer over the years. I'd give another week if she had asked."

My mind starts to run in circles.

So, what the hell is going on?

Who is Shephard Sudler and where is my mother?

"What would you do then?" I ask.

"I never get anyone's family involved in their business dealings. My debtors have to come up with the money on their own or else deal with the consequences."

"I don't know what's going on," I admit.

Marlo narrows her eyes and lights a cigarette. Leaning

on the railing, she takes a drag and then turns
toward me.

"One option is that this Shephard Sudler found out
about your mother's debt, researched you, found out
that you could in fact pay her debt, kidnapped her,
reached out to you, and now wants you to pay my debt
to *him*."

I nod, not really understanding everything.

"But that seems unlikely. If he's this sophisticated of a
criminal, he'd probably know that it is unwise to
pretend to work for me and to do business deals on my
behalf," Marlo says, taking another drag.

Making an O with her lips, she lets out her breath in
little puffs.

"The other option, and the most likely one, is that your
mother is the one who is behind all of this."

Her words are a punch to the gut.

Even the wind gets knocked out of me.

"She hired some unsuspecting idiot to pretend to be
someone who works for me. That guy has no idea who
it is that he is impersonating. She wants you to pay her
the money that she owes me either to pay off her debt
or to just keep it and start a new life somewhere."

"You really think she made this up?" I ask.

I feel the color draining out of my face.

34

WHEN WE TALK...

MARLO'S WORDS ping-pong around in my head.

Is she telling the truth?

Is my mom lying?

She has lied about a number of things but never anything this big.

Is she really trying to just steal the money from me? Why?

I told her I would help her.

No, I told her I would help her, but only if she went on the run. If Marlo is telling the truth, then my mother has no intention of going on the run.

"There are two things I can tell you for sure. One is that I did not order anyone to kidnap her or threaten her life. The other thing is that I do not have a

Shephard Sudler working for me," Marlo finishes her cigarette and looks around for somewhere to throw the butt.

"There's no trash can up here," I say.

She takes the cigarette butt and tosses it in her purse.

"I never litter," she says in response to the surprised look on my face. "So, what do you want to do?"

"What do you mean?" I ask.

"You have the money. You can keep it and let Eleanor's debt ride. I'll find her on my own, it shouldn't be too hard."

"Or?" I ask.

"Or you could pay it off like you wanted to. Unless, this little development changes your mind about whether or not your mother is someone you should help."

She's not.

I know that now.

I knew that a long time ago.

But ties with toxic mothers are the most difficult ones to break.

We, their children, can never really fully do it because our mothers never really taught them how to be adults.

We are always looking, striving, seeking that approval that we never got as children.

We don't trust our strength.

We don't trust standing on our two feet.

I saw a therapist for over two years to help me come to terms with everything she has put me through. I know all of these things intellectually, but my heart still aches for her.

"You seem like a nice kid, Olive," Marlo says, walking away from me. We get into the elevator.

"You have a good job. Nice apartment," she continues. "You seem to have your life in order. Why don't you just take that money from wherever it is that you got it from and not get involved in your mother's business?"

I lift up one of my eyebrows.

"Is that your *professional* opinion?" I ask.

"You could say that."

The elevator stops on my floor and I invite her inside.

"It's just for a second," I say. When the door closes behind us, I ask, "*What* makes you say that?"

"You don't look like someone who has an extra fifty grand laying around. It's probably what you make a year at your job."

"So?"

"Well, people who have that much aren't usually particularly generous human beings. I don't know where you got it but if your mother set you up like this, she's not worth your time."

I take a deep breath and walk over to the kitchen island where I hid the envelopes of money. Before opening the drawer, I look at Marlo.

"If I give you this money will you wipe her debt?"

She hesitates.

"She doesn't owe you another cent," I say.

"If you hand me fifty-thousand dollars in cash then her slate is clean," Marlo says with an exasperated sigh.

I hand her the envelopes. She counts the stacks and then points a finger in my face, "You're too good to her. Some people have to learn the lesson the hard way."

I feel like I have to explain.

"She's my mother," I whisper.

"She fucked you over and she'll keep doing it until you put your foot down. Trust me. I know. I had a mother just like her."

Marlo spins on her heels and walks out of the door. I descend onto the sofa wondering if I have made a terrible mistake.

I paid her debt even though she tried to steal from me.

I paid her debt even though she tried to con me.

The thing is that I didn't do it for her.

I did it for me.

I did it to finally, once and for all, be free of her.

35

WHEN HE STARTLES ME...

IF THERE IS one perk to taking your time unpacking a suitcase, this is it, you don't have to pack it all up again when you decide to go back.

I throw in a few toiletries that I took out and dress in my favorite pair of leggings and slip-ons.

My ride share should be here in a few minutes, but since I'm all ready to go and it's a beautiful afternoon, I go to wait outside on the curb.

"Where the hell is my money?" Someone grabs my arm. My body tenses. A couple walks by giving him a disapproving look and he lets me go.

"I had a little chat with Marlo," I inform him. "She told me you don't work for her."

Now, it's his turn to recoil. This is the last thing he was expecting.

"You're in a lot of trouble, Shephard Sudler," I say his name extra loud so that any passerby hears me clearly.

"I don't know what you're talking about. Don't you care about your mother?" he hisses under his breath.

"No, I don't. I have a feeling that none of what you said to me was true," I say sternly. "How much did my mom pay you to pretend to work for Marlo? 'Cause guess what? Whatever it was, it wasn't enough."

My words land like a punch.

I smile at my own power.

Then I look out at the cars driving down the street, praying that my ride will be here soon.

Shephard takes a step away from me, at a loss as to what to do next.

"Marlo is a very dangerous woman to fuck around with," I continue. "She did not like hearing that you were out there using her name to do your bad deeds."

I watch his Adam's apple move up and down as he swallows hard.

"Oh, wait, my mother has no money. You probably did it for free, huh?" I ask.

Talking to him like this is a risk. Just because he doesn't work for Marlo, it doesn't mean that he wasn't holding my mother hostage and wanted a ransom to be paid.

I wasn't sure how I was going to find out the truth about

what my mother did but seeing his reactions to my questions, I'm starting to get it.

Marlo was right.

It was my mother who hired Shephard to make the threats.

"Or was she just going to pay you something on the back end?" I ask. "How much exactly?"

Shephard shakes his head and looks down at the ground.

"I've never done anything like this before," he caves. "But I needed money. I got fired and I couldn't find another job for months. My family is getting evicted and Eleanor said that this would be an easy two grand."

Shephard stumbles over his words as he talks and I practically feel sorry for him. Then I remember looking down the barrel of that gun he shoved in my face and my pity hardens.

"There's no such thing as easy money, no matter what anyone says," I say. "You threatened me. You tried to blackmail me. I could report you to the police..."

"No, please don't," he pleads, touching my arm again.

I snap it away from him.

There are tears in his eyes.

"Don't ever point a gun in anyone's face like that again.

In fact, don't ever do anything like this again," I say. "Otherwise, I will go to the cops."

"Thank you, thank you," he says over and over, a wave of relief rushing over him.

"But you've got bigger problems than the police. My mother got you involved with some really bad people."

"I thought that Marlo was just someone she...made up."

I furrow my brow.

How could he be so stupid?

"What do you do for a living?" I ask.

"I'm a bus driver. I drive kids to school. They laid off a number of people and all I can get is a substation gig."

Then it occurs to me that it's not that he's stupid, it's just that he's totally out of his element. He has never dealt with the underworld and my mother was selfish enough to put his life and his family's wellbeing in danger for her own gain.

"Marlo is very much real and she is one of the most powerful people around these parts that you have never heard of. It was more than unwise for you to go out there and pretend to work for her. People have been killed for a lot less."

I don't really have any knowledge of this but I get a feeling that it's probably true. Besides, I need to put the fear of God into this man so that he never messes with my mother again.

I see a car with the Lyft sticker on the side pull up to the curb.

It's my ride.

"What do I do now?" he asks. The question catches me by surprise.

"Go try to find a real job," I say. "And get rid of that gun."

"But what if I need it for protection?" he asks.

I shake my head. "I'm the last person you should be getting advice from."

"I know, but you're the only one I can trust. Please tell me."

I shrug my shoulders as the driver puts my bag in the car.

"Is the gun registered to you?" I ask.

"I bought it just for this," he says.

I laugh.

I am not sure that you need that many street smarts to know *not* to use the gun that belongs to you to commit crimes. That just seems like something you could learn from a cop show on television.

"What do I do if your mom comes looking for me?" Shephard asks.

"She's harmless...physically I mean," I add. "But if you do see her, tell her that her debt to Marlo is paid and she can go fuck herself."

36

WHEN I GO BACK...

MY FLIGHT BACK TO MAUI, thanks to the elusive Mr. Crawford, is much more comfortable than my flight here and I sleep almost the entire way there, lying flat on a seat that's almost the size of a bunk bed, in my first class cabin. I wake up rested and refreshed and have time to fix my hair and makeup and make myself look presentable.

I thought that coming here would make me anxious and sleepless but in fact, I feel the complete opposite. Leaving Boston and everything that happened with my mother behind seems to infuse me with energy. By the time we land my worries all vanish and I'm excited to see Sydney.

While I wait for my bags, watching the carousel in the baggage claim go 'round and 'round, I know that seeing Nicholas again should give me some pause. He made an absurd proposal to me, one that only a crazy person would entertain. Yet, a tingling sensation spreads throughout my body at the thought of seeing him again.

Luckily, with the time change, I have the whole day to think about it. I won't be seeing him until this evening.

"Olive!" My mouth drops open.

He's standing outside the double doors, right on the other side of the baggage claim, holding a sign with my name on it.

"I...I thought that Sydney was picking me up," I say.

He folds the paper up and slides it into the pocket of his muted Hawaiian shirt. It hangs loosely around his broad shoulders, but it's not so baggy that it completely obfuscates his chiseled body.

"I asked her for a favor," he says, taking the handle of my large suitcase away from me.

Left with just the backpack that I took on the plane as my carry-on, I feel naked. When we get outside, the sweltering humidity overwhelms my senses.

He leads me toward a new BMW 8-series convertible in gray metallic and opens the passenger door. I place my backpack in between my legs and fish out a pair of sunglasses to shield my eyes both from the sun and his eyes.

Through the side view mirror, I watch him put my suitcase into the trunk and the way his hair falls into his face with each move. It is only after we pull out of the short-term parking garage that I realize that I've been holding my breath.

"Thank you for coming," Nicholas says, smiling at the corner of his mouth. I give him a slight nod.

"How's your mother?"

I shrug, not really wanting to get into any of the details. "Thank you for helping me. She's fine."

"I'm glad to hear it."

"I don't really know how long it will take me to pay you back."

He glances over at me as we turn onto the winding two-lane highway going along the razor's edge of a cliffside.

"Don't worry about it."

We sit in silence for a while.

I wait for him to say something but then think that maybe he is doing the same thing.

Still, the silence is comforting. Usually, I am very uneasy being in a small space with someone without saying a word, but not with Nicholas.

He has an easy energy to him. He doesn't demand me to perform or pretend. I like that.

"I need you to do something for me," he says as we turn off the main road and into a development.

There is a large gate out front and a security guard who

waves us through as soon as he sees Nicholas' identification.

"Where are we going?" I ask.

"You like to play games?" he asks, igniting a spark deep within me.

"I don't know. I guess it depends on the game."

"I think you'll like this one."

He pulls up to a five-star resort and hands his keys to a valet who is waiting out front. Another employee opens my door and helps me out. They place our bags on a rolling suitcase cart and I follow Nicholas to the front desk.

After checking in, they show us to a two-bedroom penthouse suite with a large wrap-around balcony.

"That will be all, thank you," Nicholas says, handing the bellman a tip in the palm of his hand.

"Thank you for staying with us, Mr. Landon. Mrs. Landon. Please let me know if there is anything that you need."

I look out at the impossibly vast ocean through the floor-to-ceiling sliding doors that span the entire west side of the suite.

Nicholas walks up to me from behind. He stops short of touching me but I can feel his breath on the back of my neck.

"Why did he call you Mr. Landon?" I ask.

Nicholas runs his fingers up my arm, sending shivers down my spine. The comfort that I felt only fifteen minutes ago is replaced by a sense of free fall. But I'm not afraid.

"Why am I Mrs. Landon?" I ask, turning to face him.

"Those are our names here at the Wailea Lani Resort and Spa," he says, moving the hair off my neck and bringing his lips so close to mine I can almost feel them on my skin.

I close my eyes to enjoy the moment. I wait for him to come closer. I wait for him to touch me. I open my eyes when he doesn't.

He takes a step away from me, smiling with his eyes. My body yearns for his but I don't dare make the first move.

"In my line of work, I am required to use a number of aliases. Here, I am Mr. Landon and you are my wife, Mrs. Landon."

I straighten my back and broaden my shoulders.

"So, this is the game you *want* me to play?" I ask.

He takes another step closer to me. Tilting my chin up to his face, he runs his finger down my neck. My eyes grow heavy from the anticipation that builds in the pit of my stomach. I move an inch closer, waiting for his lips to touch mine.

But instead he brings them over to my ear and whispers, "This is the game you are *going* to play."

37

WHEN WE PLAY A GAME...

HE UNZIPS the garment bag and pulls out a short black cocktail dress.

"What's that for?" I ask.

"My assistant picked it out for you."

"I don't have any shoes to go with it."

He pulls out a pair of nude pumps and unzips another garment bag with his own newly pressed suit. Without even turning around, he begins to unbutton his shirt. Our eyes make contact and I'm the first one to look away. Not really away, more like down. My gaze drifts down his perfectly round pectoral muscles.

Once his fingers unbutton the last button, his shirt falls open and onto the bed. I stare at the way his biceps flex and relax with each move. His sun-kissed skin is perfectly mocha brown. It looks so delicious that I almost want to lick him. My tongue runs over my bottom lip in anticipation.

As my eyes focus back on his, I notice those flecks of gold again. When he smiles, they sparkle. He unbuttons his belt and lets his pants drop to the floor. I get a glimpse of his black, hip hugging boxer briefs that accentuate every part of him.

My cheeks burn and I look away.

"It's okay, you can look if you want to," he says.

My mouth salivates as I stand facing the ocean, waiting for him to put on his suit. I hear him pull up his pants, buckle the belt, and tuck in his shirt. Only then do I feel like it's safe to turn around.

"All decent," he says, cocking his head to one side.

I press my tongue to the roof of my mouth, blocking it from touching my lips.

I know exactly what he's doing.

He's teasing me.

Playing with me.

Toying with me.

He is trying to seduce me. Well, I'm not going to be the one to crack first.

"You look nice," I say, running my eyes over his well-tailored exquisite suit. It fits him like a glove, emphasizing all of his best features.

He sits down on the bed and waits. From the positioning of his body, I can see that he's challenging me. Nicholas leans back on one arm, propping up his head with the other, as if to say, "you wouldn't dare change in front of me like I did in front of you."

For a moment, I consider going into the bathroom for some privacy, but I can't bear to break this sexual chemistry that's brewing in between us. Besides, I want to show him that I'm a formidable opponent. That two can play this game.

With my eyes fixed on his, I take off my cardigan and step out of my shoes. He moves his fingers closer to his mouth and leans a little bit closer to me. I can see his anticipation building and it infuses me with power. Even from across the room, I can feel the energy that's building between us.

I slide down my leggings and let my tank top drop down over my panties. A moment of truth.

A part of me is tempted to turn around for a semblance of privacy but another part pushes me to go on.

I want to make him sit up.

I want to make him stand up.

I want to make him push me down on the bed and kiss me.

I pull my shirt over my head, tossing it onto the floor. He sits up and moves to the edge of the bed. That's a good boy.

I watch him as he looks my body up and down. Without uttering a word, he makes me feel desired.

I reach back to unhook my bra. His mouth drops open and he raises to his feet.

Come on over, I say silently. Put your hands on me. I hold my chin upward, elongating my neck.

He licks his lips.

He walks over. I close my eyes to brace for impact. But nothing happens. When I open them a moment later, he's standing in front of me holding the dress.

Nicholas hands me the hanger.

I thought that I had broken him, but he turned the game on its head. I tense my jaw and steel my eyes.

He smiles in that self-satisfactory way that makes me both want to punch him and fuck him.

"You remember what I said earlier when I made my offer?"

I take the dress off the hanger.

"Remind me."

"You said that you wouldn't have sex with me," Nicholas says.

I exhale trying to expel the anger out of me.

Taking his finger, he runs it down my neck and then around the outside of my breast and down my side.

"And I promised you that before our time is up, you'd be begging me to do it."

I clench my fists around the hanger until I see the whites of my knuckles. I hate him. I hate him for being right. I hate him for how much I want him.

"Why don't you try on the dress," Nicholas says. He takes a step away from me and sits down on the bench at the edge of the bed.

I shouldn't like the way that he speaks to me but I lose myself in the nuance of *how* he says everything. He makes demands instead of requests and he teases me by seducing me with his gestures.

I pull the dress over my head, slipping it on. I straighten it out in front of the full length mirror and admire how well it hugs my body.

I can only pull the zipper halfway up and turn back to him for help.

Feeling his hands on the small of my back makes every part of me shiver. His hands slide expertly up to the nape of my neck making my head tilt back from pleasure.

Slipping on the pair of pumps that Nicholas' assistant picked out for me, completes the look. I don't know who she is but looking at myself in this outfit makes me want to ask her to be my permanent stylist. Imagine never having to worry about picking out something to wear again. As someone who isn't very keen on clothes shopping, this is a dream come true.

"Your assistant is very good at what she does," I say without taking my eyes off myself in the mirror. "It's a perfect fit and it looks...amazing."

"*You* are the one who makes the dress look amazing," Nicholas corrects me. I smile at the compliment and thank him.

He hands me a small purse and I move some of the contents of my backpack into it, phone, lip gloss, wallet.

"You won't need that tonight," Nicholas says, pointing to the wallet. "Or for the rest of your time here, for that matter."

"Why is that?"

"I'll take care of everything."

"Is that part of the deal that you mentioned earlier?" I ask.

He nods.

"Is tonight part of the deal, too? Me pretending to be your wife, Mrs. Landon?"

He shakes his head.

"Tonight is a trial," he says. "I want to see what you're capable of."

My heart jumps into my throat and my hands get ice cold.

Nicholas walks up to me. He stands so close that I can smell the mint Tic Tac that he has just popped into his mouth.

When I take a step back, I realize that my back is all the way against the front door.

"Who are we supposed to be?" I ask.

"Newlyweds from Boston. We are madly in love and are here on our honeymoon," he says. He takes another step closer to me and I straighten my back against the door.

"Why are we from Boston?" I whisper. My body yearns for his but I don't let myself touch him first.

"The best lies are those that are closest to the truth," he says, touching a strand of my hair and twisting it around his finger.

His eyes drift up to mine and watch me as I watch him lick his lips. I can almost feel the tension that builds between us. I can't take it much longer. I bite my tongue to keep myself from screaming. Give in. Give in, I say. Give in so you can put your hands on him.

His hand makes its way up my neck and toward my

lips. My mouth falls open. He runs his finger across my lower lip and whispers, "Tell me to stop."

My knees start to buckle. I can't say no even if I wanted to.

He presses his mouth to mine and a wave of relief sweeps over me.

Finally.

It's finally happening.

I reach out for his face pulling him closer. Our tongues collide, hard at first, and then quickly find their rhythm. I bury my hands in his hair. He wraps his arms around my waist.

I reach for his tie. When I try to untuck it, he grabs my wrists and pulls them apart.

"No," he whispers just as I think he's going to kiss me again. He lets go. My hands drop to my sides.

"What's wrong?" I ask, trying to hide my disappointment.

With a wink, Nicholas says, "We have a job to do first."

38

WHEN WE ARRIVE...

I GLANCE over at Nicholas Crawford as we ride the elevator to the penthouse of the Wailea Lani Resort and Spa.

He gives me a wink. He looks excited.

I'm consumed by terror.

Nicholas Crawford is an enigma. I don't know what he does for a living. I don't know how he makes his money. I don't know why he made me that offer. What I do know is that my desire for him is so strong it feels like an addiction.

The other thing that I know is that he likes to play games.

Not long ago, he sent me a check for almost one hundred and sixty-eight thousand dollars without leaving his name. It was only after I deposited it and paid off my student loans that he invited me to his home in Hawaii.

Then he made me an offer.

Spend a year with him, traveling, pretending to be his date, his girlfriend, whatever he needs, and in return he will pay me one million dollars. When I told him that there was no way I would ever sleep with him, he promised that before our time was up, I'd be begging him to do it.

His offer frightened me. But it wasn't because I didn't want to accept, it was because I did. Overwhelmed by feelings that I couldn't handle, I ran back home only to discover that my mother had made a mess of her life, only this time she'd put herself in real danger. The only thing that would save her was fifty-thousand dollars and Nicholas sent me the money without me even having to ask.

Why did I come back to Maui?

Sometimes, standing still isn't enough.

Sometimes, you have to take a chance.

Sometimes, doing something that scares the shit out of you is the only way to move forward.

I don't know if his offer is still available.

I don't know if I would accept it even if it were.

I don't know why we are pretending to be Mr. and Mrs. Landon.

What I do know is that when he touches my hand, he rouses every cell in my body.

What I do know is that when he intertwines his fingers with mine, I never want to let him go.

A woman with a long mane of curls comes up to us. "Thank you for coming," she says, shaking Nicholas' hand.

"Albert Landon. This is my wife, Olivia Thom... Landon," Nicholas says, correcting himself as if he had made a mistake using my maiden name instead of my married name.

The lies flow out so naturally, they feel like the truth.

Nicholas smiles at me, almost giggling, giving me a warm squeeze. We are supposed to be newlyweds staying at this resort for our honeymoon.

"It's a pleasure to meet you. Can I get you something to drink?"

"No, I think we'll walk around first," he says.

"Yes, of course. The bar is right over there."

Nicholas nods and pulls me toward the center of the room by my hand. Intimidated by all of the people in their cocktail attire and accurate life stories, I grab onto his arm and stay close to him. I want to ask him what we're doing here. I want to ask him who I'm supposed to be even though we already went over this.

A waiter walks around with glasses of white wine. Nicholas grabs one for himself and one for me. Now, we look like everyone else in the room. The penthouse is huge with various seating nooks arranged just so, giving the place an inviting feel.

I rest my glass on a tall cocktail table, but Nicholas nods for me to follow him. We smile as we walk past groups of people sitting on couches and around tables.

What mesmerizes me most is the view through the floor-to-ceiling windows of the wrap-around balcony, which looks over the ocean. Water goes all the way to the horizon and I yearn to be out there somewhere, instead of in this room.

"This is my wife, Olivia Landon," Nicholas introduces me to a group of people standing around a roulette table.

He thought it would be best that I use my real name so that I wouldn't forget to respond when he called me.

Nicholas purchases chips directly from the dealer and places six of them just on the outside line of two rows of three numbers. The point of roulette is to place the chips on the numbers you think that the ball will land on and this way he is betting on the whole block of six numbers. The dealer spins the wheel, releasing the ball. I watch the board and other people's bets. When my eyes return to his bet, all I know is that he lost some and won others.

"Oh, well." He shrugs and repeats the process.

"So, where are you two from?" the woman standing next to me says.

She has big hair and long nails and a thick nasally accent. She's also not playing and looks as bored as I feel.

"Boston," I say. "We're here on our honeymoon."

This is only partly a lie.

"Oh, how wonderful! I'm Kathy. My husband and I are celebrating our ten year anniversary. Second marriages for both."

"Congratulations," I say, shaking her hand.

"We're fellow East Coasters. We're from New Jersey."

"Oh, nice," I feign interest. "I used to vacation at the Jersey shore all the time as a kid."

"Really? Where?"

Shit.

I haven't practiced this.

I've never been to the state but I try to remember a city that I heard of from television.

"Cape May?" I say, but it comes out more like a question than an answer.

"Yes, of course! Great place. We're not too far from there."

I nod, letting out a sigh of relief.

"What do you do?" she asks.

"I'm an assessment writer."

Nicholas and I have practiced this. Just tell the truth, he said. You have an interesting job that you can talk about a lot and that's exactly what we need.

"Goodness, what does that mean?" she gasps.

I laugh.

"Basically, I write test questions for all of those standardized tests that kids have to take in schools."

"Wow, I had no idea that was a job."

"Somebody's gotta do it," I say with a shrug. "I write the math ones."

"Math?" She puts her hand over her mouth. Her whole body shudders. "I think I need another drink just to get over the PTSD that I still suffer from high school algebra."

I laugh. This reaction is nothing that I'm not used to.

Most people hate math and they aren't afraid to tell me to my face.

"C'mon, let's let these guys play their game. Get a drink with me," she says, tugging at my arm.

My eyes search for Nicholas'.

I'm not sure what I'm supposed to do.

"Oh, get me some whiskey," he says, placing another bet. "You know what kind I like."

My blood runs cold.

Though I may know math, I know nothing about whiskey. Not even a name of a company that makes it. But Kathy waves at me again and I have no choice but to follow her.

39

WHEN HE TELLS ME THE TRUTH...

KATHY IS TALKING my ear off as if we have known each other for ages. I walk up to the bar only half listening.

I'm not a very good liar and I do not think well on my feet.

My heart is pounding out of my chest.

I am cursing at myself for ever coming back here.
To him.

"What's the best kind of whiskey that you have?" I ask.

"We have Johnny Walker Blue. Macallan Rare."

I've heard of the first one so I opt for the second.

"Great choice, ma'am."

"Wow, your husband has expensive taste," Kathy says, taking a glass of Pinot Grigio.

It feels like the moment when I should complain about something, so I roll my eyes and nod.

"I know, right?" I say. "He complains about how much I spend on my shoes, but then has no problem spending money on stuff like this. At least, after it's all said and done, I still have my shoes."

"My husband is the same way with cars."

We laugh as I deliver his drink back to the table.

"Thank you, honey," Nicholas says, reaching his hand out for the glass.

He takes a step toward me, bumping into Kathy.

She collides with me and the drink goes crashing down to the floor.

"Oh my God, I'm so sorry," I say, kneeling down over the mess.

Ice cubes mixed with glass and a puddle of whiskey are spreading over the wreckage.

I reach to pick up a piece, but the group of waiters push me away.

One of them carefully sweeps all the shards up with a little broom while the others blot away the liquid with a dishrag.

A moment later, it's as if nothing happened.

Nicholas helps me to my feet.

"You really didn't need to help," he whispers.

"I can't help it," I say, more for Kathy's benefit than my own. "I'm not used to having servers around."

She laughs and joins her husband around the roulette table.

"Well, it was nice to meet you, Paul," Nicholas says, tugging at my arm. "We'll have to get a round of golf in sometime."

"Yes, of course," Paul says without looking away from the table.

Nicholas gives me a small smile on our way out.

"What was the point of all that?" I ask, when we get back to our room.

Nicholas goes directly to his bag and packs up the few things that we have scattered on the bed.

"We're not staying here?" I ask.

"No," he says.

I pack up my stuff and follow him to his car.

It is only after we drive out of the resort and disappear onto the highway that zigzags along the cliff that Nicholas opens his mouth.

"Thank you," he says without taking his eyes off the road.

"Thank you for what?"

He reaches into his pocket and pulls out a tennis bracelet.

There are six rows of diamonds with a delicate clasp in the back.

My forehead creases.

Where had I seen this before? Oh, yes, of course.

I shake my head.

Of course!

"But...that's Kathy's!" I gasp.

He smiles.

"What are you doing with Kathy's bracelet?" I take it from him and examine how the high grade quality diamonds twinkle even in the faint light of the setting sun.

"This bracelet belongs to Theodore Grabinsky who bought it for his wife for their fortieth anniversary. She loved it dearly until her death seven years later from breast cancer. When Mr. Grabinsky decided to sell his home in Cincinnati and retire to his vacation home on Marco Island, he sold off his wine collection but kept most of his wife's jewelry, especially the pieces that she really loved."

Shaking my head, I try to figure what any of this has to do with the woman I met at the resort or why Nicholas lifted it off her.

"What does this have to do with Kathy?" I ask, raising my eyebrow.

"When Mr. Grabinsky went through his late wife's jewelry box," Nicholas continues without answering my question. "He was shocked to discover that this bracelet was no longer there. His property had not had a break in, not one that he knew about. So, he hired a private investigator to help him get it back."

A new song comes on through the car speakers. Nicholas skips it using the control panel on his steering wheel.

"Kathy Moreno's husband, Paul, is a dentist who spends his off hours running a pretty sizable bookie operation. One of his clients didn't have enough money to pay his debt so Paul accepted that bracelet in exchange and gifted it to Kathy on Mother's Day."

Nicholas taps his finger on the steering wheel and looks out in the distance.

"Of course, he couldn't tell her that the diamonds are all real and are of the highest quality because then he would have to explain how he could afford a piece of jewelry that costs more than a million dollars," Nicholas says.

"She doesn't know what he does?" I ask.

"Unfortunately, Kathy Moreno doesn't know much about her husband." He smiles mischievously.

I lean toward him eager to hear more.

"Paul's girlfriend is pregnant with their second child and he is filing for divorce as soon as they get back home."

"But they are here celebrating their anniversary!" I point out.

"Paul got burned in his first divorce so he was smarter the second time around. He wants Kathy to think that the four thousand a month she will get as alimony in addition to keeping the house will make him suffer."

I shake my head.

"How do you know *all* of this?" I ask. "*Any* of this?"

40

WHEN HE MAKES ME CHOOSE...

"It's my job to know," Nicholas says.

I wait for him to elaborate, but he doesn't.

"So, why did you take her bracelet?"

"Mr. Grabinsky *hired* me to retrieve his bracelet for him."

I nod as if any of this makes any sense.

"This is what I do, Olive," Nicholas says. "A part of it anyway."

"How did ..."

"This is what I used to do," he interrupts me. "Back home, I developed a special set of skills ..."

"To steal?" I interrupt him.

"That's a crude way of putting it."

"How would you put it?"

"I learned how to separate people from their property without them noticing."

"Maybe not in the moment," I point out. "But Kathy will notice that she doesn't have her bracelet on when she gets back to her room. And her husband will know that it was the real one that went missing."

A speck of gold in Nicholas' eye twinkles.

He smiles out of the corner of his lips.

"This is a big deal, Nicholas. They may not know our names, but they saw our faces. The resort probably has cameras all over the place. We weren't in that room for longer than half an hour. We were the only ones who left."

My heart starts to beat a mile a minute.

I see the police knocking at my door.

They place handcuffs on my wrists.

They take me to the station, take my mugshot.

My boss sends me an email asking me not to come back. She doesn't care that my trial is pending. She doesn't care that I haven't been convicted of anything yet.

Two months later, my landlord sends me an eviction letter. I haven't paid the rent and I can't afford to do it anymore.

I have nowhere to go except my mother's place.

"How dare you bring me into this." I say. "I had no idea what you were doing. And I'm going to tell the police everything you told me. I'm not going down for this shit."

Nicholas' face remains expressionless.

"Can you hear me?" I ask, grabbing his arm. "Are you even listening to me? You have money, you'll be able to get out of this mess. But it's all going to land on me and I've worked way too hard to lose everything."

He can hear me, but he doesn't look like he's listening. I need to wake him up.

If he weren't driving, I'd smack him.

"Everything is going to be fine," he says.

"No, it's not. They're going to catch you."

"Kathy won't notice a thing because she still has a bracelet on her," Nicholas says slowly, savoring every word. "It's identical to the one that she thinks her husband gave her, dotted with Swarovski crystals and worth just under five hundred dollars. About the same amount of money that she thinks her husband spent on it."

I stare at him, trying to process what he just said.

"You switched her bracelets?" I ask.

"Yes, and you assisted by providing the opportunity."

"But how?" My mouth drops open.

I replay the events in my head.

I walk up to him with his drink.

Someone bumps into him.

He bumps into Kathy, who bumps into me.

The drink shatters onto the floor.

"You created the little bit of chaos that I needed to make the swap. It's all a game."

I scratch at the leather on the arm rest.

"Paul will only find out when he files for divorce and tries to take it from her. By then, he will assume that it was Kathy who is trying to pass Swarovski crystals off as real diamonds."

I nod.

"None of this will ever come back to me," Nicholas says. "Or you."

I can't resist the temptation to roll my eyes. That's what men like him always say.

They believe they are impervious.

They believe that nothing can touch them.

And maybe they're right.

Maybe nothing will happen to them because they're

too powerful. But there are others, the ones that help them, who will lose.

Others like me.

"You don't trust me," Nicholas says. It comes out as a statement rather than a question.

"Am I so obvious?" I ask sarcastically.

I cross my arms and stare out of the window.

A bird flies in the sky somewhere in the distance. The jealousy that I feel toward her right now is difficult to describe.

Nicholas doesn't say a word.

Instead, he leaves me alone and lets me stew in my anger.

"You are not a stranger to this, Olive."

"Is that why I'm here?"

The road looks familiar now and I know that we're getting closer to his house. I'm regretting coming here again. I look down at my phone and wish that I had cell reception so that I could call Sydney.

"Sydney is staying at James's," Nicholas says, reading my mind. "You can call her when we get to my place."

"I'm not staying with you. This was a terrible mistake."

Nicholas turns down the music just a bit. "Do you want me to take you back to the airport?" he asks.

I take a deep breath.

Is that what I want? My thoughts all mash together, making it impossible to separate one from another.

"Yes, I do," I say.

A part of me expects him to beg me to stay, but he doesn't. Instead, he pulls over at the nearest turnaround and flips the signal that he's turning back.

"You're going to take me back now?" I gasp.

"That's what you said you wanted."

Our eyes meet.

I want him to plead for me to stay but his eyes remain cool and collected as before.

Not exactly dead, but completely free of expression.

The blinker makes a steady dinging sound.

As all other sounds disappear, it seems to get louder with each passing moment.

"Tell me to go," Nicholas says, motioning toward the road back.

My jaw clenches up.

My nail makes a deep indentation in the leather.

I don't want to go home, but I can't bring myself to say it.

He is so infuriating.

Anyone else would pressure me to make my decision quickly. They would urge me to hurry up already, but Nicholas has infinite patience.

Sitting back in the driver's seat, he stares straight ahead as the cars whiz by us in both directions.

"I'm really tired," I finally cave. "I don't want to go on another long flight."

"Does that mean you're staying?" he asks.

A dimple forms in the lower part of his cheek.

"Tonight, yes."

"Good." He steps on the gas.

41

WHEN I WAIT FOR MORE...

YOU'RE NOT a stranger to this. That's what Nicholas said to me in the car. It was supposed to sound like a throwaway line when in reality it was anything but that.

I asked him if that's why I'm here but he didn't answer. He changed the topic to Sydney and he never went back to it.

But why?

How much does he know about me?

We don't speak the rest of the way to his house. After parking the car, he shows me to the same cottage I stayed in before.

"Where is everyone?" I ask, looking around.

None of his staff are here now and the property feels almost deserted.

"They're off work for two more days."

I nod.

"We'll just have to fend for ourselves."

I nod again.

He smiles when he says that but it's a bit different from his other smiles.

There's a mischievousness in this one. A glint of hope, even.

I can feel his gaze on my body.

I know that he wants me.

I want him, too.

I've never felt this much desire for anyone before.

"Would you like to join me for a drink on the porch?" Nicholas says.

"Let me freshen up first and then I'll join you."

I use the bathroom and then look at myself in the mirror as I wash my hands. The woman looking back at me is tired but energized. There are few things in the world that are as exciting as taking something that doesn't belong to you. My only regret about today is that I wasn't in on the con.

I don't know how much Nicholas knows about me but he seems to be the type to do his research.

I am not here by accident and it is not just his affection for his dead sister that got him to reach out to me.

I knew there had to be something more to this. The thing that I didn't know was that anyone knew about my past.

"You used me," I say when he hands me a martini.

I stare at the slice of lemon that he placed on the edge and my mouth waters.

"Everyone uses everyone," he says, bringing his martini to his lips.

"Is this why you made me that offer?" I ask.

He stares out to the ocean. Somewhere around us, crickets and frogs start to sing their evening songs.

"What do you know about me?" I ask.

He turns slowly toward me. Glaring into my eyes he opens his mouth, pauses, and then says, "Enough."

"I doubt that." I shrug.

I'm acting smug but in fact, for all I know, he knows everything.

"Anyway, it's not a secret," I say, trying another angle.

"I doubt that." He smiles.

We drink our martinis in silence, unwilling to be the first one to speak up and show a sign of weakness.

"You used me," I start. "You told me the story but not the mark."

"You didn't need to know who I was after or why."

"It's best when everyone involved knows what's going on," I correct him.

"It may be preferred, but you handled yourself quite well going in on it blind," he says.

"You did that on purpose," I say.

It's less of a statement and more of an accusation.

"It was a test. I wanted to see how you would do under less than ideal circumstances."

"You had no right," I hiss.

Nicholas walks up to me, places his index finger under my chin, and lifts it up in the air.

"I had every right to know what the people who work for me are capable of," he says stoically.

Of course, I think to myself. How could I be so stupid?

None of this is real.

He brought me here, told me a sob story about his sister, and made me think that we had some sort of sexual chemistry that we never really had.

That's the thing about confident men (and women), they *not* only lie, but they make you think that it's not a lie at all.

The best cons are those in which the mark, the person being taken for a ride, doesn't even know that they have been swindled.

Like Kathy Moreno. She didn't know that her bracelet was worth a million dollars and she didn't know that she'd lost a bracelet worth a million dollars. For the conman, it's a win-win.

"What do you want from me?" I ask.

"I need a partner. I have a number of projects that need to be executed in the next few months. You are the best person for the job...or so I've heard," Nicholas says.

"From whom?" I ask.

"Does it matter?"

I lean on the railing and turn my body to face his. "Of course, it does. No one knows about my past. No one is supposed to, anyway. How do you?"

"Like I said before, I am very good at research." Nicholas inhales deeply, clearly agitated. "Now, if you're interested, I have one more test for you."

"I'm not," I say, narrowing my eyes. "My days of lying and cheating and stealing are over."

"My real offer is this. You travel with me, pretend to be my girlfriend, wife, ex, whatever I need for 365 days. In exchange, I'll pay you one million dollars for your services."

If he's offering me this much money then, not only must he really need me but these jobs must be bringing in a lot more than that.

"And forty percent of the take," I say.

He shakes his head, giving me a laugh.

When he focuses his eyes on mine, I show him exactly how serious I am.

"Ten," he says after a moment.

"Ten percent? Are you kidding me?"

"Don't flatter yourself. You're not the only pretty girl who can run a con out there," Nicholas says to deflate my ego.

But I know that it's just another bargaining tool.

"Thirty percent," I say after a beat.

There's a long pause.

I wait while he thinks.

"Fifteen," he says after a moment.

"Thirty," I insist.

Nicholas takes a step closer.

I can feel his breath on my skin.

His plump luscious lips are relaxed.

He opens his mouth a bit and I see his tongue.

A flash of heat rushes through my body. It takes an enormous amount of effort to keep myself from reaching over and kissing him.

He leans over and whispers, "Fifteen."

What a son-of-a-bitch.

"Twenty-five percent," I whisper, feeling my knees getting weak.

He takes his hand and runs it down my side.

A bolt of electricity rushes through me.

"Twenty-five percent and no sex," I say as sternly as possible once I catch my breath.

I state the no sex clause out loud more for my benefit than for his, as a reminder.

"Sex is not part of the deal. I already told you that you'll be begging me for it before our time is up," Nicholas says nonchalantly. "Fifteen percent. That's my final offer."

Angry with how the negotiation went, I give him a slight nod. He puts out his hand for me to shake.

"This handshake is contingent on how everything goes tomorrow night," Nicholas says.

"What's tomorrow night?" I ask.

"Your second test. One word of advice: leave your prudishness at the door."

42

WHEN I RECEIVE THE PRESENT...

AFTER SLEEPING for fourteen hours straight, I wake up in a strange bed and try to remember exactly what I had agreed to the previous night. Things slowly come back to me.

The bracelet. The lies. The show.

A good con always requires a bit of a show.

It's not about brute force.

It's a sleight of hand.

It's about telling an outlandish story with a smile on your face or tears in your eyes, depending on what's required.

I stumbled upon this world by accident.

In high school, I spent my Friday afternoons at the mall stealing fashion jewelry, makeup, and the occasional pair of jeans.

Then one day, a security guard at Marshall's stopped my friend Jamie Van Camp, took her to the back room and found that she had three unpaid for shirts on underneath her hoodie.

Back then, our modus operandi was to take a bunch of clothes into the changing room, put the ones we wanted to keep under our clothes, place a big pile on the clerk's table, and tell her that we are buying the rest.

If you were chatty and had a big enough mess of clothes, she rarely bothered to make sure that you had the same number of pieces to match the number with which we went into the dressing room with.

But one day it didn't work. The manager called the police and Jamie's parents, but her parents' lawyer convinced them not to press charges.

The following weekend, Jamie was ready to try her luck at Target but I was done with it.

If that had been me, I would've been arrested and my mother wouldn't have paid my bail so I would be stuck in jail until my hearing. No, I didn't have two caring parents who would save me from whatever mess I got myself into so I couldn't risk so much anymore.

I take a walk around Nicholas' estate. There is no one outside but the weather is marvelous and the crystal blue water of the pool calls to me. I slip into my bathing suit and dive in.

"One million dollars," I say when I reach the other side.

I spent all of my years in high school, and especially in college, working as hard as I could just to give myself a chance.

I wanted to get as far away as possible from the life that I grew up in.

I wanted more than anything to *not* be like my mother.

There is nothing wrong with government assistance and most people who receive it really do need it. But I knew that I could make my own way in life. I don't have any children and I wanted to make a career that I could be proud of.

I thought that after working for two years at a job that I would have some prospects.

I know that I'm due for a promotion to a position with more responsibility and maybe more money, but is this really what I want to do for the rest of my life? More responsibility and an extra thousand dollars a year still means writing assessment items all day long. And now that I have spent two years doing that, I don't have experience in another related field, meaning that I would have to start at the bottom at whatever new job I take.

I lie down flat on my back and float with my head half submerged in the water.

I have a good salary, that many people would give anything to have.

I have a nice apartment, a great roommate.

My student loans are all paid for.

So...why am I still considering this?

One million dollars plus fifteen percent of whatever our partnership brings in.

This is the kind of money that changes things. It's no longer just getting by. It's no longer living paycheck to paycheck waiting for your annual, one-week vacation.

This is the kind of money that makes a boss obsolete. If invested and allocated properly, this is the kind of money that could set me up for the rest of my life in a very comfortable life.

I fold my arms on the edge of the pool and rest my chin on top.

A tall white bird walks confidently among the lush landscaping outside of the wrap-around porch.

Given the prices in Maui, this house costs a lot more than one million but that million will go a long way toward getting me here.

I take a deep breath.

It's not just the monetary perks that make me yearn to say yes.

It's something else.

I have an itch that I haven't scratched since I gave up replacing sorority girls' Tiffany jewelry with knock-offs at Wellesley.

I walk back to my cottage to the sound of squeaking rubber as my flip-flops collide with the bottoms of my feet.

There was a time when an opportunity like this was all I ever wanted. But back then I didn't have much of a life.

To take this chance, I will have to give up my apartment and put my career on hold for a year.

And what happens if something goes wrong?

After taking a shower, I find a large box on the bed.

The note placed on the top reads:

BE READY BY 7. *Wear this.*

NC

THE BOX IS BEAUTIFUL, decorated in ornate swirls of turquoise and gold. I lift up the lid carefully and place it to one side. The contents are packed in perfectly folded tissue paper with a large gold sticker holding everything in place.

My hands shake as I try to peel it off, eventually giving up and just ripping through it.

When I see what's inside, I gasp.

43

WHEN HE SEES ME...

No wonder he told me not to be prudish, I say to myself, looking at the contents of the box. This isn't exactly something that a nun would wear.

I take the bra and panties that lay on the top. They are a matching set with the same light gothic design. They are both made from ultra-fine Bobbinet tulle and crisscrossing silk bindings.

The items are so beautiful, I can't stop myself from trying them on.

Looking at myself in the full length mirror, I admire the way the plunge underwire bra enhances the cleavage without the need for padding.

I run my fingers over the delicate tulle and lace motifs of the thong and linger over the gold rings and double elastic rouleaux sides.

Below another layer of tissue paper, I find the corset. It has a curved front hem with diamond-shaped paneling that wraps all the way around the back.

There's a knock on the door. A rush of adrenaline courses through my body. I look around for something to cover myself up with. The only thing big enough is the towel.

"It's not seven," I say.

"I thought you may need some help," Nicholas says.

Dressed in a two piece blue suit with a notched lapel and a three-button front, he looks me up and down with a smile.

"I'm not ready yet." I straighten my back.

"I'm not sure that's part of the outfit," he says, touching the welt pocket on the right side of his chest.

I adjust the towel to make sure it's tighter.

"Drop the towel," Nicholas says.

"No."

"This is part of the deal."

"What? You seeing me in provocative clothing?"

"No, you wearing *this* to tonight's event," Nicholas says. "All of it."

He motions to the corset.

I clench my jaw.

"This is part of the deal. The mark will be there and we both have to fit in."

I cross my arms and sit down on the edge of the bed.

"What's wrong?"

"I'm not going anywhere wearing that. I look like an escort."

"You're not an escort but this job may require you to look like one on occasion. So what?"

"So what? I don't need this," I say.

"Actually, I have a feeling that you do," he says boldly.

There's a rush that comes with doing something like this.

The anticipation alone is intoxicating.

It's like waiting for sex.

The foreplay that goes on and on...in some ways it's better than the orgasm.

But then, when you get away with it, a wave of relief sweeps over you consuming everything in sight...that's why I have to put on these clothes.

The anticipation starts to build. This is a costume that I need to be the person that the mark needs me to be.

I walk up to the mirror and let go of the towel.

Nicholas' eyes are on me.

They make their way up my body carefully but without a tinge of desire.

He is in work mode and he isn't looking at me like a woman wearing provocative lingerie.

He's looking at me the way that a designer looks at the set that he has just constructed. There's a window out there and a table to the left and a door leading backstage. All of the pieces are fake but the question is, do they look real enough for the audience to suspend their disbelief enough to get through the show?

Without another word, Nicholas hands me the corset.

It's a deep-cut, timeless, sexy piece made of Chantilly Leavers lace with satin panels and boning. The lining is made of tulle and it comes with four detachable suspender straps. He helps me fasten the hooks, trimming my waist and forming my body into the ideal female hourglass figure.

"Perfect," he says.

I glance at myself in the mirror.

Whatever insecurities I have about my body seem to vanish even though I am not wearing much when it comes to clothes.

Everything about the outfit is flattering and alluring. It

draws the eye only to my best features while minimizing the rest.

"I don't have any pantyhose," I say.

"We'll just have to fix that," Nicholas says, getting down on one knee.

He gets so close to me I feel his slow deep breaths on my thigh.

Shivers run down my spine.

I shift my weight from one foot to another.

His fingers run up the side of my leg and tug at the first suspender strap.

It unfastens quickly, dropping into his hand. Instead of leaning over, he places one hand on my butt and another on my stomach and twists me slightly.

Another strap is off.

He twists me again, only this time his hand lingers a bit on my naked buttocks. I love the feel of my ass in his strong hands and revel in the moment.

He takes off another strap and unfortunately there aren't ten more.

I glance down at him.

Our eyes meet.

I can see his professionalism wavering.

I lift up his chin higher and sweep my fingertips across his lower lip.

My heart rate speeds up. He opens his mouth and wraps it around my finger, pulling it inside.

My knees get weak.

When they start to wobble, Nicholas grabs my butt cheeks again and spins me again.

"Two more straps to go," he says. "Stand up straight."

My legs feel weak as if I'm about to fall down. I take one step to the side and then another.

Instead of going up my side, this time, his hands hesitate just below the small of my back.

I clench my butt and then relax, allowing my cheeks to fall naturally into his cupped hands.

My body jerks and another strap comes off.

One last twist.

I adjust my stance so that he actually has to put some force into it.

He places one hand on top of the panty line and runs the other one down my butt, outlining the contours of each curve.

Fire starts to build within my core. His fingers run down the inside of my thighs and then back up.

He stops for a moment, touching the thong right

between my legs for just a moment before continuing on and removing the last strap.

My body deflates from disappointment.

Nicholas smiles, pleased with his power, and gives me a little slap on my ass. "Let's go," he says.

44

WHEN IT'S TIME TO PLAY...

Luckily, the drive to this place isn't far because sitting in this corset makes it nearly impossible to breathe. The bones that keep the corset tight and in place, shaving inches off my normal waist and giving it an unattainably small diameter is the same thing that makes bending at the middle futile.

"How did you find out that I have a history with this kind of...work?" I ask.

I've never been arrested or convicted of anything before. I never told anyone, not even Sydney.

I always worked alone so telling others was an unnecessary risk.

By the time Sydney and I got to be close friends, I'd put that part of my life behind me.

I locked the secret up in a little box and promised myself never to open it again.

But that's the thing about secrets, if they are forced into a dark place, they find a way out.

"I already told you," Nicholas says. "I'm very good at research."

"But there is no one who knew anything about this."

"Just because there were no charges doesn't mean that there weren't people who had their suspicions about you."

My fingertips turn to ice.

"Who?" I ask in a whisper.

"It doesn't matter."

"It matters to me."

Nicholas shakes his head. "I do not reveal my sources. All I can say is that they're not after you. It was just a Tiffany necklace. She married a man who could buy her twenty of them a day."

I search my mind for names. The problem is that I had gone through so many dorm rooms and so many jewelry boxes that I couldn't possibly know every owner's name.

None of the women confronted me.

None of them even acted suspiciously around me.

"Why did you stop?" he asks as we pull up to a large manor house.

"I got close once. Close to getting caught. There was a big fraternity party that all the Kappa Kappa Kappa girls were obviously invited to. It wasn't going to be a lavish affair, more like the exact opposite. Raunchy and dirty with a mud wrestling pit for those who really wanted to impress the guys. None of the women were going to wear their expensive jewelry to this party and I had some time to break in and go through the merchandise carefully."

I've never told anyone this story before.

It feels good to share it now, especially with someone who understands the desire to take what's not yours.

The expert way that he lifted that bracelet off Kathy Moreno and replaced it almost simultaneously with a fake made me realize that he might be one of the few people in the world to know how I feel.

"What happened?" he asks.

"That night I got away with about ten thousand dollars' worth of stuff. I replaced them with good quality replicas that cost me about a grand, so that was a good night's work," I say. "But when I got home, something happened. No one suspected a thing and it had nothing to do with getting caught. I just felt...bad. I'd occasionally have these pangs of remorse over what I was doing, and they were debilitating."

Nicholas nods to keep me talking.

But I don't need any additional encouragement.

"One part of me would say that I wasn't doing anything wrong. It's not like these women deserved to get ripped off but they wouldn't even know that anything happened, so who was I really hurting? What was the big deal? But another part of me, the one that kept me up at night, would gnaw at my conscience. It doesn't matter if anyone knew what I was doing, it doesn't matter how much money they had or how little money I had, all that mattered was that stealing was wrong and I was better than that."

A valet opens the door for me and I step out in my sky high stilettos.

I am not an expert heel wearer by any stretch of the imagination, so I take each step with care and deliberation.

This way I don't look like I don't know what I'm doing, instead, I look like I'm just taking my time getting there.

"So, you haven't run a con since?" Nicholas asks, taking me by my arm.

I cinch my trench coat a little tighter around the waist and shake my head.

"I went to counseling to stop," I say. "But in order for it to work, I needed to divulge details, which I wasn't ready to talk about. So, I quit cold turkey."

He leads me up the steps and I lean on him for support.

"Is this something I should be worried about?"he asks

as we walk inside a glamorous modern house with minimalist furniture.

A woman standing at a podium next to the double doors at the entrance asks for our names.

"Thank you for coming, Mr. and Mrs. Puglisi, the coat check is right over there."

There is no one else in the foyer besides us and the thought of taking off my trench coat makes me sick to my stomach.

I cross my arms, tightening my hands around my shoulders to make sure that nothing can take my cover away from me.

But when we enter the adjacent room with a bartender and couples in various states of undress lounging, drinking, and laughing, my anxiety lessens.

The women are dressed in a lot more provocative clothing that I am and the men are hardly wearing anything except for tight underwear that leave very little to the imagination.

"Feel free to get a drink and explore the house. Different things happen in different rooms. This room over here is for socializing. Then when you want more privacy, you can go into the back rooms. Some are just for women. Some are just for men, others are for couples and another is for everyone to enjoy themselves together."

I hand over my trench coat and Nicholas takes off his suit jacket and loosens his tie.

Something comes over me and I reach over and unbutton his shirt.

He smiles.

"You getting in the mood?" he asks without stopping me.

I lick my lips.

It's not so much the others that get me excited, it's really just him.

Once his shirt falls open, I move the tie out of the way and run my fingers over each defined pectoral muscle.

They relax and flex with each breath and I bite my lower lip to hold back the excitement that starts to build in my core.

At the bar, I take my martini and watch Nicholas take a sip of his whiskey.

We make firm eye contact before he gazes down at my breasts. This very expensive bra does make them look amazing.

I glance around the room.

Nicholas' eyes aren't the only ones on me.

We are the newcomers here. Fresh meat. We're here to do a job, but first, it's time to play.

45

WHEN WE MEET THEM...

CARRYING OUR DRINKS, we make our way toward the far end of the room where two groups of couples sit perched on a fat leather couch. The tall blonde has her hands on the crotch of the man next to her who is dressed in nothing but a black pair of James Bond style knickers.

I can see his massive package and she licks her lips as she feels it.

The couples are so engrossed in conversation that I wonder if they will make room for us.

They do.

The smaller brunette seizes her gaze on my bosom and immediately sits up and waves us over. Her legs part and cross at the ankles and I mimic her body position when I sit down.

Nicholas introduces us as Thomas and Meredith Puglisi.

Just a couple of everyday normal couples coming to a strange house to meet other normal couples they can hook up with. I can't help but smile at the ridiculousness of this situation. And yet...at the same time...maybe this is my chance.

As Nicholas talks and I nod and confirm whatever it is that he says, I turn my body slightly toward him and part my legs. The corset digs into my thighs but it also forces me to sit up straight and makes my breasts look fucking epic.

Danika Montezuma, the brunette, hangs on every word that Nicholas says while touching her face and lips. When he makes a joke, her skin flushes and she laughs nervously.

Suddenly, a pang of jealousy rushes through me like a bolt of lightning.

I am not Nicholas' girlfriend.

The only reason I'm here is to pretend to be his wife.

But this is not a place where regular rules of society apply. The whole point of this place is to break all rules of engagement.

Everyone here is either a couple or a single woman looking to get with someone else.

Some are into finding a third, some are into a full blown

orgy.

So, if Danika wants Nicholas, there is nothing really that I can do to stop her from having him. Right?

I don't know.

I've never been anywhere like this.

So far it feels like a bar or a nightclub just with more scantily clad people. But the fact that if you like someone all you have to do is go to another room, makes it quite unlike any other nightclub I've ever been to.

"Meredith, right?" a beautiful man with messy cool blond hair says, putting his hand on my knee.

My cheeks flush and I flash him a quick smile.

"Yes," I confirm. "What's your name again?"

"Jack Gilbert," he says, running his fingers up my thigh.

He lets his hand linger there, probably waiting for me to draw the line between what's okay and what's not.

But my eyes drift over to Nicholas and I see Danika's breasts brushing up to his arm.

He touches his jaw, and then reaches over to lift her chin.

I purse my lips, clenching my teeth.

Danika isn't the mark, and neither is Jack.

Why are we here wasting our time with them?

Why is he subjecting me to this?

Of course, the truth is that at this moment, I couldn't care less about the con. I'm again in the dark about most of it, expected to just play a part as his sidekick.

But watching him flirting with another woman, touching her...my jealousy tightens all of the muscles in my body.

My stomach hardens and my breaths become faster and coarser, getting lodged somewhere in the back of my throat on their way in and out.

Immediately my mind plays a game of comparison with my rival. I'm at least twenty pounds heavier. My thighs are much bigger. My hair isn't as shiny. My eyes aren't as beautiful.

But then she leans over to me and tucks a strand of hair behind my ear. Jack runs his hand on the inside of my thigh.

My eyes dart to Nicholas as I search his face not so much for help but for an explanation.

Instead of providing one, he just leans over and kisses my neck.

"Stay with it," he whispers.

I inhale loudly and lean back against the couch.

When Danika reaches for Jack, he brings his hands up to her face and kisses her.

They kiss each other by leaning across me.

For a moment, I lose myself in the way Jack's toned body tenses and relaxes with each breath and then it occurs to me that it's okay to touch.

I reach over to him and press my fingertips to his skin.

He moans and I let them move down his body watching his mouth move around hers.

A quick jerk snaps me out of my trance.

It's Nicholas standing in front of me and pulling me up from the couch. Danika and Jack part long enough for me to get up before falling back into each other's arms.

"What are you doing?" I ask.

"We need to go somewhere else."

I follow him but reading the expression on his face, I can tell that this isn't planned.

No, it's not like something is happening or we are about to be found out.

It's something else altogether.

His movements are quick as if he is fueled by anger rather than a strong sense of purpose.

Then it hits me.

I stop in the hallway, pulling my hand away from his. "Are you jealous?" I ask.

46

WHEN I SEE HER...

"No, I'm not jealous," he snaps back at me. I smile. He's a good liar but not that good.

"Why are you smiling?"

I shrug. "Just find it funny."

"There is nothing funny about this," he says.

He leads me down a few stairs to another room. There are couples having drinks at the far end, but he pulls me into a semi-private booth near the entrance.

"I can't sit here," I say.

"You have to," he says. "I want to talk."

"I can't sit here because if I continue to wear this corset for another minute, I'm going to pass out."

As much as I love the way my waist looks in this thing (this is the first time in a long time that I haven't felt self-conscious about my midsection), sitting in it is nearly impossible.

"Let me take it off," he offers.

He spins me around toward the group of four who were clothed only a few minutes ago and are now almost entirely nude.

As he unfastens one clasp at a time, I watch as the women kiss while the men open them wide and bury their heads in between their thighs.

My hands get sweaty and I twist my moon ring around my thumb in a circular motion.

When Nicholas frees me of my binding, he stands behind me and pushes the hair off my shoulder.

Watching the man unclasping the woman's bra, exposing her breasts while Nicholas leans over and nibbles on my earlobe, my body aches with the need to be touched.

"Tell me to stop," Nicholas whispers, pressing his mouth on my neck.

I throw my head back and expose my skin to his lips.

One of his hands makes its way down and cups one of my butt cheeks. My legs open wide on their own accord, welcoming him further. But instead, he tugs at my thong, pulling it up higher before letting it fall back in its natural position. The fire that started building deep within my core feels like it's going to explode any minute.

My hands search around behind me for something to hold onto.

It doesn't take long for me to find his throbbing dick and wrap my fingers around it. This is the first time I've touched it, and the size of it is quite impressive. I flip around to face him and reach down to unzip him.

While I fumble around with the top button of his pants, he pulls me closer and presses his mouth to mine.

When our lips touch, our tongues immediately intertwine and I press my body as close to him as possible. This is the moment I've been waiting for.

I am no longer acting.

I am just using this as an excuse to do what I want.

My tongue searches for his and I bury my fingers in his hair.

He picks me up, spreads my legs, and wraps them tightly around his waist. His hands grab onto my butt cheeks and I feel his hard, throbbing dick pressing into my pelvic bone.

I want to rip off our clothes and push him deep inside of me.

I want to ride him and I want him to take me from

behind, but all of those moves would require us to first separate and disentangle our bodies for just a moment, and that's completely impossible.

Still holding me tightly around him, pressing his mouth onto mine, Nicholas sits down.

He pulls his head away for a moment to kiss my neck again.

I open my eyes and watch as the woman across the room climbs on top of the man who has been going down on her.

Watching her take him inside of her and feeling Nicholas' body underneath mine pushes me closer and closer to the edge.

A group of three people comes into the room, already with their hands all over each other's bodies.

The woman paws at the two men who position her in between them. She unbuckles one of the guy's pants and pulls him closer to her. When the other guy is taking his time behind her, she reaches back and inserts him inside.

My mouth waters watching her take what she wants from them.

She kisses the guy in front of her, first on the mouth then down his hard body. They crowd around her and that's exactly what she wants.

The one behind her slaps her butt just as the one in the front grabs at her exposed breasts.

Jealous of the attention that I'm giving them, Nicholas tugs at my bra strap and pulls it down my arm.

My breast falls bare before him and he takes it into his mouth.

Finally, I look away from the threesome, tilting my head back consumed by my own pleasure.

When I look up again the girl is in the same position except that she's now facing me.

She looks familiar. I narrow my eyes to get a better look. It can't be her, can it?

"Sydney?" I whisper.

47

WHEN SHE SEES ME…

It takes Sydney a moment to process what she heard. I see her lift her head and look in my direction.

Her mouth falls open and she gets an incredulous stare in her eyes. The guy with his back toward me tries to pull her closer and that's what snaps her out of her daze.

"Olive?" she asks, getting up to her feet.

She doesn't rush but she does get dressed quickly. She grabs the silk robe from behind the sofa and cinches it tightly around her waist.

I climb off Nicholas' lap and take a few steps in her direction.

When she opens her arms, I reciprocate with a warm hug.

"*What* are you doing here?" she whispers into my ear.

"What are *you* doing here?" I ask.

Nicholas shakes hands with her two partners. It is only after we all take a seat around the table that I realize that one of them is James.

My eyes widen but I force myself to keep my surprise to myself.

A waitress comes around, hands each of us a menu of light refreshments.

The men quickly order a round of drinks while Sydney and I remain locked in our stare.

"C'mon," she says, tapping her fingers on my hand. "I have to go to the bathroom, why don't you come with me?"

I let out a sigh of relief.

Nicholas moves to let me out of the booth.

"You can't tell her anything about our job here," he whispers into my ear.

"I won't," I promise.

"You want a robe?" Sydney asks, stopping at the table right by the stairs, pointing to the collection of neatly folded silk robes in both men's and women's styles and a variety of sizes.

Not having noticed them before, I'm thankful to have something to cover up my bare bum.

Instead of going to the ladies' room, Sydney leads me upstairs and out onto the wrap-around porch. There are a few people there, standing with drinks in their hands, so we take the path that goes into the garden for even more privacy.

"What the hell are you doing here?" We ask each other almost simultaneously and then break out in a gaggle of giggles.

We stare at each other and wonder who will be the first one to go.

"Have you ever been anywhere like this before?" I ask.

"Yes," Sydney caves. "A few times, in Boston."

"Really?" I gasp.

I sound like I'm judging her but I'm not.

I'm just surprised. We have been friends for a long time and she has never said a word.

"I went to this club once that Tommy and Elise organized back in my freshman year. It was just in their apartment but basically you came with your boyfriend or alone and did anything you wanted with anyone you wanted," Sydney says.

"Tommy and Elise hosted sex parties?" I ask.

They met each other during orientation, a few days before the first day of classes, and have been inseparable ever since. They have two kids now and live in Connecticut.

"Some of the best ones." Sydney laughs. "They still do."

"Now?"

"They had this amazing one a month after they got back from their honeymoon when they closed on their house. It was pretty epic."

My mouth opens and I press my hand to my lips.

"Why haven't you ever told me this before?" I ask.

She shrugs. "You just never brought it up. And you were like the only person at Wellesley who didn't know about Tommy and Elise. They've slept with nearly everyone in our graduating class."

I shake my head and start to laugh.

"But I'm sorry that I didn't say anything. I should've told you. But I told my ex and he was not very happy."

"What do you mean?" I ask, tilting my head toward hers.

"One day, I sort of brought it up. Said how sexy I thought it was to watch other people have sex...you know, in porn...and I mentioned that I know about this one party. But he totally freaked out."

I give her a brief nod. Her ex was traditional and closed

off and spent ninety percent of their time together belittling her and the rest pining for her.

"I kept a lot of things away from him, as you know, so this ended up just being another thing I put into a little box under lock and key," Sydney says.

"Your sexuality?"

"Yeah." She shrugs. "I just rationalized it as I didn't need the parties. I could get what I needed from him. But that wasn't true."

"So, what happened after you broke it off?"

"The first thing I did was call Tommy and Elise." She laughs. "You remember that weekend trip I took to Vermont to pick apples and get some time to myself?"

I nod.

"Well, I went to Connecticut instead and went down on three guys while their girlfriends ate me out." She laughs. "Plus some."

"I was really concerned about you," I say, starting to laugh, too. "You were so fucking depressed. I wanted to go with you, but you wouldn't let me."

"Now, I wish you had," Sydney says, running her hand down the length of my arm.

"So...how did you end up here?" I ask, pulling my arm away from her.

"When I met James, I decided to be honest. I really

connected and I didn't want to start out another relationship with this secret. So, I just came out and told him. And he was super into it!"

"Really?" I ask.

"Yeah, I was shocked, too. I mean, I thought he would get mad or just at least push me away. But he was really into going. He has never been but it sure didn't feel like it when we were in there."

"That's awesome," I say. "I'm really happy for you, Sydney."

She crosses her arms and looks at me. When I don't respond, she sticks her chin out and waits.

"What?" I ask, shrugging my shoulders pretending to be as innocent as possible.

"Your turn."

"What do you mean?" I look down at my hands and twist the ring around my thumb in a clockwise manner.

"Why the hell are *you* here? What's the story? I need all the details!"

48

WHEN I TELL HER PART OF THE TRUTH...

I BITE the inside of my cheek. Glancing back at the porch I try to imagine what Nicholas would want me to say. I can't tell her about the con. I don't even know much about it but that part of the story must remain a secret.

"What's with the ten thousand yard stare?" she asks, grabbing my hand.

I look down at my shoes. With the weight of my body concentrating at the balls of my feet and my heels, pain starts to shoot up my legs. I shift from one foot to another, but it does very little to alleviate the agony.

"Olive, c'mon, you can tell me."

"Why didn't you pick me up from the airport?" I ask, buying myself more time to think. "You were supposed to get me."

"I know, but Nicholas asked me for a favor. You came

all the way back here. I thought that you'd want to see him as well."

I rub the back of my neck and look down at the ground.

"What happened? Did he force you to come here?"

There's a real look of concern on her face.

"No, no, it's nothing like that," I say. "You're right, I... was interested. Am interested."

She nods.

"Can we sit down somewhere? I have to take these shoes off. My feet are killing me."

We look around the garden for a bench or a rock to sit on but it is all lush bushes and wild tropical flowers. There's a dew over the grass so it would make everything wet were we to sit down. Sydney tries to usher me back to the porch but I can't manage to take another step. Kneeling over, I slip off the heels and carefully place my bruised feet onto the cool wet lawn.

"Ahhh," I moan from pleasure. "Now, this is what I'm talking about."

Sydney follows my lead.

Neither of us says anything for a while and then she kicks at me with her bare foot.

She wants to hear the story and I have no choice but to tell her.

Not knowing exactly where to start, I start at the beginning.

I tell her about Nicholas surprising me at the airport and the way I felt when our hands happened to touch on the drive down.

I skirt over the forbidden details (how I helped *him* steal the diamond bracelet to get it back to his client). Instead, I bare my soul about the chemistry that I feel burning between us.

"So, how did you end up here?" she asks.

Ah, the sixty-four thousand dollar question. We're here for a job, playing a married couple who likes to experiment in the bedroom.

"He invited me here. It's part of the game...to make me really want him."

"Oh, really?" Sydney raises her eyebrows in excitement.

"Well, you know how he made that promise to me? That he wouldn't have sex with me unless I begged him?"

Her eyes twinkle as she nods.

"Bringing me here is part of that."

"Have you ever been to this kind of party before?"

I shake my head.

"How do you feel?"

"Well, I've seen them in porn but you know how it is, it's kind of like that but completely different, too."

"Yeah, I know what you mean," she agrees. "Real sex is a bit different from how it's portrayed on the internet."

"Anyway, he didn't tell me where we were going, but I had kind of an inkling about it since he did dress me up in this outfit," I say.

"Which is *exquisite!*" She enunciates every part of the word, savoring it in her mouth. "How did it all happen? I need details."

"I found the box on the bed in the cottage. He dropped it off while I was swimming. I wasn't sure what I was going to find in there but when I saw this...it was so beautiful, I had to try it on. I've never tried anything like this on before."

Sydney's eyes sparkle and her mouth opens in a wide grin.

"Then he walked in."

"What?" she gasps. I shrug as if that sort of thing happens all the time. "So, what did you do?"

"I let him help me with the corset."

"Ohhh!" she squeals, pointing her finger at me. "You... you're a bad girl!"

"It just sort of felt...right. I mean...okay, promise me that you won't tell James..."

She nods.

"Say it out loud."

"I promise."

"Nicholas just makes me so...whenever I'm around him I feel like the ground is shifting under my feet. I never know what he's going to do next and that makes me want him so...much."

Every part of this sentence is true. I look down at my hands, which are trembling to the beat of my quickening heart rate.

"So, what happened when you got here?" Sydney asks.

"I think he brought me here not so much to be with anyone else but to seduce me," I say slowly. "We were watching people and it was so arousing. Then he started to touch me."

"How far do you think it would've gone if you hadn't seen me?" she asks, letting out a giggle.

"I don't know." I bite my lower lip. "I don't know if I wanted my first time with him to be here but at the same time, I wanted him so much that if he had stripped me and taken me right there, I would've let him."

My words come out quiet, almost in a whisper.

Telling Sydney the truth, however much of the truth I can reveal, feels like a burden is lifting off my shoulders.

The lightness in my chest and the fast pulse slow down and a wave of relief sweeps over me.

"I have only one thing to tell you," Sydney says with a mischievous glint in her eyes. "Nicholas Crawford is trouble."

49

WHEN WE MAKE PLANS...

WHEN SYDNEY and I come back inside and find our men, I know that our plans for tonight are put on hold. I don't need Nicholas to tell me this, it's basic. Sydney and James know our real names and that means that we can't make contact with this other couple, or anyone else at the party, using assumed identities. There's too much risk.

"Does anyone want to come to my place for a night cap?" James asks and Nicholas is quick to agree.

Whatever was going to happen tonight will have to wait.

"That could've gone better," Nicholas points out.

By the way he was acting back there, it never occurred to me that he was that upset by the situation. I mean, yes, our plans have changed but we can just do this again some other time, right?

"What's going to happen now?" I ask.

"The mark flew in for this party, I'm not sure that he'll be in town much longer."

"This was the only night we could do it?"

He nods, clenching his jaw.

"What should we do?" I ask.

His eyes dart back and forth as he thinks. "We couldn't have done it with James and Sydney on the premises," he says.

"Obviously," I concur.

"James doesn't live far from here. Let's stay for a drink and then you can tell them that you're tired from the flight and we can come back."

I nod. I wouldn't say no to curling up in a warm bed right about now, but I also wouldn't say no to an excuse to run my fingers over his body once again.

James's house is much smaller than Nicholas' but very cozy and loved. He has traveled all around the world and displays his collection of souvenirs proudly. He has African masks from his trip to Kenya, baskets made by indigenous Mayan women from Guatemala, and an impressive collection of olive oil from his recent trip to Spain.

"I love to visit new places, but it's hard to fit into my

schedule," James says, handing Nicholas a glass of whiskey.

"Being a pediatrician is pretty demanding work. Lots of hours," Sydney says proudly. They've only just met but she's already acting like a doting wife.

"I can imagine. Plus, flying out of Hawaii must add a ton of hours to the flights," I say.

"The long flights give me a chance to catch up on all the paperwork. Thank you WIFI, right?" James says with a shrug. "Hey, listen, let's do a toast."

We lift our glasses in the air.

"To the girls," he says. "Thank you both for coming all the way here and...into our lives."

Sydney and I exchange smiles while Nicholas says, "I'll drink to that," and clinks his glass with mine.

The conversation drifts from travel to what it's like to live in Hawaii full-time to what it's like to live in the Northeast. James is originally from Southern California, he got his medical degree from the University of California San Diego, and did his internship in Honolulu. He came here on a whim but stayed because he fell in love with the land and the sea. When he found a job at the main hospital in Maui he decided to stay for good.

"So, you'd never consider moving back to the mainland?" I ask.

"I'm not sure," he says, smiling at Sydney. "I don't really want to, but I guess I could be convinced."

Sydney reaches over and kisses him on the mouth. I haven't seen her this happy for a long time.

"On the other hand, Maui is much nicer than Boston... so maybe my girl here can be encouraged to make the move instead."

"I'm thinking about it," she lies when we both know that she is almost as good as moved here already. "I have to find a job first and tell my roommate that I'm leaving her behind."

"Oh, is that right?" Nicholas asks, his eyebrows raising. "Is that what's going on?"

I look down at the floor but the smile at the corners of my lips betrays the truth.

"I thought that we had come to some sort of arrangement?" he whispers.

"What's that?" James asks.

Nicholas asked me to never tell anyone about the offer that he'd made. I didn't tell him yet but I did reveal it to Sydney. That was before I was planning on coming back.

I glance up at him and cross my arms to see what he is going to say.

"I asked Olive to come here to give me a chance,"

Nicholas explains. "Take a break from her work for a bit and just give... *us* a chance."

He pauses before he says the word us. Without revealing exactly what his intentions are to our friends, he has to come up with an alternative explanation.

"So, it's settled then?" James asks, lifting his glass in the air. "You girls are staying in Maui?"

Sydney and I exchange glances.

"We haven't exactly gotten that far yet," she says. "Nothing is decided."

"That's too bad," James says. "'Cause I'm not sure you'll be able to find two guys like us anywhere on the mainland. And you definitely won't find this scenery."

"Ask me again in a week," Sydney says, pressing her lips onto his cheek.

"A week is good. I'll take a week." He turns to face her and their mouths collide. Their desire for one another is contagious, making me reach over to take Nicholas' hand. He gives me a little squeeze before mouthing, *we have to go.*

50

WHEN WE DISCUSS TERMS...

Just as I'm about to tell Sydney that we have to leave, Nicholas squeezes my hand and whispers, "It's off."

"What's wrong?" I ask.

He shakes his head. We can't talk now. A big part of me is relieved. I thought that I was looking forward to getting back to that house but running into Sydney and then coming here to relax has really altered the atmosphere of the whole event.

"Do you want to order some food?" James suggests and the three of us reply with a resounding yes.

"In that case, I'm going to have to change out of these clothes," I say. "Any chance you have something I could borrow here?"

Sydney shows me to the master bedroom, where half the closet is already filled with her clothes. Her suitcase is neatly put away underneath with James's shoes piled two rows high to accommodate the space.

"You don't waste much time," I joke, slipping on a comfortable pair of leggings and a loose pullover.

"Oh my God, this is heaven," I mumble, lying down on the bed and enjoying the feel of my body in something that doesn't poke and shape it in any particular way.

It's not that the outfit I wore didn't make me feel unbelievably sexy, it's more that I really hate wearing things like that. Letting the sleeves hang past my fingertips, I finally feel in my element.

"You look beautiful," Sydney says, tucking a strand of hair behind my ear.

"Earlier? Yeah, I felt pretty hot."

"Earlier...and now."

I give her a smile.

For a moment, I wonder if the fact that we ran into each other in a place without many inhibitions is going to change our relationship.

But looking at the way she gazes at me now, I realize that nothing is different. We were best friends before and we are best friends now.

There is nothing romantic or even sexual about the way she is looking at me, she is just one friend telling another friend how beautiful she is.

"You looked pretty awesome, too," I say, watching her change into a pair of joggers and a crop top.

When we get back into the living room, the men are mildly surprised.

"What happened to the thongs?" James asks, making a dour face.

"If you are going to stuff yourself fully dressed, then so are we," Sydney announces.

The food arrives fifteen minutes later. While James and Sydney head to the front door to collect it, I turn to Nicholas to find out what happened.

"It's off. He left."

"Who?"

"Our mark."

"Yes, I know." I roll my eyes. "But you never told me who he was."

"He was someone who was there for two hours and who is now gone. Probably on his way back to New York."

Shit, I say to myself. I want to ask his name again but I hear Sydney's voice and I know that the timing is all wrong.

We don't hang around James's house long after we finish dinner. Everyone is tired and overly excited from the night's activities and Nicholas says that he has an early morning.

We drive back to his house in silence. I attempt to ask more about who we were supposed to do a job on this evening, but he doesn't give me much except for a few grunts. Since there is no radio signal out here, I go through his Spotify playlists to find something to listen to.

"All you have is Led Zeppelin and the Yardbirds."

"I have at least twenty playlists there," he corrects me.

"But they're all kind of the same."

"What do you mean?"

"Classic rock. Rock anthems. Contemporary Rock. Modern Rock. It's just rock, rock, rock," I whine.

"What do you want to listen to?"

"Something...soothing."

He grabs his phone away from me, scrolls down then up before landing on the Beatles' *Blackbird*.

"I was thinking something more folky but I guess that will have to do," I say.

"What did you think seeing Sydney there?" he asks after a moment.

"I don't know...I was pretty shocked. I never thought she'd be the type."

"And you?" Nicholas asks. "Did you ever think you'd ever go into a place like that?"

I shrug.

"Tell the truth."

"No."

"Would you if I had asked you?"

"You mean, if we were like...dating?"

He nods.

"I don't know. I really don't but..." My voice trails off. I'm not sure if I am comfortable telling him this yet.

"But what?" He pushes me.

"Well, being there tonight...we were there for a job... but it didn't feel much like work. I mean...it was...really sexy."

I don't know why I feel so embarrassed admitting something like this.

It might be because I'm a woman and we are all told by society that having sexual urges is something that's wrong.

Or maybe it's just me.

My upbringing.

For men, sexuality and being aroused isn't limited to one person and no one blames them for that.

But for women? There's something wrong with it. There's something inappropriate even.

But if that were true, then who the hell are all of these men fucking?

"It is sexy," Nicholas says. "Watching you watch them...made me really hard."

His words bring me back to that moment, and I can't help but lick my lips.

"But the terms of the offer remain the same," Nicholas says.

"What's that?" I ask.

"If you want me to sleep with you, you're going to have to beg for it," he says.

"I accept your challenge," I say with a smile.

51

WHEN I GET A CALL...

THE FOLLOWING MORNING, I wake up late, head straight to the pool, and swim a few laps before Nicholas shows up. As soon as I see him, I know he's agitated. His hands move around in little jerks as he asks about my night's sleep. He rubs the back of his neck as if he has something else on his mind.

"Are you okay?" I ask, giving up on making small talk. There's no point to it if the other person doesn't play along.

"I'm just upset with myself. With how everything went down last night."

I play with the ends of my hair.

It feels like I should apologize as well but I've done that already. I had no idea that Sydney and James would be there.

Neither of us did.

"Have you made your decision?" Nicholas asks, dragging his hands through his hair. "About my offer?"

"Did I pass last night's test?"

He considers that for a moment before giving me a small nod.

"One million dollars for staying with you for one year plus a percentage," I clarify.

"Yes, yes," he says quickly.

"How will you pay me? Every other week would be ideal," I joke.

"Done," he says, surprising me.

I take a deep breath and say, "I have to send my employer an official letter of resignation."

I expect a hug or at least a smile. Instead, Nicholas spins on his heels and starts to walk away.

"Send it today," he instructs before disappearing back inside the house.

Despite the chilly reception, I can't help but feel giddy. One million dollars divided by twelve months is a little over $83,000 a month! That's more than I make a year at my old job. Divided by two, it's a payment of $41,667 every two weeks!

I dive under water and scream at the top of my lungs.

This isn't imaginary money. This isn't potential money that I will make if a con pays off. This is real money. He'll pay me this no matter what.

I get back to my cottage and open my laptop.

The words of my resignation letter flow out naturally and without much thought.

For a moment, I consider making it more formal. Then, I'm tempted to just write FUCK YOU.

Eventually, I settle in the middle and opt for not burning bridges.

The gist of it: *I am pursuing other opportunities.*

As soon as I press send, a wave of euphoria sweeps over me. My body feels lighter. My thoughts are clearer.

While I'm at my laptop, I check my email.

There are about fifty messages of promotional crap from various stores and companies I gave my email to. After I delete all that garbage, I remember that this isn't the only email account that I haven't checked.

The other one is through Corrlinks, a special email service that's reserved for communicating with federal inmates who are forbidden from using regular email accounts like Gmail and Yahoo.

I see that I have a message from *him* as soon as I log in.

Actually, there are three.

One written each day.

Owen and I have never been particularly close but over the last few years, our relationship has really blossomed. He went to prison not knowing how to read or write.

He struggled with reading since he was a kid. Mom always said he was just lazy, but in prison he learned that he was dyslexic. Luckily, the first penitentiary he was in had a program that prepared inmates for the General Education Development (GED) test. The teacher took an interest in him, helped him pass the test, and earn his high school diploma.

Owen learned quickly and now writes me long diatribes about the research he has done about the literacy rates among inmates (apparently, about 60% of prison inmates are functionally illiterate) and what can be done about it.

But that's not all we talk about.

We talk about my job.

We talk about his cellmate.

We talk about his plans for the future.

I usually write him three or four emails a week and fill them with enough detail to last him until my next message. He writes me one every day.

The first email continues the story of his cellmate's upbringing, the one he left off writing in his previous email. The second email tells me how much he's enjoying working in the kitchen and then concludes with a request to remember to write him again.

In his third email, he just writes:

OLIVE,

Where are you? Are you okay? Why aren't you writing me back? If you're mad at me, tell me, just please don't go dark. I'm your older brother and I'm worried about you.

Love,

Owen

I KNOW I can't *not* write him back again. But when I put my fingers to the keyboard, I don't know what to say. I don't even know where to begin.

I'M FINE. Don't worry about me.

I STARE AT THE WORDS. That's all I can really say without obfuscating the truth, but this is not nearly enough.

If this is all I send then he'll think something is wrong.

I never write back two sentence emails.

I never not explain.

I never not go into details.

I press my fingers to the keyboard and try again.

I MET SOMEONE. *It's a long story but I'm actually in Hawaii right now visiting him. He's great, and fun, and amazing. Sydney insisted on coming with me since it's such a long trip. That's why I haven't written earlier. I'm sorry.*

I READ OVER THE WORDS.

There is only one lie in it.

Great, fun, and amazing are not words that I would use to describe Nicholas.

A dark, dangerous enigma is much more appropriate. But how much of the story can I really tell him via email?

My phone rings.

It's a private number.

My fingers immediately start to tingle. I blink rapidly as I try to decide whether or not I should answer.

I press Accept.

I bring the phone to my ear. A robotic voice on the other line says, you have a call from the Massachusetts Correctional Institution.

52

WHEN A SECRET SLIPS OUT...

I BOUNCE my foot on the ground as the operator tells me that I will be responsible for all charges. By the time I hear his voice, my hands are damp with sweat.

"Are you okay?" Owen asks, his voice is rushed and out of control.

"Yes, I'm perfectly fine," I say as calmly as possible. "I'm sorry I haven't replied. I was just writing you now."

He takes a deep breath. A sound of metal being dragged across the floor makes me cringe.

"What's going on?" he asks.

I touch my face and clear my throat.

"I met someone. We really hit it off and we've just been hanging out for a bit."

I'm not a very good liar, especially to people who are at all suspicious.

I'm not sure why this is the case given that I'm good at sleights of hand, shoplifting, and other tricky behavior.

Or maybe I'm just not very good at lying to *him*.

I tell him a little bit more about Nicholas, staying as close to the truth as possible. My voice changes in pitch and tone from nervousness but I hope that he attributes these changes to giddiness about my new relationship.

"So, how did you meet him?" Owen asks after a while.

My mouth becomes cotton.

"At a coffee shop near work."

I rub one hand with the other, noting how rough the skin is around my knuckles and how soft it is around my palm.

"So, what does he do?" he asks.

"What's with all of these questions?" I get on the defensive.

"I'm just curious. Because you never not stay in touch."

"Listen, I doubt that any of your cellmates in there have their sisters writing them every other day. So, I got distracted for a bit. So what?" I reply, defensively.

He doesn't say anything for a moment, and we both

listen to the loud chatter going on around him. I can't make out any of the words, but there's yelling and agitation.

"Mom came to see me," he says.

Nausea shoots up my esophagus and I almost gag when I taste something on my tongue.

My hands become outright clammy.

Cold sweat drenches my underarms.

"She told me that you paid her debt to Marlo," Owen says. His tone is an odd combination, both accusatory and thankful.

"Where did you get fifty-thousand dollars, Olive?"

"Did she also tell you that she hired some idiot to shove a gun in my face so that I would turn the money over to him?" I demand to know. "Did she tell you that she tried to con me out of that money? That I had to track down Marlo on my own?"

There's a pause on the other end. Our mother, of course, never mentioned any of this.

Why would she?

In her mind, there is only one version of events - her version.

"She tried to steal the money from you?" Owen asks in a quiet whisper. "How did you find out?"

"I found Marlo and asked her. I wasn't sure how to do the exchange with that guy and make sure that he let Mom go so I thought I'd go over his head to the source."

"I can't believe that she would do that," Owen says. I clench my jaw. He has always had a soft spot for her. Maybe it's because the last time he ever saw her in the free world was almost ten years ago. Or maybe it's just nice to believe that your mother is a good person no matter what she does.

"Why did you still pay the money?" he asks.

That's the question I've been wrestling with ever since I got back. At first, it seemed so obvious but then...I started having doubts.

"Maybe I shouldn't have," I say slowly, "but I had the money and she still owed the debt. She had no way to pay it back. I wasn't sure what Marlo would do so I just paid it."

"That was a very nice thing to do," Owen says. "Thank you."

I shrug without saying a word. Tears well up in my eyes, but I push them away.

"Olive, are you there?" he asks.

"Yeah, sorry, yeah, whatever."

"So...I still don't get it...where did you get the money?" he asks.

"From this guy," I mumble.

"Wow, he must have some serious money," Owen says after a long pause. "What does he do?"

I shrug again but know that I have to answer.

"Finance," I mumble. "Real estate. He's got a few companies."

"He's not some old fart, is he? Some sixty-year-old taking advantage of you?"

I can't help but laugh.

"No, not at all. He's our age."

"So, his daddy must've set him up very nicely."

Owen's judgement makes me angry. Nicholas sent me fifty grand to help our deceitful mother out of yet another jam and here he is sitting in a penitentiary and judging him.

"He made every penny on his own," I say proudly. "Don't be such an asshole."

"Really?" Owen asks, his tone oozing in skepticism.

"He's also a local boy. From our neck of the woods."

"What do you mean?"

"He's from Boston."

I realize that I've made a mistake only *after* the name of

the city escapes my lips. But it's too late. I can't force the words back into my mouth. I can't make Owen un-hear them.

Shit, shit, shit.

I want to scream at the top of my lungs.

53

WHEN HE TELLS ME A STORY...

"WHAT THE HELL are you talking about?" Owen demands to know. "Your boyfriend is Nicholas Crawford from Charlestown?"

Earlier I had mentioned that his name was Nick Crawford but made it seem like he was just visiting Boston. It's a generic enough name to pass it off and Owen didn't question me. But now...FUCK!

I don't know what to say so I say nothing.

"Olive? Tell me you're not fucking Nicholas Crawford. *My* Nicholas Crawford."

"I am not fucking Nicholas Crawford," I say. That part is true, at least. But his name used to be..."

"You don't know the first thing about him, Olive. He's a very, very dangerous man."

Goose bumps run up my arms.

"I used to run around with Nicky C, that's what he went by back then. We had the same boss but we had different associates."

"It's not the same person," I say, trying to make him stop.

But another part of me wants to hear everything that he has to say.

"Nicky C was ruthless. I've seen him execute a man point blank. That was something that pleased the boss and he rose through the ranks quickly."

I touch my calf muscle and feel it tighten with every word that I hear come out of Owen's mouth.

"Who was your boss?" I ask, wanting corroboration, proof, something that will tell me that he's telling the truth.

"You know I can't tell you that," Owen snaps. "They listen and record everything that's being said."

I read between the lines. What he's really telling me is that *they* (the authorities) already know everything about this. Nothing he is telling me now is secret information.

"Eventually, Nicky C was in charge of all of the insurance scams," Owen continues.

"What does that mean?" I ask.

"A restaurant or a business doesn't pay their monthly

fee once, twice, three times. The boss gets agitated. The only way he'll get back the money that's owed to him is through insurance. So, he sends in Nicky C and his crew to start a little fire. It can't have multiple points of ignition, otherwise it will be suspicious. Nicky was an expert in this. Whenever he started a fire, it was always small but powerful. It spread quickly. When the firefighters arrived, they took care of the rest."

"What do you mean?" I ask.

"They'd point their hoses and spray the whole place with water. They never try to preserve anything, just put out the fire. Most damage that's caused by fires comes from water. Whenever Nicky C started a fire, the insurance company always paid out."

I lean back in the chair and take it all in.

What are the chances that he's talking about someone else?

What if he's wrong?

"I don't think it's the same person," I say after a moment.

"Nicky C vanished one day after his partner showed up dead," Owen says, ignoring me. "The boss thought that he just decided to take some time off, maybe went down to Florida for some rest and relaxation. But days turned into weeks and Nicky didn't come back."

"This isn't the same guy," I insist.

"It took a few months before we all figured out what happened. The two of them had a side job of breaking into wealthy homes out there in the country while the owners were away in Martha's Vineyard or wherever the fuck they went. At first, it was a few pieces of jewelry, some antiques but then their hauls got bigger and bigger."

I put my hand on my chest and listen to the way my breath bursts in and out.

"To say that they were good would be an understatement. They broke into secure homes with guards. They broke into safes. After casing the joint, the job took two trips. The first they would photograph and measure everything they found so that they could make replicas and, on the second, they would return for the pieces and make the switch."

"How do you know any of this?"

"They found the guy who made the replicas," Owen says.

"The police?"

He laughs. "No, our boss."

My body starts to rock from side to side. I don't want to believe this but I can't ignore the truth. His approach hasn't changed much. I've seen it in action. I was an integral part of it.

"The replicas were an integral part of the plan," Owen

explains even though he doesn't have to. "Without them, the owners would know immediately that the jewelry was missing. They'd call the police. They'd hire a private investigator. But with the replicas, months would pass before anyone noticed. The jewelry was just as heavy. It looked the same. The only thing that was different was that it wasn't made of real diamonds."

I curl my shoulders forward, caving my chest in.

This can't be true.

This can't be my Nicholas.

"My boss has been looking for him ever since he disappeared. The rule was that you were supposed to hand over seventy percent of whatever you took in on the side, since side jobs weren't exactly legal. Neither Nicky C nor his partner ever gave him a cent."

"Well, they were their hauls," I say quietly.

"The last thing that the replica guy made was a Harry Winston necklace worth over two million dollars. The night that they broke into that estate on Nantucket to make the exchange, they found his partner's body in the Belle Isle Marsh."

"I don't know why you're telling me all of this."

"Because you're with him and he's a dangerous man. He killed two people that I know of and who knows how many others," Owen says.

"It's not him," I say under my breath. "Crawford isn't even his real name."

Without missing a beat, Owen says, "He used to use his biological father's real name, Reed. But when he was in high school, he changed it."

I rub the back of my neck. I'm drowning under the flow of information unable to come up for air.

"You don't know if it's the same person," I insist. "Nicholas Crawford is a generic name. Besides, why the hell would he still use that name if everyone knew it?"

"Everyone knew him as Nicky C. Besides, he was always cocky, and an arrogant enough bastard to keep his old name. As a fuck you to the boss, to his associates, to me."

"You?" I ask.

"I've had some...dealings with him myself. We didn't exactly leave on the best of terms."

"What happened?" I ask.

There's a long pause.

"You know I can't talk about any of that here. I'm due for a parole hearing soon. I can't implicate myself in anything. But it was nothing illegal."

I furrow my brow until I realize that he had added that

last sentence for the recording. His previous statement was a sidestep, it wasn't anything that he should've said.

"You need to stay away from him, Olive. You need to just ghost him until he stops calling. He probably doesn't know that I'm your brother. You did just meet in the coffee shop, right? Just ghost him for a while until he gets the point. He has a short attention span when it comes to females."

I clench my jaw. I've always hated the way some men refer to women as females. The word is so scientific and cold.

"I can't do that," I say quietly.

"Why not? Because you have *feelings* for him?" he says in a mocking fashion. When I don't reply, something occurs to him.

"Oh, shit, I forgot. You took fifty grand from him. Fuck!"

"What are you talking about?" I ask.

"You took Mom's debt from Marlo and now you owe Nicky C a debt. That's...that's *not* good, Olive."

I hear a tinge of fear, something that I'm not used to hearing from Owen.

"I don't owe any debt to Nicholas Crawford or this Nicky C," I explain. "He doesn't even know the details of why I needed the money."

A robotic voice interrupts our conversation. "You have one minute remaining."

"Get the fuck out of the city, Olive!" Owen says. "Drive, drive out west. Buy some new documents. Start a new life. Run as far as you can!"

54

WHEN HE ASKS ME FOR A FAVOR...

Owen's words reverberate in my head long after he hangs up. It's exactly the advice that I gave our mom when I heard about her debt. I cradle my phone in my lap and run my fingers around its soft corners.

His words come back to haunt me. I try to convince myself that he's lying. No, not lying, wrong.

Nicky C is not Nicholas Crawford.

It's a common name and he wouldn't be stupid enough to use it if he were trying to live under a different identity.

But that's a big if.

My attempts to convince myself fall flat.

Nicholas Crawford is Ashley's brother. We all grew up in the same neighborhood and city.

He told me that the reason he wasn't there for her was that he was running the streets.

That's a euphemism for being in a gang, or part of some sort of organized crime syndicate.

He didn't try to hide it. In that case, chances are he knew Owen, or at least of him.

Does that mean that he wanted me to tell Owen? Does that mean that he didn't care if he were found out?

Besides these and about a million other questions, there is the undeniable truth. Nicky C worked with replicas and only stole things that he could replace with these fake trinkets. That's exactly what Nicholas Crawford did to get Kathy Moreno's bracelet.

But what about that story he told me? It came out so naturally. So effervescently. Like he didn't have to think about it once. As if it was the whole truth and nothing but the truth.

That's what people like us do, though, isn't it? We lie.

We cheat.

We deceive.

So, why *wouldn't* he lie to me?

My phone rings again. My body jolts from surprise. It's another collect call. Owen got more time.

"What are you going to do?" he asks, his words dripping with fear.

"I don't know. I'm sitting here trying to figure it out."

"You need to run, Olive."

"I can't."

"You need to get out of Boston."

"I can't."

"Why not?"

"I'm not there," I say quietly. "I'm in...Hawaii."

"What?" he snaps.

"Maui, to be exact."

He takes a deep breath. "Why the fuck are you in Maui?"

"Nicholas invited me. We're here on vacation."

"Fuck, fuck, fuck," Owen whispers under his breath.

"Listen, I'm fine. You don't have to worry about me. Nicholas is...a really great guy. He has this amazing house here and we are really getting along."

"You are so stupid, Olive," Owen says. "How can you be so smart and such an idiot at the same time?"

I purse my lips. Anger starts to rise from the pit of my stomach.

"Please don't put me down, okay? I get enough of that from Mom."

"I'm sorry. I shouldn't have said that." His tone changes immediately. "I am just so worried about you."

"I'm going to be fine."

"You keep saying that but it's not going to make it anymore true. How about this? How about you just say you have to get back home for something and come back to Boston?"

"I thought you told me to get away from Boston?"

"That's when I thought that's where you both were. But I should've known that he was a coward who was going to be hiding out in some billionaire's paradise while the rest of us rot in prison."

This jealously gives me pause for concern.

"What did he do to you exactly?"

This catches Owen by surprise. He clears his throat and then mumbles, "No, nothing. He didn't do anything to me...but the organization suffered and he killed his partner..."

I narrow my eyes and press the phone closer to my ear. Something doesn't sound right. He's hiding something, but why? Is he hiding it because he is being recorded and doesn't want to admit to any more crimes? Or is he hiding it for some ulterior motive.

"I need you to come here, Olive," Owen says after a moment. "I need to see you. I need to tell you something in person."

"What?" I ask.

"It's something I can't say over the phone."

"They record the in-person conversations as well," I point out.

"I know, but—"

"Listen," I interrupt him. "I know what you're doing. It's just a ploy to get me out of here."

"I lied," Owen says after a moment. I wait for an explanation.

"I don't need to tell you something in person. I need you to come here and testify at my parole hearing."

My mouth drops open.

"They just told me after I hung up with you. That's why I called back."

"Congratulations," I say after a moment.

"Thank you."

Getting parole is a long shot but, in prison, it's important to celebrate every good thing that comes your way.

It doesn't mean you're jinxing yourself or setting yourself up for some disappointment, it's about being in the present.

The Department of Corrections gave Owen's case a

once-over and he qualified for a hearing before the board.

Under any other circumstances, I would be jumping up and down and doing everything short of throwing him a party over the phone. But today...I can't.

"I'm sorry," I catch myself. "I didn't mean to just gloss over it. It's a really big deal, Owen. I'm really happy for you."

"Thank you. I'm happy, too."

"You should've led the conversation with that, though," I point out. "You kind of buried the lead."

We stay on the phone for a few minutes. I wish more than anything that we hadn't talked about Nicholas and he hadn't told me any of those things.

I don't want to bring it up again and force another lecture.

I just want all of that stuff to disappear.

But that's not what life is about, is it? No matter how much you want to wish something away, it doesn't go away without you actually doing something about it.

"Please come," Owen pleads.

"When is it?"

"Two days from now."

"What?" I gasp.

"They had some sort of glitch in the system. They were supposed to notify me sooner but they didn't. That's all I know."

"Are they even going to let me in?" I ask, thinking back to the one time when I drove all the way up to the prison, woke up in the dark, got in line to wait to come inside with the rest of the wives and girlfriends of the incarcerated only to be turned away for no reason.

They didn't let Owen have visitors that week but no one cared to notify either Owen or myself, even though I had registered to come.

I have been to that prison a dozen times since but it still irks me the way the guards treat the visitors, as if we are the convicts as well, as if we had done something wrong.

"They said that they will take a statement from someone on my side. I'd like that person to be you," Owen says.

"I don't know," I say, shaking my head. "I don't know if I can get back in time."

"Will you try?"

I nod.

"Olive? Will you try?"

55

WHEN I RUN AWAY...

THIS TIME, when I hang up, I put the phone on the table and leave it there. Rain which had been threatening to come down all morning finally lets loose.

Water falls in a loud steady stream, interrupted only by bolts of lightning and rolling waves of thunder.

I look at the way the rain pounds the big green bush, the name of which I don't know, right on the porch. When I open the door, my senses are overwhelmed by an intoxicating aroma of hot, wet vegetation.

I put my foot out past the awning and it immediately becomes soaked. I put it back and then stick my hand out.

Droplets run off my fingertips as if they were rain gutters.

I take a few steps forward and open my face up to the sky.

I welcome the beads of water that smash into me and even stick my tongue out.

"What are you doing?" His voice sounds muffled and originates somewhere in the distance.

I stand up straight and spin on my heels to face him. Nicholas, dressed in a casual Hawaiian shirt and khaki pants, is holding a large umbrella over his head.

"Just enjoying the warm rain," I say. "Haven't you ever done this?"

"Not recently. C'mon," he says, walking past me into my cottage. "I have to talk to you about something."

The air-conditioning feels cool on my skin and goose bumps immediately cover my body.

My clothes are soaked.

I step out of my soggy flip-flops. Nicholas gets a towel in the bathroom and hands it to me. I use it to wipe my face and dry my hair. The towel is too fat to pile on top of my head.

"Do you want to change?" he asks, sitting down on the couch in the living room. "I'll wait."

It's a request that's in the form of a question. Not long ago, I found this to be incredibly charming and not at all threatening. But knowing what I know now...I am not so sure.

I go to the other room and change into another long sleeve shirt and a cropped pair of yoga pants.

When I come out, I see Nicholas at my computer. My account has logged out but the screen is still up.

"Who do you know in prison?" he asks.

I crack my knuckles.

"Why are you looking through my stuff?" I ask.

"I wanted to check what the weather will be tomorrow. I forgot my phone back at the house."

His explanation is plausible enough the way that good explanations typically go.

I consider lying, pretending that it's someone else I know who is in prison but what if I told him truth? Would that turn the tables? Would it catch him off guard?

"My brother, Owen, is doing a stretch for an armed robbery charge," I say.

My chest swells with pride using the right lingo just like the incarcerated do.

"Do you know him?" I ask.

The question slips out before I have a chance to really consider it. His eyes snap back and focus on mine. His face remains blank, devoid of all expression.

"Your brother?" he asks, buying more time. I nod and wait.

"Same last name? Owen Kernes?"

Again, I nod and wait.

"No." He shakes his head. "I don't think I do."

Our eyes remain locked on each other. He lies so effortlessly it makes my skin crawl.

"Why, did he say something?"

"No, not at all." I shake my head trying to be as nonchalant as he is.

Nicholas invites me back to his house for some dinner and I feel compelled to go. I don't have any plans with Sydney and he knows full well that I have nothing else to do. We both have to eat. Plus, I don't want to raise any suspicion.

As we devour the meal that his chef has prepared, we don't speak.

My thoughts focus on the way his body tensed up just a bit when I asked about Owen. I don't know if that means anything, or if I'm just reading too much into everything. Still I can't shake this feeling that he's lying.

There isn't another Nicholas Crawford from that area of Boston. And there's definitely not one who steals valuables by making replicas first. Owen knew his original last name. He knew too much about him for this to not be the same person. Then there's the flinch.

When I asked him if he knew him, his shoulders tightened. He tried to cover it up. He took his time answering me. Those were all signs of deception.

"I have to go back to Boston tomorrow," I say, biting into the end of an asparagus spear.

"Tomorrow? Why?"

"I'm going to be a character witness for Owen at his parole hearing."

"Did you know about this before?" he asks, taking his time chewing every last bit of his arugula before bringing his fork up to his mouth with another bite.

"No, I just talked to him today. He didn't know before either. They were supposed to notify him but apparently he never got the message."

Nicholas takes a sip of his whiskey.

"Why aren't you saying anything?" I ask after a moment.

"Just trying to give you the opportunity to reach your own conclusion."

"About this," he says, taking another sip. I furrow my brow.

"I don't know understand what you don't understand," I say, taking a more stern approach. "I am not asking your permission. I am just notifying you about what I'm going to do."

Nicholas takes another bite. And then another. Then he finishes his drink and pours himself another. Still, he doesn't talk.

I put my plate in the sink and head toward the door.

"How are you going to get back to Boston?" he asks. "On what money?"

"I have enough for a ticket, don't worry about it."

"And what about our...arrangement? You promised to be at my disposal."

I slip into my flip-flops by the entrance and turn around to face him.

"I don't understand why you are making this so difficult," I say. "Don't you get what's going on here? My brother who has served years in prison finally has a chance to get out."

"Most inmates don't get parole during their first hearing," he points out.

I want to smack him across the face for saying that but instead I just ball up my fists.

"You're an asshole for saying that."

He shrugs.

"You know what, I can't talk to you when you have that

smug expression on your face. Why don't you find me when you aren't so closed off."

I swing the front door open and step onto the porch. Water is falling in sheets but I have made too much of a scene to not leave.

"You're going to get soaked!" he yells so that I will hear him over the rain.

"I'm not made of sugar!" I scream back.

56

WHEN WE PLAY A GAME...

I'M ABOUT HALFWAY DOWN toward my cottage when he catches up to me. He grabs me by my arms from behind.

I fight to break free, but he holds me tightly. At first, I'm incensed.

Upset.

But the more we struggle, the more aroused I get.

He towers over me, clasps me firmly. I have nowhere to go and that's the way I want it.

When he spins me around, I stand on my tiptoes and press my lips to his. The kiss catches him by surprise, but it only takes a moment for him to respond in kind. His mouth opens wide, welcoming me in.

His arms release their grasp. But instead of pushing me away from him, they now pull me close.

I run my fingers up his neck and bury them in his hair. It is thick and soft even though it is completely waterlogged.

His hands get lost in my own mane. They go in circles and then pull down just as his tongue rushes into my mouth craving to intertwine with mine.

Wrapped in each other's arms, we let the rain fall onto us. To move or go back to a drier place would be to break the spell. Neither of us is ready for that yet.

His fingers grab my shoulders and then sweep down my arms. Another move and they are on the small of my back. I press my mouth harder against his. With our chests together, I can hear the thunder of our combined heartbeats.

Nicholas leads me back to my cottage. As soon as we are somewhere dry, he pushes me against the nearest wall.

His body is solid and defined. Muscles protrude against his shirt, which he quickly peels off.

I run my fingers down his six pack, as he flexes and gives me a wink.

Licking his lips, he pushes me into the wall again. It's cold and smooth against my back. Then he starts to undress me.

A moment later, I'm in nothing but my bra and panties. He takes a step back to get a good look at me.

He objectifies me and it feels damn good. He wants me and he wants my body. As much as I want his.

I grab onto his belt and unbuckle it.

His pants fall to the floor and he tosses them to one side.

I look down at his substantial package. It's throbbing through his boxer briefs, which are so tight that I can see the vein running down it.

He's the biggest man I've ever been with. It's the size of the ones I've only seen in porn.

"You like?" he asks.

I nod.

My tongue finds the corner of my mouth and slowly slides along the bottom lip.

"I like, too," he says, grabbing the front of my bra and unclasping it with one quick move.

My breasts fall open for him. My nipples stand up erect, waiting for him to devour them.

He takes one in his mouth.

I press my head to the wall, enjoying the sensation.

His tongue is hard but his mouth is soft, filling the space between my legs with heat.

After pulling down my panties, he takes my hand and leads me to the bed.

This is it.

No more foreplay.

No more games.

Just thrust yourself in me and fill me up like no man has ever filled me up before.

I lie down on my back.

He climbs on top of me. He's naked now, too.

When his body touches mine, I run my fingers down his muscular back and then toward his butt.

I take two big handfuls of his glutes and squeeze hard.

My legs open for him and wait.

Hovering slightly above me, he doesn't make a move to get any closer. I open my eyes.

"What are you waiting for?" I ask.

"You," he says without missing a beat.

"What do you mean?"

"If you want me to fuck you, you have to beg," he says, with a smug crooked smile on his face.

I furrow my brows and cock my head.

"Are you serious?" I ask.

Pulling himself away, he lies down next to me and

props up his head. "I'll accept a please, or a pretty please. But you have to ask for it. Demand it even."

"No," I say, shaking my head.

"A promise is a promise," Nicholas says, his eyes lighting up. "You don't beg. You don't get this."

I grab the sheet and cover myself up.

"Get over yourself," I say, twisting away from him and turning off the lights.

57

WHEN HE MAKES ME CRY...

I WRAP my sheet around my chest and prop up my head. My eyelids feel heavy, but I try to keep them open. Waves of emotion are no longer taking me on a rollercoaster ride. I look at him, but really somewhere past him in the distance.

Nicholas is just as relaxed. He lies flat on his back with his arm tucked behind his head. His hair is infused with body but not a mess. He stares at the ceiling. His chin is tilted upward, away from his body, as his chest moves up and down with each deep breath.

I have met my match. He wants me as much as I want him. We lust after each other, and yet, neither of us can give up the game. I will not beg and he will not give in until I do.

"So, are we actually ever going to *do* it?" I ask, teasing him.

"That's up to you," he says without moving a muscle.

"Oh, is it?"

"You ask me to, I comply and send you to the moon."

"Or the next time, you can just *not* stop," I suggest.

He turns to his side. His eyes focus on mine. After a bit, I'm the one who blinks first.

"So, there will be a next time?" he jokes.

"Maybe. Maybe not," I say smugly.

But if we keep talking like this, I can't be too sure that it won't happen again really soon.

I've never thought of myself as a competitive person but Nicholas seems to bring out that side of me.

Especially when it comes to this. He had set up the rules. When I agreed, the rules made me feel safe.

But now, I feel anything but that. Every time I touch his arm, every time he brushes up against me, the bolt of electricity that surges through me makes me weak in the knees.

It's almost as if my body aches for his and there's nothing I can do to keep that sensation at bay.

I lie back and look up at the ceiling tiles, which have thick crown molding around each one.

I've never seen anything like this except in magazines. As much as I want to keep them out, Owen's warnings about Nicholas and his true identity creep back in. He lied to me about not knowing my brother, and Owen wouldn't have any reason to lie.

But does knowing that change anything about our deal? I'd suspected that he had a past, with his skills, it would've been ignorant not to.

But what about the people that he has supposedly killed. Did he do it or are those just rumors?

"I have to go back to Boston," I say definitively.

Nicholas doesn't reply.

"I have to testify on my brother's behalf. He's all I have."

Again, Nicholas doesn't reply.

"If I don't go and he doesn't get out, I will never forgive myself."

He doesn't say a word.

"Are you listening to me?" I ask.

"I can't let you go," he says after a moment. There's that possessiveness rearing its ugly head.

"I don't need your permission," I remind him.

"You do, if you want to get paid. If you want to stick to the terms of our arrangement."

I sit up.

I feel tears of frustration and anger welling up in my eyes.

I had just quit my job.

The money he's offering me is more money than I will ever make in a lifetime. But is he really going to make me choose between all of that and my brother?

"I don't understand why you're making this so difficult. I can fly there and fly back right away. I will only stay there for the hearing."

Nicholas says nothing. His face is expressionless and empty. He continues to lie on his back staring at the ceiling. I touch his arm to try to shake him out of his trance, but again he doesn't respond.

"Why? Why can't I go? Our arrangement will remain the same. This is just a two day trip on a personal matter."

"You don't have the option to take personal days," Nicholas says slowly. "This isn't a normal job. If it were, then you would be paid normal money."

I get off the bed and take the sheet with me.

It slides off his naked body but he remains motionless. The muscles in his stomach move up and down with each breath. His legs lay slightly apart, relaxed.

His calmness makes me even more agitated. When it reaches a boiling point, I grab my pillow and toss it in his direction.

"What the hell is wrong with you?" I demand to know. "Why are you such a robot?"

Nicholas turns his head only slightly in my direction.

"What do you want to talk about?"

"I'm going to Boston," I say.

"Fine. Go."

He rises out of the bed and pulls on his trousers.

"What does that mean?" I ask, as he buckles the belt.

"It means we're done," he says. "I will buy you your ticket home and you will never hear from me again."

"Why?" I ask.

"Because I don't need you," he says harshly. His words are like a knife through my heart. My body trembles.

"But what about...the offer? Why did you even ask me here?"

He puts on his shirt. His hands are slow and meticulous, pushing every button through its designated loop.

"I thought we could help each other out," he says, finally meeting my eyes. "I thought we could have fun doing it. But I see now that you were never committed to me."

Still grasping onto my sheet, I walk up to him and grab him by his shoulders.

"I am committed. To you. To this deal. I just need a day. He's my brother and he has been in prison for years. This is his chance and if there's anything I can do to help him get parole...I have to do it."

"If it means giving up a million dollars?" Nicholas challenges me.

"I will do everything you want. Why do I have to?" I plead.

"Because I said so," he says.

58

WHEN I HAVE TO MAKE A CHOICE...

HOT TEARS START to stream down my face. I can barely see a thing through them. Nicholas doesn't put his arm around me. He doesn't comfort me in any way. The man that created so much heat inside of me now fills me with nothing but ice.

How could he do this?

Who is he?

Why is he doing this?

What is the big deal with me taking this short trip? Why is he being so unreasonable? The questions keep coming but the answers stay away.

"You have to make a choice, Olive," Nicholas says, walking up to me. He touches my chin and pulls it up to his eyes. "It's either Owen or me."

"Don't you see how ridiculous this is?" I ask. "I don't

need to make a choice, you are making me. Why? Why are you being so...unreasonable?"

"I have my reasons," Nicholas says.

"Please," I beg. "You wanted me to plead, you wanted me to demean myself, to beg. I'm begging you now."

"I never wanted you to do anything you didn't want to do," he corrects me. "It's offensive that you think I wanted you to demean yourself."

I don't say a word.

Even though he is trying to remain calm, I see anger building up within him. I have finally gotten through.

He takes a deep breath.

His icy demeanor returns.

He only gave me a glimpse, but now it's gone.

He walks toward the door. I run after him and trip over my feet. I let go of the sheet that's wrapped around me but it's too late. The fabric is taut and it pulls me down to the floor.

"Nicholas, please," I say. I rise up to my feet and stand before him naked and totally vulnerable. "Can we talk about this?"

"There's nothing to talk about," he says.

"I want to spend the year with you. I want to go with you wherever you want to take me."

"But?" he finishes my thought.

"There is no but. That's the end of the sentence."

"What about Boston?"

I shrug. He knows my answer to that.

"Is there anything I can do to change your mind?" I ask. "I don't want this offer to be off."

Nicholas is about to say something but then he shakes his head. I can see that something is on the tip of his tongue, but what?

His lips open again and then purse shut.

"What? What is it?"

"It's...too dangerous."

"What are you talking about?" I ask.

"No." He shakes his head. "You should go back to Boston and our relationship is over."

"You have to tell me," I say, putting my hands on my hips.

I have never been so naked and felt so clothed before. It's like my nudity no longer exists.

This is who I am and this is what I look like. You can take it or leave it.

"If there's anything I can do, please tell me," I ask again.

He looks me up and down, I freeze.

But then I realize that he's not really scrutinizing me. Instead, he's gazing somewhere past me at nothing in particular. Thinking.

Am I really getting through to him?

"I have a job to complete. There's a dangerous man that I am after who has taken something very dear from me."

I nod.

"He was supposed to be at the party when we ran into Sydney and James."

A wave of relief starts to sweep over me.

I don't know where this story is going or what it will require me to do but at least we are talking.

At least, me going to testify at Owen's hearing is now a possibility.

"He is staying on the island tonight. He called a number to ask for an escort to be sent to his room," Nicholas explains.

My throat cinches up. I rub my index finger on my hip bone but remain motionless. He cannot see fear in my eyes. Then he will never let me do it.

"I've intercepted the call and I know that he's expecting her there at eight."

"What do you want me to do?" I ask, raising my chin in the air.

"No," he says, shaking his head. "This is a bad idea. I will just have to track him down and try again. It's too dangerous."

"I'm fine with dangerous," I say as bravely as I can. "Anything I can do to help." What I really mean is that I will do anything to prove to you that I'm in.

He hesitates.

I watch him think, analyze, assess the situation.

"If you do this, then I will take you to the prison to testify. But you have to stay by my side the whole time. You will not leave my side and you will not question my decisions."

I furrow my brow. He tilts his head toward mine waiting for an answer. I'm not sure I can get anything more out of this negotiation so I agree.

Without another word, he walks back to the front door, leaving me standing in the middle of the room, unsure as to what to do.

"Get dressed and come with me," Nicholas says. "I need to make sure you know what you're getting into before you agree to do this."

I swallow hard and put on my clothes.

I follow him to the main house and into one of the guest rooms.

Nicholas opens the large armoire and pulls out a hanger.

"You will have to wear this," he says.

To say that it's a bra and a pair of underwear would be a grave understatement. The cups are cut out completely, leaving nothing but straps. The panties are low rise bikini bottoms but also missing that ever important area that covers the crotch.

"Can you wear this?" Nicholas asks.

59

WHEN WE MAKE A PLAN...

I TAKE the lingerie into my hands and examine it closely. The lace and the stitching is exquisite and expensive. The back of the panties is nothing but a long string.

"Why this?" I ask.

"He requested that the escort show up wearing this."

"So...you want me to have sex with him?" I ask, trying to hide the disappointment in my voice.

"No. Absolutely not," he says quickly. "I don't want him within a mile of you let alone touching you."

My heart swells a bit.

He does care about me.

Nicholas sits down on the bed.

I find a spot next to him.

"What is this? You have to talk to me," I say.

"No, this is a very bad idea," he says after a moment. "I can't let you do this."

"Why?"

"This guy is not anyone you want to mess with. He has killed a lot of people."

"What do you need to get back from him?" I ask.

"Something valuable."

I wait for him to continue but he doesn't.

"You're not going to tell me anything more than that?" I push.

"Not now."

When Nicholas gets up to pace around the room, I pick up the hanger with the lingerie and stare at it. There are lace and straps but to call it a complete *outfit* would be a grave understatement.

Still, if this is the only way I can get back to Owen and keep my end of the deal, it's worth it.

I quit my job.

After just two weeks of this, I'll get almost forty-two thousand dollars in cash. After a month, I'll have over eighty-three thousand. That's more than I would have made at my old job in a year.

And if I'm still with him for three hundred and sixty-five days, I'll have a million dollars. Cash.

That's enough to set me up for life. It's not about never working again, of course I will work. I love working. But it's about doing something that I'm really passionate about. Maybe I'll finally get that Masters or PhD in mathematics, anything other than write assessment items.

It's also about never worrying about bills again. So, if that requires me to wear this for one evening and not have sex with this guy...why not?

"What's the plan, Nicholas?" I ask. "I need to know what I have to do."

Nicholas stops mid-step and looks back at me.

"You show up in his hotel room. You distract him, make small talk. That will give me the opportunity to let myself in and take what I need. He's staying in the suite so you can lead him to the bedroom. What I'm looking for should be on the desk in the living room."

"Should I leave the door open for you?" I ask. What if I can't, I think to myself.

"You won't have to, I have the master key."

"You really planned this out."

"For bigger jobs like these, there are a lot of moving parts. On the back end."

I bite the inside of my mouth. There is so much I don't know about him and his line of work. But I'm kind of eager to find out.

"What happens then?" I ask. "After you take what you need to take?"

"I leave," Nicholas says.

"What about me?"

"You will receive a call and then make an excuse and leave as well."

"It sounds too easy," I say.

"It won't be," Nicholas assures me. "You will have to play a role. You will have to read him. Put him at ease. Then let yourself out without hurting his pride or his ego."

"And what if something goes wrong?" I ask.

"That's when we go to plan B. I really don't want to do plan B."

Again, I wait for him to explain but talking to him about this is like pulling teeth. He gives me the bare minimum of information and that's nowhere near enough.

Whenever I did my previous jobs, I always made sure that I thought of at least five escape plans; things I would say and things I would do in case A, B, C, D, and E happened.

This isn't how I operate.

I'm going into this blind and it doesn't feel safe.

But I don't have much of a bargaining position if I want to hold on to the deal we made. I can see him hesitating about getting me involved. He wants this thing that he took but he's wondering if the risk is too great.

"Nicholas, I need to know more. I need to know what his suite looks like. What he's like. I need to know what I'm getting myself into so I can protect myself against him in case anything happens."

Nicholas swallows hard.

"If anything happens, you won't be able to protect yourself. That is the *fucking* problem. That's why this is such a bad idea."

He starts to pace again.

His body makes short, jerky movements.

He rubs the back of his neck. Closing his eyes, he takes a calming breath and turns to face me.

"No," he says after a moment. "This isn't a good idea. Too many things can go wrong."

"But you had everything planned out."

"I don't. You are right. I don't know the layout of that hotel room. I don't know anything about him but his first name. Jobs are only successful when you are prepared. I was prepared back there in the club. I had intel that he was going to bring the laptop with him and leave it in his locker. He always felt safe there."

Laptop.

The word slips out of his mouth before he realizes what he's saying. Nicholas and I make eye contact.

No, it wasn't a slip.

Nothing with him is by accident.

He wanted to tell me so he did.

"This is a good plan. I'll distract him while you go in and take the computer," I insist. "You were planning on switching it? You already have a replica, right? A laptop that's identical in every way except one."

I want to ask him what's on it but that's not important now. What's vital is to go through with the plan so I can get back for the parole hearing.

"It doesn't look like it but I'm good with people. Small talk, that kind of thing. I'll put him at ease," I lie. "I'll take him to the bedroom, everything will be fine."

I'm so positive and confident that I manage to convince myself that this job is going to be no different from walking into a department store and taking a dress off the rack.

I ask Nicholas to lay out all of the details.

He shows me the laptop.

He tells me the name of the hotel. The guy's room number.

I already know the time that I'm supposed to be there.

It sounds like he's starting to ease into this plan. It sounds like he is starting to believe that it's, in fact, possible for us to get away with it. But then he throws a bombshell.

"No, absolutely not," Nicholas says. "I'm not letting you do this."

60

WHEN THE PLAN CHANGES...

I TRY to change his mind for a bit longer but then give up. There's no use. He has made his final decision.

Angry and upset, I go back to my cottage.

It's seven o'clock. I only have one hour before the deal is officially off. My mind starts to race.

I'm in free fall and my adrenaline is on high. A nagging thought keeps popping up in the back of my mind. *What if I do this by myself?*

I don't need Nicholas' permission. I have done plenty of jobs entirely only my own. Now, he knows only a little bit about my past but he doesn't trust me.

If I were to do this and get the laptop to him then it will take our professional relationship to a whole new level.

I sneak back to the main house.

I hear falling water and I know he's taking a shower. I

open the drawer where he keeps the laptop and place it into my backpack.

Tiptoeing into the guest bedroom, I grab the lingerie off the hanger and stuff it into my pockets. The shower stops and I freeze for a moment, holding my breath.

Snap out of it, I say to myself, forcing myself to focus. The worst thing you can do in a situation like this is to do nothing.

On the console table near the front door, in a porcelain bowl, I see five pairs of car keys.

The door creaks.

There's no time left. I grab the first one and carefully turn the knob so that it makes the least amount of sound possible. Once I'm on the other side, I close it with the same meticulousness.

I slip down the stairs.

Running my fingers along the house and sticking as close as possible to the siding, I make my way to the garage.

Luckily, it's open and there are a number of cars parked right in the front. I click the button on the key chain, pointing to one car at a time.

A silver Mercedes responds.

I climb in, press the accelerator, and drive out slowly, praying that Nicholas doesn't hear me.

I arrive at the hotel five minutes before eight. After being barefoot since I walked up the stairs to Nicholas' door, the wedges that I got from Marshall's feel heavy and cumbersome.

I say hello to the valet and walk straight to the bathroom in the lobby.

First rule of a good con, if you want to act like you belong somewhere then act like you do.

I don't look around.

I don't look like I have any questions.

I hold my head up high. I have to look like I know exactly what I'm doing even if I don't have a clue.

The stalls are all empty. I consider using the one meant for disabled people or families with the changing table. Since I don't fit into either category, I decide against it.

Second rule of a good con, never break unnecessary rules and regulations.

Never speed.

Never park in the wrong place.

Never use a stall not meant for you.

It may not seem like a big deal but it's little things like these that will come back to haunt you later on.

I change out of my clothes in the smaller stall, stuffing

my other clothes into the backpack that I hang on the hook above.

Once I clasp the bra in the back, I look down and bounce my naked breasts in the air. The space between my legs is equally unsupported by the crotchless underwear. I wrap myself up in the trench coat and apply a coat of red lipstick in front of the floor length mirror.

"You can do this," I say to myself.

I stretch out my fingers as a rush of excitement courses through me.

I should be afraid but instead I'm strangely turned on.

Perhaps, it's the lingerie or how amazing it makes me feel.

I've never worn anything like this before.

It makes me feel sexy and alluring. The only disappointing thing is that Nicholas won't be the first person to see me dressed in this.

When I knock on his door, I take a step back noting that familiar feeling I had every time I took something that didn't belong to me.

It's difficult to explain to someone who hasn't ever done it, except to say that it feels dangerous and exciting at the same time.

Your breathing speeds up. Your pulse rate goes through the roof, but your hand remains still.

Calm.

Under control.

The man who answers isn't who I expect. Even though Nicholas told me that he has killed before, I still assumed he would be kind of meek, small, maybe even bald and unattractive. This man is nothing like that. He's tall, with broad shoulders, an expensive haircut, and a cut body.

Dressed in a tight white t-shirt, he gives me a young Marlo Brando vibe circa *A Streetcar Named Desire*. He even smells manly.

"Dallas Stone," he says, looking me up and down.

"Abigail Sanders," I say, giving him a strong handshake.

Touching his jaw and licking his lips, I can see that he likes the way I look. I let out a little sigh of relief and walk into the living room.

With his eyes burning holes in my ass, I look around the suite.

There's a couch to one side and a small worktable on the far end.

The laptop sits squarely in the middle with the lid closed.

"Would you like a drink, Abigail?" Dallas asks.

"Yes, please, vodka with spritzer water and a wedge of lemon."

Dallas goes over to the bar.

"Do you go by Abigail or Abby?" he asks, cutting the lemon.

"Abigail," I say.

I practiced the name earlier in the car so that when I said it out loud it would come off as natural as my own name.

"What should I call you?"

"Dallas for now," he says. "Mr. Stone later."

I turn around to let him see my eyes light up.

My mouth forms a little smile.

The thing is that it's not all an act. I'm strangely attracted to him.

Well, maybe there's nothing strange about it.

He oozes sex and he knows it. There's an arrogance to him in the way he is already undressing me with his eyes.

My tongue touches the roof of my mouth when I have a dirty thought. He looks like a good lay. What if I were to fuck him first?

61

WHEN THERE'S AN INTERRUPTION...

DALLAS GIVES me the drink and I take a sip. It's slow and deliberate. I lick my lips and enjoy him watching me do it.

I know that I should be scared, but I'm not.

I'm here to do a job, but would it be so terrible if I had a little fun along the way? I don't owe Nicholas a thing. We have a professional relationship and I want to have sex with him as well but he's playing games with me. And two can play this game.

Another part of me is angry with Nicholas.

I'm pissed off that he was so unreasonable as to forbid me to go back to Boston and help my brother.

Who the hell does he think he is?

What gives him the right?

I look Dallas up and down. Maybe fucking him is the

best thing for me. I haven't been with a man for a while now, all of the way that is, and this guy may be just what I need.

The fact that it will also go a long way to piss off Nicholas would just be the icing on the cake.

I take another sip and take a step toward Dallas.

The glass makes a loud clinking sound when it touches the marble table.

I'm so close to him, I smell his minty fresh breath.

I appreciate the preparation.

"What would you like to do with me?" I ask slowly.

His eyes are blue, the color of the ocean, with flecks of green.

"Something bad," he says after a moment.

Reaching over, I run my fingers up his neck and along his jawline.

He takes a step forward and kisses me on the mouth.

His lips are demanding. They part mine and immediately make their way inside.

His hands pull on the belt of my trench coat. Then he pulls away from me.

"You want to see?" I ask, raising one eyebrow.

He nods with a wide smile.

I grab it by the lapels and toss it off me.

I stand before him exposed.

Naked but not naked at the same time.

His eyes slowly leave mine and travel down my elongated neck, down toward my chest.

They pause as he looks at my nude breasts before looking further down.

I suck in my stomach a bit and stand up as straight as possible. This should be Nicholas' eyes on my body, but Dallas's will do for tonight.

My pulse speeds up as I anticipate all the bad things he will do to me while I imagine that he is Nicholas.

He's about to say something but I beat him to it.

I spread my legs in a wider stance, for him to take a better look at the apex of my thighs.

Then when I think he has had enough I turn around and fold my body in half.

Keeping my arms straight, I place my hands on my knees and extend my butt outward and into the air. I feel his eyes on my body and a warmness starts to radiate from my core.

He takes a step toward me and runs his fingers up my thighs.

My legs open wider for him, aching to be touched, but

instead of pulling them inside of me, he wraps them around the cheeks of my ass and goes up the sides toward my breasts.

I stand up straight.

Cupping both of them at the same time, he presses his body to mine with the bulge of his pants directly on my coccyx.

It's thick and wide and it feels like it's made of wood.

Grinding my butt against it, my thoughts return to Nicholas.

If only he were to see us now.

If only he were to be forced to watch, unable to stop a thing.

My imagination is so vivid, I can almost taste his jealousy.

A knock on the door forces him to pull away. I wipe the sweat off my palms on my thighs.

Maybe it's just room service.

Maybe it's nothing to worry about.

From where I'm standing, I have a clear view of the door.

It's a beautiful woman.

"Oh, hey! I didn't realize that they were going to send

both of us," I say, taking two large leapfrog jumps toward them.

"Um...I thought..." the woman starts to say.

I interrupt her by reaching toward her and pulling her inside.

"The more the merrier, right?" I ask, raising one eyebrow and biting my lower lip. I drape myself over both Dallas and the woman.

The escort is a natural at playing characters so she quickly puts her bag on the counter and starts to undress.

But Dallas rubs the back of his neck, concerned.

"Looks like I have some catching up to do," she jokes, turning around for him to unclasp her bra.

Do it.

Do it. Do it, I say silently to myself.

He reaches for the straps instead and pushes them off her shoulders. By the time I see her nipples, Dallas's face relaxes and he starts to believe.

I let out a little sigh of relief.

That was close.

But now...I have another problem.

The escort has Pantene commercial hair with legs that

go on for miles. Her booty is as perky and perfect as her breasts.

Still, I have never even kissed a girl and my desire for Dallas has evaporated with the prospect of getting caught.

It's not that she isn't sexy. It's more like whatever trance I was just under has vanished and I know that the best thing to do is to get the job done and get the hell out of here.

Dallas gets down on his knees and puts her breasts in his mouth.

"C'mon, join us," he mumbles and waves me over.

I glance over at the table with the laptop.

My bag with the copy is all the way across the room. This is going to be quite a challenge.

Focus, I say to myself. You can do this. Just think.

It's not a problem unless there is a solution.

And there's a solution here.

"Let's move over to the bed," I suggest.

62

WHEN HE SURPRISES ME...

I walk over to the bedroom and stand with my legs and arms apart holding on to the two French doors. The sections of each door are made of glass but luckily, they are also covered in curtains for a semblance of privacy.

"You must be new," the escort says. "I don't think I've caught your name."

My heart drops. Dallas can't suspect that I'm not who I say I am.

"I'm not new," I say, taking my finger and running it down one of her breasts. When I reach her nipple, I give it a little pinch. "I just switched over from another outfit. I'm Abigail."

"It's a pleasure," she says, opening her mouth and grazing her tongue along the edge of her teeth. "I'm Rosemary."

"Okay, ladies, I'm ready," Dallas says, lying down spread eagle on his back.

"I don't think you are," Rosemary says, climbing onto the bed.

I wait a moment for them to lose themselves in each other's bodies.

"I'll be right there," I say. "My mouth is a desert."

That part is true.

I want to clear my throat, but I cover it with my hand instead to not mess with the mood.

I open the door and then quickly close it behind me, but not all of the way through so that the lock doesn't make a sound.

Once I'm outside, I don't waste any time.

I grab my bag, rush across the living room to the desk with his laptop and make the switch.

In the kitchen, I turn on the water in the sink to make it seem like I'm pouring myself a glass and then slip through the front door.

Holding the handle so that it doesn't make a sound as it closes behind me, I only let out a small sigh of relief once I get to the fire escape.

Running down the stairs, I put on my trench coat, only slowing down my gait when I reach the lobby.

"What are you doing here?" I ask when I run into him in the parking lot.

"Get in," Nicholas says from behind the wheel of his BMW.

"No, I drove your car here."

Without missing a step, I unlock my car and I get in.

My phone rings when I pull out of the hotel's parking lot and disappear down the winding highway along the coast.

"What the hell were you thinking?" He demands to know as soon as I answer.

"Thanks for sending in the other escort," I say sarcastically. "That made things a lot easier."

"You weren't supposed to go. The deal was off."

Anger starts to build up in the pit of my stomach.

"Who the hell do you think you are, talking to me like this?" I demand to know.

"I'm...I'm," he says, stumbling for the right word. "I'm your fucking boss."

"No, you're not. You're my partner."

"Oh, is that right?" he asks, his tone oozing in derision.

"Yes, that's right."

"The last time I checked, one partner usually doesn't

arrange everything and pay the other a salary. Only a boss does that."

I hang up the phone, hitting my palms on the steering wheel. As expected, he calls back.

I don't answer.

He keeps calling. I refuse to answer.

After three attempts, he gives up.

I drive in silence around a few bends. The GPS lady on my phone warns me that I have to turn in 0.2 of a mile. That's the exit onto his property, but that's the last place I want to go right now.

When she tells me to turn, I keep going. She tells me to do a U-turn so I turn her off completely. Not going anywhere in particular, I press down on the accelerator.

I don't see Nicholas behind me and it seems like he either turned onto the road toward his house or just fell behind. Either way, I wait for a phone call but it doesn't come.

I take a few more turns around the cliffs before pulling onto a turnout and parking the car. There's a narrow path leading down to the beach. I make my way down carefully since I'm no expert in walking in heels, even if they are wedges.

The beach is wild and deserted.

It looks like man hasn't touched it in centuries.

The sand is soft but covered in naturally occurring debris.

I find a spot away from the splinters and driftwood. I pull my knees up to my face and rest my chin on top. I listen to the swishing of the water as it comes and goes in a continuous rhythm and then take off my shoes, burying my toes in the sand.

"I'm sorry," Nicholas says, walking over to me.

His voice breaks my concentration but doesn't frighten me.

"What do you want?" I ask.

"I want to apologize."

"For what?" I ask. "I thought you were never wrong."

This seems to hurt him, but that's exactly how I mean it.

I do want to inflict pain. I'm angry at him for following me here.

I'm angry at him for ruining my surprise. I'm angry at him for lecturing me as if I am a kid who did something wrong.

I turn my face toward him. Shrugging my shoulders and lifting my chin, I wait for him to talk.

"I'm sorry for saying that I'm your boss."

I nod.

"But...

"But what?" I ask. "You realize, of course, that this 'but' negates your whole apology."

"Well, that's not what I mean to do."

"Well, that's what *you are* doing," I say. "You're justifying and that means you're not really apologizing."

Nicholas sits down next to me.

"Why did you go there?" he asks.

I bite my lower lip and stare into the distance.

"I knew I could do it and I did," I say, sitting up straight.

"You did?" he asks.

By the tone of his voice, I can tell that something is different. Slowly, I turn my head toward him. His eyes are lit up like it is Christmas morning.

"That doesn't change anything," I point out.

"No, that's where you are wrong," he corrects me. "It changes everything!"

63

WHEN WE TALK...

NICHOLAS and I sit on the sand for a bit staring at the waves crashing just below our feet. There are so many things I want to ask him.

There are so many questions that I need answered.

Just not at this very moment.

I bury my hands in the sand. I bring my palms together and scoop up as much of it as I can.

"You calling that escort to go to his room didn't help much," I finally say. Nicholas' mouth drops open.

"What happened?" he whispers.

I prop up my head with my hand and rest it on my knee.

"It kinda killed the mood," I joke.

He furrows his brows, looking perplexed.

"Dallas isn't a bad looking guy," I explain.

My lips form into a little smile that I can't force off my face.

"What are you talking about?" Nicholas asks.

I don't respond. He turns his body toward mine, grabbing me by my shoulders.

"Don't tell me you were thinking of...what exactly? Actually, going through with *it*?"

I shrug, reveling in his jealousy. "I was expecting some troll but he and I had real heat. Besides, I haven't had sex, proper sex, in a long time."

"You wanted to *fuck* him?" Nicholas asks.

"Yeah, maybe." I smile.

"Don't you know who he is?" he says, shaking his head.

"No, I don't. That's the problem. You didn't tell me anything about him."

"That's because I wanted to protect you. I called this whole operation off."

I shake my head and turn away from him.

He forcibly turns my face toward him.

"What happened?" he asks.

The fire in his eyes is still there but it no longer feels like just jealousy. It's something more than that.

I go over the broad strokes.

"You're lucky that you slipped out of there when you did," Nicholas says.

This irritates me.

"I don't need you to tell me that. I'm not an idiot."

"I wasn't implying that you were."

Shaking my head, my eyes follow the seagull that wanders around the edge of the water looking for a snack.

When he puts his hand on my arm, I brush it away.

"I didn't want you to go because I was worried that something might go wrong and then..." Nicholas' voice trails off. "I didn't want anything to happen to you."

"What do you care?" I ask. "I'm just your employee."

"Why are you making this so hard?"

"Because you make me angry," I say. "You put me into an impossible position. You refused to let me go back home and be there for my brother."

"That wasn't fair," he says.

"You can say that again."

I don't know if he really doesn't understand or if he is just trying to be difficult, but the emotional rollercoaster that I have just experienced is all because of that choice.

"It wasn't really a choice. It was an unfair thing to ask me to do," I continue. "You know that. I don't have any other family but Owen. My mother is an asshole. She doesn't care about me or anyone else but her. She won't be there for him, and even if she were, what would she say? He's all I have."

"I'm sorry," Nicholas says quietly.

"When you suddenly and arbitrarily, mind you, decided that suddenly I wasn't experienced enough to do this job, I had to prove you wrong. I'm sorry I snuck out and stole your car but I did what I needed to do. I don't have a fucking job anymore and you are going to pay me my first paycheck if it's the last thing you do."

The words fly out of my mouth without much editing for content, meaning, or impact. It's almost as if they have a mind of their own.

"I was never *not* going to pay you," he says.

I let out a mocking chuckle.

Nicholas scooches over to me. Our arms touch. He turns his body to face mine. Placing his finger under my chin he turns my face toward his.

"There is still a lot you don't know about me," he says.

I meet his eyes and don't look away.

"But I always pay my debts."

"Okay," I say.

"Also..." He leans over and kisses me.

My mouth opens up to welcome him inside before my mind can stop it. He buries his hands in my hair. Shivers run down my body each time he tugs.

His lips are soft and powerful, devouring mine. Our tongues touch and intertwine. His hands make their way down my neck and to my back. They look for a way to my flesh, but I'm sitting on the bottom of my coat.

His hands find the belt and unwrap it moving quickly. When he pushes the sides of my coat off my shoulders and away from my body, he realizes that underneath I am dressed in that lingerie that he had showed me on the hanger.

His mouth waters and he licks his lips.

He positions himself right in front of me, and I spread my legs slowly for him.

My nipples get hard from the way he looks at them and the wind feels nice against the crease in between my thighs.

I'm completely exposed, surrounded by only the strings of the crotchless bikini, and now also somewhat covered in sand.

"Oh, wow," Nicholas whispers, taking off his own shirt. I run my fingers down his hard body, pausing briefly over each washboard ab.

Nicholas leans over and picks up my leg.

"Lie down," he says. "I want you to enjoy this."

I do as he says and close my eyes.

His lips make their way from my toes up to my knees. Then up around the outside of my thighs before dipping down on the inside.

My body throbs for his. I arch my back and open my legs even wider.

Touch me. Touch me down there. You know where, I say silently.

But he doesn't. Instead, he does the same thing up my other leg. When he reaches the inside of my thighs, his kisses get more frantically. My body burns for him even more. He reaches up, taking one of my breasts into his hand.

The other remains down below.

"I want you," I say. "Now."

He leans over me. His substantial package presses against my pelvic bone. I wrap my legs around him.

"Are you taking birth control?" he asks.

I was, but I've given it up. They always made me feel kind of off and bloated and I haven't been having sex with anyone to make them worthwhile.

"No," I say.

"I don't have any condoms," he says.

He tries to kiss me again, but I stop him.

"I can't have sex without protection," I say.

That's a rule I haven't broken since I became old enough to have sex.

I'm terrified of getting pregnant by accident or possibly getting some sort of disease. No matter how aroused I have felt in the moment, I have never broken this rule.

When, or rather, if I ever get pregnant it will be because I want a child. There are enough unwanted children in this world and I know that I couldn't handle a baby that I didn't really want to have.

"I don't want to have sex without using anything either," Nicholas says, lying down next to me.

I turn on my side, laying one leg over the other and propping my head up with my hand. He mirrors my position. Scooping up a handful of sand, he slowly releases it onto my thighs.

Some of it blows away in the breeze, but most of the grains land and either go down the front or the back of my body.

I reach over and touch his penis. It's big and as hard as a rock. I unbuckle his shorts and he slides them off him.

I look at the large vein that runs the whole way down it

and the way it moves every time I give it a little squeeze.

I wait for him to push me to do it anyway, even without protection, but he surprises me. He doesn't press.

Instead, he continues to play with my body, covering it in sand.

Laying me down on my back, he makes little mounds of sand on my stomach and in between my breasts.

The sexier he makes me feel, the harder I squeeze his penis. After a while, we both start to moan.

"I want to watch you pleasure yourself," he says.

His words send a shock of electricity through my body.

My legs open as if on their own. I touch my breasts and then quickly make my way toward the center of my body.

The sand feels rough, but I manage to flick off most of the grains as my fingers find their way inside. The pleasure forces my butt off the ground.

When my eyes drift over, I see that he's touching himself, too, watching me. His eyes are glued to my hands.

Watching him watching me pushes me over the edge. The warm sensation in the pit of my core spreads quickly throughout me. My hands move faster and faster and then a wave of exhilaration rushes over me.

When I turn my eyes to Nicholas, his hips move faster and faster until he comes as well.

Afterward, we walk into the water, hand in hand and completely nude. The water isn't very warm, but my well-heated body welcomes the refreshment. Nicholas takes me into his arms and kisses me again.

Then he leans over and whispers, "This doesn't mean that you can go to Boston by yourself though."

64

WHEN HE SPEAKS...

THE ROOM SMELLS like bleach and sharpened pencils. It reminds me of my sixth grade classroom, minus the wall decorations.

There are large plastic tables set up against the windows on the far end where the panel of judges sit. The parole board consists of four men and three women, all over the age of forty-five.

I don't know what requirements you have to possess to get yourself this position but none of them really look like they could relate to the kind of upbringing that Owen and I had.

The only advice that Owen gave me when I was trying to figure out what to say was to speak from your heart. Not exactly useful.

Owen sits at a table directly in front of me with his attorney. This isn't the same guy who represented him all of those years ago. After losing the case, that lawyer stopped returning his calls.

This one is a woman, who looks like she's barely out of high school. She has a meek voice and she's dressed in an outfit that's way too big for her small frame.

The parole panel speak among themselves in hushed tones. The way they shuffle papers back and forth makes me wonder if this is the first time that they are reviewing his case.

The guards brought Owen in twenty minutes ago and no one has spoken yet. Unlike the inmates on television, he is dressed in his usual garb; hunter green pants and a matching button-down shirt with a white t-shirt underneath.

He has short light brown hair, cut short, as if he's in the armed forces. Before prison, he had always worn it long, and the first time I saw him with his new haircut I worried that he had been forced to join some Aryan Nation gang.

When I asked about it, he denied it. It's hard to know if the person on the other side of the plexiglass is ever telling the truth, so I would scan his body for tattoos hoping to find out the truth. No swastikas or other hate symbols appeared so I decided to take his words at face value.

Under the harsh fluorescent lights, everyone's skin is

sallow and pale, including Owen's. But otherwise, he looks healthy. Well-rested even.

He gives me a big, white, toothy smile as soon as he sees my face. I know that no matter how long he spends in here, no matter how old we get, that smile will always remain the same. It will always belong to the happy go lucky little kid who never used to have a worry in the world.

Owen was convicted of armed robbery. He didn't stick up the liquor store but he was in the car waiting for his friends who did. This whole time he's maintained that he had no idea that they were going to do that.

They had all been drinking. After running out of alcohol, they drove down to the Five and Dime. It was after two a.m. and the cashier was busy watching television.

He didn't speak much English so his friends thought it would be funny to just take some stuff. They lined their pockets with chips and soda and anything else they could find.

They were laughing and joking around too loudly and the guy at the counter noticed that they were trying to sneak out. He pulled out a baseball bat and started yelling at them in Korean. Two of them dropped everything they had, but one of them pulled out a gun from his back pocket.

The video they showed in court didn't have sound, but

it did capture the fear in the guy's face. Being a convenience store clerk on the graveyard shift is one of the most dangerous jobs in the world. Suddenly, the gun went off. The bullet missed the target and lodged itself in the wall behind the cashier.

After gathering the stuff they'd dropped onto the floor, they ran out and told Owen to drive. He didn't even know there had been the robbery. Of course, that's not the way the prosecutor had put it. To him, they had planned this whole thing out. They went in there to steal five packets of chips and four bottles of soda. And they were all in on the shooting. The jury gave them all the same sentence. If the cashier had been killed, Owen would have probably received life in prison.

After shuffling the documents in front of them from one person to another and familiarizing themselves with my brother's case, they give him the floor. One of them asks him to go over what happened that night.

I don't see why this is necessary, but Owen isn't fazed. He starts at around seven o'clock and the drinking.

"And why did you decide to stay behind in the car?" the oldest parole board member asks.

Because it was freezing and he didn't want to leave the warm car or turn the engine off. That was what Owen always did whenever we went anywhere together. He hated running errands and would always prefer to stay inside the vehicle even if the shopping trip would take an hour.

"I had a hunch as to what might happen," Owen says.

My eyes open wide. What?

"Can you please elaborate?"

"It was late and we were all joking around and had been drinking quite a lot. No one mentioned doing it directly but I had my suspicions," he says.

"And you didn't want to stop them?"

"I wasn't sure. Those guys say a lot of things."

His attorney nudges him. She whispers something into his ear and he starts to elaborate. He tells them that they have never done anything like this but they were talking about it for a bit back at the house.

This answer isn't satisfactory. One of the members flips through his file and then asks, "Why did you say during the trial that you wanted to sit in the car because it was cold out?"

65

WHEN I SPEAK...

BECAUSE THAT'S the *fucking* truth!

I want to yell out and have to bite down on my tongue to stop myself. My hands start to tingle and I rub one with the other. My stomach feels heavy like I had just eaten a five-course meal even though I had nothing but a power bar this morning.

"My attorney told me to plead not guilty," Owen says and then stops himself. "No, I was pleading not guilty. And I lied."

"Do you often lie to get what you want, Mr. Kernes?" one of them asks. It takes actual effort to not run over there and smack that smug look off his face.

"No, I don't, but in that situation I did," Owen says, keeping his composure. "I was a kid. I was scared. I was facing a lot of time."

"It says here that the prosecutor did offer you a deal."

"It would've required me to testify against my friends and put them in jail for a very long time. I couldn't do that."

"What about now?"

"The trial is over. They are serving their time. This is a parole hearing and I want to be as honest as possible. I want to apologize to the Kim family for causing them all of this distress. I know that Mr. Kim must've suffered severe PTSD from going through what we put him through and I am very sorry for that. My apology doesn't come with any qualifications or explanations. I did a bad thing and that's what I have realized after all of this time in prison."

I put my hand over my racing heartbeat but it doesn't slow it down one bit.

Why is he saying all of these things? After all of this time, why is he lying like this?

Then I answer my own question.

Of course. How could I be so stupid?

He's telling them what they want to hear.

If he comes up there and makes excuses for what he did or minimizes his role in the robbery then they will think that he hasn't learned his lesson.

It's a chess game and he's finally playing to win.

I can still remember how much my tears burned while I begged him to testify for the prosecution.

They were offering one year in jail and three years probation. I pleaded for him to take their deal. They had everything on video and the law on their side. He had waited for them in the car while they committed the robbery. That meant that he was as guilty of whatever they did as they were.

But Owen refused. It wasn't that he didn't believe that he would be convicted. It was more that he couldn't turn on his friends. But now that everything is said and done, now that he's at his first parole board hearing, he can speak as freely as he wishes. Or rather, he can tell them whatever they want to hear.

After Owen finishes his statement with another impassioned plea, it's my turn. I came here thinking that I would stand behind his old story one hundred percent and plead for them to let him go because he wasn't really part of what transpired.

But now, as I walk up to the front, I have no idea what I'm going to say.

My hands shake along with the rest of my body. I am thankful for the blazer that I wore over my button-down shirt.

With every step I take, I can feel the wetness under my arms spreading.

I have always been terrified of public speaking. Whenever I would see a podium set up in the classroom, my body would shut down and I would often pretend that I had some sort of illness. If I knew a speech was coming up, I would skip that class or school altogether. But right now, I wish to God I had a podium to lean on.

I stop in the middle of two tables. Owen and his attorney sit to my left and the prosecutor to my right. There are chairs set up behind the prosecutor for the Kim family but they are all empty.

I clear my throat and take a deep breath.

"I'm Owen's younger sister. He asked me to be here as a character witness," I start. That's all that I can use from my previous speech.

Shit!

Okay, focus. Just speak from the heart. But don't say too much that's contradictory with what he has just said.

Shit! Shit!

"I came here with everything that I was going to say memorized, but now I just want to tell you about my brother. We did not have the best childhood. Our eldest brother died in a car crash sending our mother, who wasn't much of a mother, into a downward spiral. Then our father went out to the store for milk and never came back. This crushed her even more and she stopped getting out of bed. She never really had a job or did any of the cooking or the shopping or cleaning so it was just us doing everything. I am not telling you this as an excuse for what Owen did, but I just want you to know what kind of world we were living in at the time. When Owen got older, he started hanging out with the wrong kind of people. There aren't very many good types of people running around the streets of Boston late at night. He was young and didn't think that anything could happen. Well, it did. I am very sorry to Mr. Kim and the rest of the Kim family for what happened. I know that he has suffered from post-traumatic stress disorder and I can imagine how hard it must've been for him to return to his job. My only consolation is that he was not physically hurt."

66

WHEN WE LISTEN TO HIM...

WHEN I SPEAK TO THEM, I focus on their eyes so that they know that I am being genuine but I'm not really looking at them. More like through them.

It's a trick Nicholas told me about on the flight here. Looking into people's eyes while speaking terrifies me but avoiding eye contact will make me appear deceitful.

So, he told me to just look behind them. Through them and at some inanimate object right over their shoulder.

"As you can see, Owen is not here pleading his case," I continue. "He's not saying that he's not guilty. He's not trying to make you believe something that the jury didn't. He is telling you that he is guilty and that he is sorry for what happened. Very, very sorry. And that means that prison has taught him exactly what it was supposed to. It rehabilitated him."

My speech doesn't come to a close the way it goes in movies. It doesn't finish on an uplifting piece of music that tells the audience that the right side will prevail at the end. But I sit down with a quiet feeling of satisfaction nevertheless.

It's over. I have made my case.

I have pleaded for leniency and I did it off the cuff and from my heart.

The parole board continues to shuffle their papers and then it's the prosecutor's turn. Instead of focusing on who Owen is, his speech is more about the purpose of doing time.

"Prison has four purposes: retribution, incapacitation, deterrence, and rehabilitation," he says. "Owen Kernes sits before you, telling you everything that you want to hear. You don't want to hear excuses. You want him to give you a categorical apology. But the Kim family are not the only people who Mr. Kernes has hurt. He has committed a crime against society. He is a criminal, and depriving him of his freedom is the way to make him pay a debt to society for his crime."

What fucking crime? Sitting in the car while his idiot friend waves a gun around until it goes off? What exactly did he do that gives you permission to take his twenties away from him? And now you want even more?

"Incapacitation is the removal of criminals from society so that they can no longer harm innocent people. We did that with Owen, it is up to you to decide if we did it for long enough. Deterrence refers to preventing future crimes. Given Owen's upbringing and his past," the prosecutor says, "it is unclear whether prison will deter him to not commit crimes in the future. But if he remains incarcerated, you will be able to rest soundly at night."

I stare him down without trying to make it too obvious.

Who the hell does this guy think he is saying all of this shit? Making all of these assumptions. He doesn't know a thing about Owen, or our family, or what he will do a month from now, let alone a year from now.

I glance over at Owen whose expression remains calm and detached.

This isn't his first time in court and this isn't his first time being judged by complete strangers by a few sentences printed on pieces of paper.

After years of prison, he is used to it.

I, on the other hand, am not.

"Finally, we reach rehabilitation," the prosecutor says.

He doesn't need to state the definitions of any of these terms to either the parole board, the defense attorney, Owen, or anyone else in this room except maybe me.

But he does so for effect.

He uses these words to make a point and to prove it at the same time.

"The last but not least important purpose of our penal system is to rehabilitate criminals to make sure that they become law abiding citizens. As we all know, Owen has taken advantage of the opportunities that we offer. He learned to read and write and has gone far in his education. But as you take that into account, don't forget that with education comes knowledge. Knowledge as to how to manipulate the system and knowledge about what he should and shouldn't say to you to get what he wants."

So, in other words, there is no way to win.

If he hadn't learned to read, then you would be standing here saying that he hasn't taken advantage of any of the resources available to rehabilitate himself.

But now that he has, you are saying that he has done so only to advance his own agenda.

My blood feels like it's starting to boil.

My throat closes up.

I start to cough. The sound echoes around the large room, filling it with my contempt and disappointment.

Finally, his speech is over.

Every person on the parole board gives the prosecutor a little nod, a courtesy that neither Owen nor I got when we spoke.

By the time it's Owen's attorney's chance to speak, they are barely listening.

I can see their eyes glazing over and two of them check their phones. This is the most important moment in Owen's life and these people, who are supposed to make their decision about his freedom, can't wait to get out of here.

Once his attorney sits down, silence falls.

"Well, thank you all for coming. We will make our decision and notify you all accordingly."

"Wait, what?" I whisper under my breath. Owen glances back at me, shrugging his shoulders.

"They aren't going to decide now?" I ask his lawyer.

"No," she says. "They never do."

67

WHEN I TALK TO HIM...

OWEN DOESN'T SEEM AS SURPRISED by this as I am. I reach over to him to give him a hug, but a guard blocks me.

"I am sorry, there is no touching."

Owen shrugs his shoulders. He is used to this kind of treatment, but after all of these years somehow, I still am not.

Why can't we even hold hands? They are afraid that I will pass him something illegal, but I promise that I won't. That's not enough, of course.

The incarcerated are in there for many reasons, which all boil down to one; they are liars.

They will tell anyone anything they want to hear to get what they want. At least, that's what prosecutors, guards, judges, and the parole board think.

"How long will it take them?" I ask his lawyer whose name I already forgot.

"I have no idea," she says. "It depends. Sometimes, we hear by the end of the day, sometimes it takes a week."

I shake my head. It's almost as if this whole system is designed to make prisoners and their families feel completely out of control.

Perhaps, that's the point, huh?

But Owen isn't guilty.

Technically, he was in the car while the robbery took place. Still, there's the truth that exists on paper and then there's the real truth. I'm not saying he's completely innocent. He's just not guilty the way other people in there are.

Owen's hands are shackled in the front attached by a long chain to his feet. Dressed like this, he looks like a scary person to let back out into society.

If I were sitting on that parole board and this was the first time I saw him, I'd have a hard time saying that the world would be a safe place were he walking among us.

I watch the guard lead him away and listen to the loud clinking sound that the chain makes with each of his laborious steps.

I watch the parole board shuffle out the side entrance near the front, leaving all of the paperwork on the table in front of them.

I wonder whose case they will hear next.

"You know that he got a shitty deal," I say, turning to the prosecutor.

Up close, he doesn't look like he's even in his forties, but he already has a head full of gray hair. Hereditary or an occupational hazard?

He puts the papers in front of him into a briefcase without acknowledging me.

"You don't agree?" I ask.

"It's not up to me to say," he says, getting up.

"What do you mean?"

"Much of this case is out of my control. There are statutes that govern what sentencing he got. He refused to cooperate with the prosecutor's office, so our hands were tied."

His voice is robotic and detached. He wasn't the one who originally prosecuted the case and I wonder how much he knows about any of the details.

"Please, there must be something you can do," I plead, touching his arm.

He looks down at my hand on his suit jacket and then up at me. I pull away.

"It's not up to me," he says. "It's up to them. But for what it's worth, you made a really nice speech."

"You think it helped?" I ask.

"It didn't hurt," he says, walking past me. "Listen, I have another hearing in here in half an hour. I have to run to my car to get my sandwich."

I've always thought about lawyers living the high life.

Fancy apartments. Nice cars.

Definitely, not people who stuff their faces with smelly bologna sandwiches on their short breaks.

"Glamorous life of a district attorney," he says, reading my mind.

He takes a gulp from a can of soda that he also brought from home. "From what I read here, your brother should've turned state's evidence when they made him the offer. That was the only way he would've avoided such a harsh sentence."

"He didn't want to snitch on his friends," I say, using his words. "I tried to convince him but he wouldn't budge."

"Well, his friends aren't exactly the easiest people to testify against, but if he had then he wouldn't have spent so much time in prison."

I narrow my eyes.

"Wait, what do you mean?"

"They are pretty connected. Organized crime," he

explains. "Not exactly the type that's easy to testify against. Especially if you're from Charlestown."

This is news to me.

"Was my brother also involved?"

"Yes, of course. You didn't know?"

I shrug. "I knew that he hung around with some bad people but I didn't know that he did anything...illegal."

"He was a well-known dealer of meth and opioids," the prosecutor says. "Ran a small crew, with four guys under him. The ones he was with that night were also a bit higher up in the organization. They called each other managers. The ones who worked for them were entry level associates."

I shake my head.

"None of this is on record, of course," he continues. "But it was well known in the department. The cops never had enough to really put him away, so when he was arrested on this charge, they threw the book at him, so to speak."

It's hard to explain how it feels to find out that something is a lie after years of thinking it was the truth.

All I can say is that it tastes like bile.

I feel like Owen and I have gotten very close recently.

He wrote me every day telling me everything about his life. The thing that he neglected to share was his past.

"You didn't know?" the prosecutor asks.

68

WHEN WE WAIT...

I STARE AT THE PROSECUTOR, hoping that I don't look too bewildered. He asks me again if I knew any of what he had just told me about Owen. Do I look like I do? I want to ask him. Instead, I just shake my head no.

"Well, pretty much everyone in prison has a past. That doesn't change the fact that he might have been rehabilitated."

This piques my interest. "You think he should be released?" I ask.

"That's not what I said."

"That's what you argued."

"It's my job to argue for the state, whether or not I agree with their position."

I shake my head, unable to fathom what it would be

like to make arguments that I didn't believe in. I can hardly make arguments that I do believe in.

"What are you saying?" I ask.

"I'm saying that there are a lot of people who are serving time they probably shouldn't be. And there are a lot of people who are living the good life on the outside, who probably should be incarcerated for life. The system isn't perfect but it's all we have."

"Where does my brother fit in?" I ask.

"Somewhere in the gray area. He did something wrong. He got convicted. Should he be paying for that misdeed all of these years later?" He sighs deeply. "I'm not so sure."

I look down at my shoes not sure what else to talk to him about.

"Listen, I have to get back inside and review my notes. But it was nice talking to you, Olive, right?" He extends his hand and I realize that I don't know his name.

"Yes, Olive Kernes. And you are?" I ask.

"Bradley Bookout." He gives me a firm handshake. "It has been a pleasure."

Watching him walk back into the room, I wonder if the next argument he makes for the state he will actually believe in.

Or maybe, he has done this for so long, that he's past the point of caring.

Our legal system is based on the assumption that if both sides fight hard, then the truth will emerge.

How does that saying go about what happens when you assume? You make an *ass* out of *u* and *me*?

I texted Nicholas as soon as the hearing was over so that he could drive from the hotel. There was no point in him waiting for me in the parking lot because I had no idea when everything would come to an end.

"How long have you been waiting?" I ask, climbing into the rental car, a new model Range Rover.

"How did it go?" he asks.

He starts the engine but doesn't move the car from park. He turns his body toward mine and waits.

"It was in the administrative part of the building but I still had to go through all the checks like I was a visitor," I start. "Those can take an enormous amount of time, depending on how many guards are on duty and how many visitors show up. In the past, I had to wait in a lineup of cars at three a.m. just to get in at six. But today, because I had an appointment, they actually let me through."

This isn't really what he is eager to hear but I can't bring myself to tell him the rest. Not yet.

"Let's just get out of here," I say. "I'm starving."

We don't talk much on the way to the restaurant. I'm so famished I want to ask him to pull over at the nearest fast food place so I can order everything on the menu, but I keep my cool. It's the anxiety talking.

Besides, I've made a promise to myself to eat clean and healthy for thirty days. No processed food. No sugar. No bread.

I haven't eaten meat in years and, for this challenge, I quit dairy as well.

What's left? Greens like asparagus and celery and kale. Fish - salmon and tilapia are my favorites, and eggs.

I've been cooking with olive oil instead of butter for a while now and have taught myself to snack on sunflower seeds and walnuts in moderation.

This morning I broke the rules and had a power bar. But this evening, I'm going to stick to them.

I scan the menu and quickly order sautéed salmon with asparagus and green beans on the side. Technically, green beans are also not allowed, beans are a processed food, but the cheating here isn't out of control. It's when Nicholas suggests a dessert of chocolate cheesecake that my mouth really starts to water.

Chocolate has always been my downfall. A few years ago, I switched to very dark chocolate like eighty-five or ninety percent instead of milk because those bars have a lot less sugar in them. I developed my palate and now I can throw back one or two of them on a bad day, quite easily. I love the bitterness and the tartness as well as the complexity in the taste.

"You've been quiet all evening," Nicholas says, as I stare at his gigantic plate of pasta, yearning for just one bite.

"Just thinking about your food. It looks delicious."

"It is," he says, taking a bite. "You want some?"

"Yes, but no."

"It's okay if you have some."

No, it's not. I have made a commitment and this time I'm going to stick to it. I have started and stopped this thirty-day challenge about five times already, always giving up just a day into it. Beans and a power bar are not such bad cheats, but if I take even one bite of pasta, I know that I won't be able to stop.

"You look beautiful just the way you are," Nicholas says.

"Thank you, I appreciate it." I give him a nod.

I'm glad that he finds me attractive but it's not really him who I'm doing this for. I appreciate and love my body but at the same time I know I need a change.

I want to get out of this spiral where whenever

anything bad happens, I immediately turn to food to make it better.

Today is a hard day to say no, but if I can stay strong today then I can do it on all of those other days as well.

"So, are you ever going to tell me what happened?" Nicholas asks.

69

WHEN WE EAT...

BACK IN HAWAII, Nicholas didn't want to let me come back here. We had a fight about it. I did something that was probably stupid and too dangerous. The only reason I'm here at all is that he chartered a private plane and traveled with me.

I look into Nicholas' eyes. Under the candlelight, the flecks of green are almost gold. Owen's warnings echo in my head.

Can I really trust him? I don't know much about him.

But then again, I don't know much about Owen either.

"The prosecutor told me that he was a lot more involved in the gang than I knew," I finally say.

Owen's going to be my metaphor. I don't know what Nicholas is hiding from me but I want him to know that I don't appreciate it.

"I'm sorry about that," he says nonchalantly.

"He lied to me. All of these years. It doesn't feel good," I say.

"Well, maybe he had a good reason."

I clench my jaw. "Like what?"

"Isn't every conversation you had recorded? Don't they check all the mail and the emails?"

I nod.

"Well, there you go. He didn't want to implicate himself in anything by telling you the truth."

That is such a convenient explanation. It's almost too convenient.

I've played enough games for one day. I've heard enough untruths.

"You wouldn't lie to me, would you?" I ask.

"It depends," he says without missing a beat.

"On what?"

"On what it was about. You already know that you do not know much about my business."

"But I will in the future?" I insist.

"No, I can't say that you will. Some things you just can't know. It will be too dangerous."

I lean over the table. "You know, I'm a big girl. I'm

getting really sick of all of these men in my life trying to decide what I should and shouldn't know."

Nicholas sits back, completely unfazed.

"I'm sorry you feel that way but it's not going to change," he says. "There are certain parts about my life that you just cannot know about."

"Like what?" I challenge him. He narrows his eyes and gives me a wink.

"Like what's on that laptop you got for me," he says.

"That's the first and last job that I'm doing for you without knowing everything."

The smirk vanishes suddenly. Nicholas leans forward over his plate. "That's not up to you. You agreed to do as I say, whatever I need you to do. If you don't comply, if you demand answers that I can't provide out of fear for your safety, then I rescind my offer."

Each word of his statement lands like a punch. I didn't want to get into this now. My day has been too emotional as it is.

He sees the disappointment on my face. "I am sorry. I don't mean to be so harsh in my language, but I just want to be very clear about what is going to happen," Nicholas adds.

The only thing that I am clear about is that I am tired of all of the lies.

I have spent the day listening to Owen lie on the stand.

For years, I believed that he was wrongfully convicted, or at the very least, doing way too much time for the crime that he had committed.

But today, I found out that he was actually a criminal for a long time, one that eluded the police. That's probably why he refused to testify against his friends. Not out of some perverse sense of loyalty but rather out of obligation. Who knows what they had on him that they could use as retribution?

And now...sitting here across the table from Nicholas, the man who stirs the kind of emotions within me that I have never felt before, I am being forced to accept more lies from him.

Only this time, he is warning me about them.

He will hide things.

He will lie to me.

He will obfuscate the truth.

I just have to accept it because that's part of our agreement.

Well, fuck that!

"No, absolutely not," I say.

Nicholas rubs one of his temples with his index finger. "What are you talking about?"

"That's not our agreement and if that's what you want to make it now, then I am not going along with it."

"You can't," he says.

"Yes, I can. I'm back home. Just get on your plane and get the hell out of here. I don't need you."

The waiter comes over to our table and we both sit up straight and force polite smiles. This a nice restaurant with a water view and no entrees under twenty bucks.

"Let's calm down," Nicholas says after the waiter leaves.

"I am calm." I look straight into his eyes without flinching one bit. "I am just done with listening to lies."

He takes a deep breath. He looks away first.

"I don't mean to lie to you. There is just certain information that I am not privy to discuss."

"What does that mean?"

HIs eyes widen as if he is surprised by my question. I tilt my head to one side and wait for him to explain. But he doesn't.

"What do you do for a living?" I ask. Again, he doesn't reply. "It's a simple question. Some people are lawyers. Doctors. Firemen."

"I am none of those things."

"So, what is it that *you* do?" I have no idea where all of

this pent up energy and anger is coming from but it's just rushing to the surface and out of my mouth.

"You know what I do, Olive," Nicholas says quietly.

I have some idea, of course. I know that he's a thief and a con man. What I don't know is who he works for and the extent of what it is that he does.

"I think you need some rest. Today was a very emotional day for you," he says, putting his hand on mine. I jerk it away.

"Don't tell me what I need," I say. "I know what I need. The truth."

Somewhere in the back of my mind I know that he is right. The reason I'm so emotional is because of everything that happened at Owen's hearing and the fact that I still don't know what the resolution was.

But I can't admit that to him. Not now.

My pride won't let me.

"You want to know something true?" he asks, cocking his head.

I nod.

"That woman who surprised you at Dallas's hotel room..." his voice trails off.

"What happened?" I ask.

"She's dead," Nicholas says.

70

WHEN I FIND OUT THE TRUTH...

His words reverberate in my head over and over again but I still don't understand. How could she be dead?

"Rosemary?" I ask.

"You know her name?" Nicholas hisses. "How do you know her name?"

I shrug. "She introduced herself when she came in."

"Okay, tell me everything that happened."

I run through the story that I told him earlier. Only this time, my mind doesn't immediately go to my lust for Dallas or the jealousy that I wanted Nicholas to feel. I keep my voice low and speak in metaphors because I don't want anyone around us to hear.

When the waiter comes back and asks us about dessert, I refuse to see the menu to not even give myself the chance to be tempted by something dark and delicious. Nicholas asks for the check and hands him his card without even looking at it. Neither of us says anything while we wait for it to come back for him to sign. Once he does, we promptly exit the restaurant.

In the privacy of his rental car, Nicholas wants me to go over everything that happened that night with Dallas yet again.

"Do not neglect to mention a single detail," he insists.

I take a deep breath and start at the beginning. Once I describe how I felt the first time I saw Dallas, Nicholas' face contorts for a moment and then relaxes. He clenches his jaw.

"You found him attractive?" he asks, stroking his Adam's apple. I nod.

"Why?"

"I don't know. He was hot. WE had this...chemistry."

He smooths down the cuffs of his shirt and then looks at me again.

"Why is this important?" I ask. "I mean, why do you even care? Tell me what happened to Rosemary."

"Rosemary's real name was Caitlyn Montgomery Sudik," he says without missing a beat. "She grew up in Florida and trained at the Bloom Academy."

Is that a school? I'm not sure why this is relevant. I give him a blank stare.

"The Bloom Academy is a secret and very elite private school that teaches men and women about the art of seduction," Nicholas explains. "She was recruited and taught well and has since traveled the world and made a lot of money for the organization."

"What organization?" I whisper.

He shakes his head. He is telling me a lot more than he did before so I don't push for now.

"So, what happened to her?" I ask.

"She never came back after meeting with Dallas. She texted her boyfriend that she was meeting up with a friend of hers but they never met and her friend didn't know a thing about this supposed meeting. Her body was found yesterday, deep in the rainforest by a couple of hikers. The police are clueless but my sources suspect that it's Dallas's doing."

I put my hand over my mouth.

If the police don't know who did it, what sources does Nicholas have that tell him that it was Dallas?

"You were the last person to see her alive," Nicholas says as if he can read my mind. "Well, not the last, but you were the one who left them in that room together. Alive and well."

"Are you saying that this is my fault?" I ask.

"No, not at all. It's mine."

"How is it your fault?"

"I should have never told you about that laptop or that job," he says. "I'm just glad that it wasn't you."

I hope that whatever was on that laptop was worth it, I want to say. But I immediately catch myself.

What could that laptop possibly contain that would be worth a human life? A young, healthy life of an innocent at that?

"Do you really think Dallas did it?" I whisper.

Nicholas gives me one conclusive nod.

I shake my head, no, no, no.

"What do you think happened?" I ask.

"He might have seen that the laptop was switched and thought that she was in on it. Or he might have found it suspicious that you just suddenly left and again took it out on her."

I look down and rub the outside of my knuckles on my left hand.

"I'm not saying this was your fault, not at all."

"You don't have to."

"But I am involved in some serious shit, Olive. With some serious people. And the less you know about it the better."

My stomach begins to roil.

Doesn't he realize that this whole thing happened because I didn't know *enough*?

He should've told me that I was going there.

He should've trusted me enough to let me handle it.

If we had followed his original plan, Rosemary would still be alive.

"Dallas Stone is a savage. He has killed many people. I only know of a few, but that's enough. That's why I didn't want you doing that. Not for me. Not for any offer."

Owen thinks you killed a few people as well, and yet here we are, I want to say. But I bite my tongue.

Growing weary of second-guessing and going over every regret from that night, I pivot our conversation.

"How long have you been tracking him?" I ask.

"For about a year. That's why I set up my headquarters in Maui. I knew that he was going to be there to go to one of those parties, just not when."

"I'm so sorry," I say.

"For what?" he says. "That your friend and my friend are frisky and decided to go to a sex club together? You didn't know what they did together. And neither did I."

I nod. We sit in silence for a while staring into the distance.

My thoughts return to Rosemary.

She was so beautiful and perfect and now she's dead.

It's all because of me.

Dallas might have done it but were it not for me, she would still be drawing breath.

I glance over at Nicholas. His mind is likewise occupied.

Rain starts to fall and we both watch the droplets smash into the windshield.

How did everything get so complicated? I wonder.

71

WHEN WE KISS...

NICHOLAS BOOKED a few nights at the Ritz, but I don't feel like staying at a five-star hotel. Instead, I invite him over to my place.

We have the lease for six more months and I have no idea if we should give it up. Frankly, the world has been spinning so fast recently that it's hard to find solid footing.

After giving Nicholas a brief tour around the living room, the kitchen, and my bedroom, I glance down at my phone and realize that I hadn't texted Sydney back since this morning. She even left me a few voice mail messages, and she never leaves voice mails.

Scanning the transcriptions instead of listening to her frantic voice, I know that I can't *not* write her back. I need to put her mind at ease even though all I want to do is to curl up in my sheets and not come out of bed for days.

"Make yourself at home," I say, standing in the middle of the kitchen.

I quickly type up a long paragraph summarizing everything that happened and press send. I add another text for good measure: *can't text anymore tonight. Will message you tomorrow for sure.*

Instead of long paragraphs, Sydney has always been a rapid fire type of replier. Every thought gets its individual line.

OMG, seriously?

I was thinking about you all day.

Btw, James is amazing!!!

Okay, let's talk tomorrow.

How's our apt?

I READ them quickly but want to not write back but I can't stop myself.

Everything's great here. Still have to figure out what to do about the lease. R u moving to HI?

MAYBE?? Yes! No! I don't know.

Shrug emoji.

. . .

NICHOLAS PARKS himself on the couch and buries his head in his phone. After I put mine down, I see him swiping through emails and checking different apps for who knows what.

"So, what now?" I ask.

He mumbles something without looking up.

"What's going to happen now?" I ask again.

He finishes typing something and looks up. "What are you referring to?"

"I mean, we came here for the hearing. I really appreciate you letting me do that."

I cringe at my use of the word *let*. He didn't let me. I don't need his permission.

Yet, I still want to thank him for what he did: bringing me here on his private plane in all of the comforts that kind of lifestyle affords.

"Thank you for not rescinding the offer," I say. "I still want to do it."

"One year with me? You sure you can handle that?" he jokes.

"It's you that you should worry about." I smile. His hand grazes his temple just as he drops his chin.

"Yeah, I'm getting that sense."

Our eyes lock on each other's and we share a moment.

Suddenly, nothing else exists except the two of us. I don't know much about him and he doesn't know much about me but that's part of the attraction. It's the mystery that gives me all of the feels.

I take a step toward him, he takes two closer to me.

He brings his hands to my face. They smell like lemon.

He squeezed one into his drink over dinner.

The scent is intoxicating. I stand up on my tiptoes and press my lips to his.

I bury my fingers in his hair. It is so soft and luxurious I can lose myself in it.

He opens his mouth and our tongues intertwine. But only for a moment. Then he starts kissing my neck.

Warmth starts to radiate from somewhere in between my legs and course through the rest of my body.

My hands search for an entrance into his flesh. I peel off his jacket, dropping it to the floor.

His shirt is tucked in. Tightly. His mouth returns to mine as I tug on it trying to keep our lips together. I laugh. Then he laughs. He pulls the shirt up from the back and helps me unbutton the front.

I do one button for his two.

Once the shirt is shed, I take a second to admire the body underneath. I run my fingers down his washboard abs. Then I run them back up again. I kiss his nipples, one at a time.

He takes off my cardigan and kisses my arms, from the shoulders down to the crook of my elbows. Instead of letting him, I wrap my arms around his neck. He tries to unbutton my blouse, but I don't even let him untuck it. Instead, I just pull up my skirt over my butt and place his palms on my cheeks.

"Hmmm," he moans, squeezing them gently.

"In case there's any confusion," I say slowly. "This is me begging you to do it."

He pulls away from me. His eyes light up. Even twinkle. I roll mine.

"Oh, is that right?" He squeezes me tightly.

"Please, fuck me," I whisper into his ear.

"Yes, ma'am," he says, spinning me around.

There's a perfectly good bed right over there.

My roommate is six thousand miles away.

We have all night to enjoy ourselves and our bodies.

But I don't want any of that right now.

I have been teased enough by this man. I want him to take me from behind. I want him to fuck me. I want him to do it so hard that I see stars.

Nicholas' hands grasp onto my thighs and fold me over

the kitchen island. It's the perfect height for this exact activity.

I grab on tightly to the edge, bracing myself for impact. But then I remember that I'm still wearing underwear.

It's not really much, just a black thong that can easily be slid to the side.

Instead of doing that, he tugs at it slightly and watches it fall down to the floor. By the time, I step out of it and press his body to mine, I realize that it wasn't just my thong that he had removed. We are now flesh to flesh. I can feel his hard dick against me.

I spread my legs. I lean over. I wait.

"Get the fuck off her," a stranger's low deep voice says.

72

WHEN THERE IS AN INTERRUPTION...

For a second, I think that the voice might belong to Nicholas. But it's raspier, older than his. When I turn back, I see a man in all black. Black long sleeve shirt, black pants, black combat boots, black gloves, and a black ski mask.

He's pointing a gun with a long barrel right at Nicholas' head. My throat closes up. Nicholas takes a step away from me.

On instinct, I pull down my skirt but Nicholas doesn't make a move to get dressed. His pants are still at his ankles and he just stands there, motionless. His shoulders spread wide, his arms at his sides.

It takes significant effort to pull my eyes away from the weapon. But after a moment, I focus on him instead. The guy with his finger on the trigger.

Who are you? I wonder.

I can't make out a single distinguishing characteristic except for his height, which is way over six feet. I don't even know what race he is because the slits in the mask are too small to distinguish the skin color.

"What do you want?" Nicholas says.

"The girl is coming with me."

"No," Nicholas says, but then the perpetrator points the gun at him.

"I'm not here to kill anyone, but I'm ready to do it," he says. "Don't get in my way."

My head is spinning. He's here for me? Why? Who is he? What does he want with *me*?

"You mind if I pull up my pants?" Nicholas says.

His voice sounds strange. Casual somehow.

Sing- songy even.

The usual intensity is gone.

But why? Maybe to appear calmer or not so threatening. Though why would *he* seem threatening?

The guy shakes his head no.

"C'mon, man," Nicholas whines. He actually elongates the a in man so that it resembles a sound that a sheep would make.

The man grabs me by my arm and pulls me toward him.

I look back at Nicholas. My eyes open wide. His hands are strong and powerful and they pinch at my neck. I try to resist but he keeps waving his gun over my head.

The gun goes off piercing my ear drum.

When my head stops pounding long enough for me to open my eyes, I see the guy lying on his back with a little black dot in between his eyes.

"Are you okay?" Nicholas says, throwing his arms around me.

Tears stream down my face making it impossible for me to speak.

He holds me for a few minutes and lets me cry on his shoulder. I feel safe in his arms, even though I had just watched him execute a man in front of me.

"Should I call the police?" I ask, keeping my eyes closed. Nicholas pulls away abruptly.

"Absolutely not."

I reach out for him again, but he just walks away.

"Not now," he says curtly.

Nicholas picks up his phone. Okay, he wants to make the call to the cops. That makes sense.

I don't even know how to begin to explain what just happened.

"Yes, I'm calling for Katherine Hepburn. Urgency level 9," he says and hangs up.

Katherine Hepburn, the dead movie star? Is that someone's name? Why did he call her instead of the cops?

He walks over to the sink and opens the lower cupboard.

"Do you have any...?" he asks, turning around all of the bottles and searching through the mess of crap underneath there.

Before I can answer him, he pulls out a pair of Sydney's canary yellow cleaning gloves.

"Why do you need those?" I ask.

My blood runs cold. He needs them to hide evidence.

"But you did nothing wrong," I plead.

My voice gets really high and uneven, even cracking, as a result of my disappointment. "He burst in here and pointed his gun at us. He was going to kidnap me. I'm sure that the police will understand."

As I talk, Nicholas continues to work.

He pats down the body and checks his pockets.

What is he looking for?

"No identification," Nicholas says. "He's a professional."

"Professional what?" I gasp.

"Killer."

The word ping-pongs around my head like an echo.

Professional killer. What did a professional killer want with me? I don't know anything. I haven't done anything. Why would someone even bother to hire someone like this?

Nicholas grabs a bottle of bleach from under the sink and puts it on the counter. There isn't much blood.

Actually, there's hardly any at all. I should probably offer to help him clean up, but I can't make a single muscle in my body budge.

The buzzer goes off. I nearly jump up in place.

My heart starts to race.

I get drenched in sweat, and I start to shiver at the same time.

"Don't worry," Nicholas says. "It's Katherine Hepburn."

When he opens the door, a well put together woman in her fifties comes in. She has an expensive haircut and she smells of Chanel No. 5 perfume. Dressed like a lawyer on television, she carries a large leather purse on her shoulder. She doesn't look anything like the movie star, yet she somehow gives off a similar vibe.

Nicholas is about to close the door behind her, but then

two men appear. Outfitted in hoodies with the word, Daly Moving Company, and back support belts with suspenders on top, they are carrying flat boxes as well as large bags big enough to fit a huge living room rug. Or a body.

73

WHEN THEY TAKE CARE OF THE PROBLEM...

My breathing slows down along with my heartbeat. A little bit of fear dissipates with each exhalation.

Without saying a word, the movers just get to work. Katherine Hepburn gives them instructions and they do as they are told.

First, they unzip the rug bag and lay it flat on the floor. It's black canvas on the outside and plastic on the side. Very convenient in case there's bleeding. The bag looks expensive, exactly the type of bag that this type of woman would have.

They place the body inside the bag and zip it closed. I am surprised by how little blood there is on the floor.

The woman motions to Nicholas and he kneels down and soaks up the blood with the paper towels. Afterward, he pours bleach on the spot and rubs until all of the visible residue is gone.

Katherine Hepburn opens her bag without taking it off her shoulder and pulls out a small device. Someone kills the lights. She sprays something onto the floor. The device emits a cool blue light.

"Is it not out?" I ask him.

"The Luminol is reacting with the bleach right there," Nicholas says. "That's why it's all bright like that."

Katherine Hepburn takes slow careful steps away from where the body was lying.

"What is she doing?" I ask.

"Checking for hidden blood splatter," he explains.

Nicholas, the movers, and I wait while she carefully makes her way around the perimeter, spraying and illuminating as she sees fit.

Once she is satisfied that there are no particles of blood anywhere else in the apartment, she turns on her heels and tells the movers to get started.

Her voice is low, quiet, and authoritative.

The movers take the boxes that they brought with them and fold them up. They tape the bottom and the top but don't put anything inside.

They make a total of four of them. Even though the boxes are empty, there is visible strain on their faces once they lift them. Katherine Hepburn opens the door for them and they disappear down the hallway.

"What are they doing?" I ask.

"You are moving some of your stuff to storage," Nicholas says. "You hired the Daly company to help you. You are also selling this rug here to a buyer from a rug clearinghouse in New York. You don't know her name but you found her through her advertisement in the Boston Magazine."

I nod. The story comes out of his mouth so naturally I almost believe it even though I know the truth.

Katherine Hepburn pulls out a copy of the magazine and places it on my coffee table.

"Is your ad really in there?" I ask.

"Of course," she says.

Taking out a large plastic Ziplock bag from her purse, she opens it for Nicholas who places all of the blood-soaked paper towels into it.

He sprays some bleach on the spot where they were laying, wipes it with another sheet, and places that into her bag as well.

Everything about this operation is so professional and efficient that it makes my head spin. I pick up the magazine and go to the back where most of the ads are.

"Page one thirty-five," Katherine Hepburn says.

The movers come back.

Arguing about the Patriots, they leave the front door wide open and grab the black bag, one on each side.

"Shit, this rug is no joke," one of them says.

They let the door slam behind them.

I flip to the page that she told me and there at the bottom I see that someone had circled Prestige Rug Company's advertisement in thin blue ink.

"Thank you very much, ma'am," Katherine Hepburn says, handing me a check for $700 made out in my name. Prestige Rug Company's name and address are prominently displayed at the top. It's signed by K. C. Prestige. "It was a pleasure doing business with you."

"Thank you," I mumble. "You, too."

She walks out of the door, just at the movers come back for their last load.

"We'll drive this right over to the storage unit," one of them says. "Thanks again."

They let the door slam again and then Nicholas and I are alone.

Their smiles and their acting are so convincing that I have to look around for a second and remind myself of what really happened.

Or maybe I shouldn't.

Maybe it's better to just pretend and improvise a different outcome just like they are.

"Well, that was...efficient," I say slowly, not entirely sure if that's the right word for it.

"I need a drink. You want one?" Nicholas asks.

"Oh, God, yes!"

Nicholas pours us both generous amounts of whiskey and we sit down on the couch.

The amber colored liquid ignites my taste buds with a pleasing combination of leather, cedar wood, and candied almonds.

It burns my throat as it slides down and leaves a bit of an orange pith aftertaste.

"Why didn't you want to call the police?" I ask even though I suspect that I already know the answer.

"Olive, I have to tell you something," Nicholas says.

74

WHEN I FIND OUT WHY...

I NOD. I don't need to brace myself for impact. I already know what he's about to say.

That guy, the professional killer, wasn't really after me. He may have wanted to kidnap me but this whole thing has to do with Nicholas and the kind of business that he's in.

"Someone is after you," he says. "I killed this one but they aren't going to stop."

I turn to face him. His words don't make any sense.

"What are you talking about?" I ask when he doesn't elaborate.

"I was foolish enough to think that I could protect you," he says without turning toward me.

"Remember when I told you that Ashley asked me to

watch out for you?" he asks. I nod. "There's a contract out on your head."

I sit back into the couch. I press the nails of my hand into the palms of my other until they leave creases.

"The reason why Owen got a parole hearing is that he provided testimony against someone over something that happened in prison. I don't know the details but that's why the district attorney arranged for his hearing."

"What does that mean?"

"It means that the people he testified against are out for blood. He doesn't have a wife or children, you are the closest living member of his family. He loves you and they want him to hurt."

"How do you know this?" I ask, shaking my head in disbelief.

"I'm a pretty well connected guy, Olive. I have feelers set up on the streets. They tell me what they hear."

"And what is that?"

"These guys want to make him pay."

No, something doesn't make sense. Owen loves me. He would never set me up like this. He's not our mother. He would never betray me.

"He doesn't know about this," Nicholas says. "If that's what you are thinking. He thinks that his life is in danger in prison but I doubt that he knows that they would go so low as to try to kidnap and kill his sister."

That makes me feel good but only momentarily.

"That's why I didn't want you to come back to Boston," Nicholas continues. "I know that you must've thought that I was some sort of possessive asshole, but I didn't want to tell you this and I didn't know how else to protect you."

My mind quickly reviews the highlights of everything that has happened ever since I met him.

"So, this whole time, this offer you made me...I thought you needed me to be your partner. I thought that's why you were paying me." My words rush out all at once, in fragments, barely making any sense.

"I couldn't very well kidnap you against your will," Nicholas says. "But I needed to protect you."

"For Ashley?" I ask.

"At first, but then...for me."

"For you?" I ask. I feel an invisible feather tickle the back of my throat and cough.

"Yeah, I kinda grew to like you," Nicholas says, giving me a little kick with his foot. The flecks of gold in his eyes light up.

"So, what now?" I ask.

"I don't know but we need to be very careful. These

men that he testified against have very powerful friends. That guy I killed, he is one of the best assassins out there. The only reason I got the upper hand was that he got distracted."

"What exactly happened?"

"It's always difficult when you have two people to keep the gun on, especially if you're not exactly willing to kill immediately," Nicholas explains. "He wanted to take you somewhere. Probably to his boss who would use you as leverage to get Owen to do something."

"To take back his confession?" I ask.

"Maybe." He shrugs. "Or something else entirely. I have no idea. The problem was that he didn't want to kill me. He didn't know I would be here and he definitely didn't know who I was. That's why I was acting so aloof."

I nod my head, processing everything that he's saying.

"When I saw him look at you, I grabbed his gun out of his hand and shot him."

"Just like that?" I ask.

"You wanted me to talk to him first?" He laughs.

I run my fingers around the rim of my empty glass. The whiskey makes me feel warm and cozy, slowing down my thoughts to something less than the speed of sound.

My phone rings. I look at the screen. It's a private

number. I'm tempted to make it go to voicemail, but at the very last moment I don't.

As soon as I hear the robotic voice on the other end and wait for it to make the connection, I know that it's Owen.

"Guess what?" he says. He is so excited he can barely contain himself. "They granted my parole."

I'm stunned. My tongue touches the roof of my mouth. He says my name over and over again before I can bring myself to respond.

"Are you okay?"

"I'm fine," I lie. "I'm just really happy for you."

Nicholas furrows his brow, confused. I hold out my palm to tell him to wait.

"Is this normal for them to grant parole so quickly?" I ask.

Nicholas nods, understanding immediately what I'm talking about.

"I don't know, but who cares, I got it!" Owen says. He takes a beat. "You don't seem very excited."

"No, no, it's not that," I say quickly. "I am very excited."

I shift my weight from one side to another and cross and uncross my arms. Nicholas puts his arms around me. Having his body so close to mine calms me down a bit.

"So, what happens now?" I raise my voice, forcing the excitement.

"They told me that they will be releasing me tomorrow. Actually tonight. They always do it in the middle of the night, starting the process around one a.m."

"Why is that?" I ask.

"There are a bunch of steps," Owen says. "They take me to a series of waiting rooms. There is a lot to process. The stuff that I collected in prison. Books, writings, things like that. And then they have to return the belongings that I brought here as well."

I nod along pretending that any of this makes sense.

"Okay, don't take this the wrong way," I say. "But isn't it a little bit suspicious that you're getting released so...soon?"

There's a long pause. "What exactly are you saying?"

I shake my head. "Did you....do something to make this happen?"

I know that this is the wrong thing to ask just as the words come out of my mouth.

"What the *fuck* are you saying, Olive?" Owen demands to know. The tone of his voice shifts from loving brother to convicted felon.

"Nothing. I'm not saying anything."

"What the *fuck* are you *implying* then?"

Owen's education has come a long way since he first went in. When he started doing time, he was an angry young man who couldn't formulate a coherent sentence about his feelings or anything that was happening to him.

But when he learned to read and write and then spent years educating himself in his cell and the prison library, he developed words for his thoughts and feelings.

He was no longer the irate toddler who knew what he wanted but couldn't quite express it.

"I am just surprised by how this whole thing has unfolded, that's all," I play dumb.

I want to ask him who he ratted on, but this isn't the right time or place. Everything we are saying is being recorded. He knows it as well as I do. Besides, as soon as he is out, he will have plenty of time to explain himself.

"You're not the only one," Owen says. "But it has happened to a few of my friends. There's a major overcrowding problem so they're letting out some non-violent, well-behaving inmates on parole earlier than they probably would have otherwise. The new governor has done a lot to make it happen."

"That's great," I say under my breath.

Oh, hmmm. Maybe this is it then. Nothing suspicious. Maybe the guy who broke into my apartment had *nothing* to do with Owen. I was so quick to judge him and to put the blame on him. Nicholas' explanation seemed so plausible, but what if I was wrong? What if that guy had something to do with Nicholas instead?

A robot voice comes on the line and tells us that we only have a minute left.

"Will you be here to pick me up?" Owen asks.

"When? Where?"

"At the front gate of the prison. Six a.m.," he says. "Be there at six but it may take longer. Sometimes there's a delay and it's out of my control."

"Yes, of course, I'll wait," I say. "After all of these years I'm pretty used to working around their schedule."

Owen sighs and then chokes up. When he gathers his composure, he says, "*We* won't have to work on anyone's schedule after tomorrow."

"No, we won't." I smile.

When I'm about to say goodbye, Owen interrupts me.

"You have no idea how much it means that you were there for me all of these years. I know that we were never very close as kids, but you taking the time to write me all the time and talk to me...it really made the time bearable. I love you, Olive."

"I love you, too," I say, tears welling up in my eyes.

I hang up the phone and stare at the blank screen, wiping a rogue tear from my eye.

"He's getting out," I say. "He's really getting out."

Nicholas doesn't reply. Standing up, he paces in front of me in a circular motion. His nostrils flare. His chest thrusts out with his elbows firmly planted away from his body.

"Are you...upset?" I ask.

He cracks his knuckles. Glaring at me, his eyes tighten and then turn to ice.

"You can't go there," he finally says. "You can't meet him when he gets out. Absolutely not."

***

Thank you for reading OBLIGATION!

I hope you enjoyed continuing Nicholas and Olive's story. Can't wait to find out what happens next?

One-click TELL ME TO STAY Now!

DECADENT and delicious 3rd book of the new and addictive Tell Me series by bestselling author Charlotte Byrd.

If you love brooding men, a thrilling romance filled with lust, turmoil, secrets, and explosive drama, you can't miss this ride.

Official blurb coming soon...

One-click TELL ME TO STAY Now!

SIGN UP for my **newsletter** to find out when I have new books!

You can also join my Facebook group, **Charlotte**

Byrd's Reader Club, for exclusive giveaways and sneak peaks of future books.

I appreciate you sharing my books and telling your friends about them. Reviews help readers find my books! Please leave a review on your favorite site.

CONNECT WITH CHARLOTTE BYRD

SIGN UP for my **newsletter** to find out when I have new books!

You can also join my Facebook group, **Charlotte Byrd's Reader Club**, for exclusive giveaways and sneak peaks of future books.

I appreciate you sharing my books and telling your friends about them. Reviews help readers find my books! Please leave a review on your favorite site.

Follow me on BookBub and Goodreads!

ALSO BY CHARLOTTE BYRD

**All books are available at ALL major
retailers! If you can't find it, please email
me at charlotte@charlotte-byrd.com**

Tell me Series
Tell Me to Stop
Tell Me to Go
Tell Me to Stay
Tell Me to Run
Tell Me to Fight
Tell Me to Lie

Tangled Series
Tangled up in Ice
Tangled up in Pain
Tangled up in Lace
Tangled up in Hate
Tangled up in Love

Black Series
Black Edge
Black Rules
Black Bounds
Black Contract
Black Limit

Lavish Trilogy
Lavish Lies
Lavish Betrayal
Lavish Obsession

Standalone Novels
Debt
Offer
Unknown
Dressing Mr. Dalton

ABOUT CHARLOTTE BYRD

Charlotte Byrd is the bestselling author of many contemporary romance novels. She lives in Southern California with her husband, son, and a crazy toy Australian Shepherd. She loves books, hot weather and crystal blue waters.

Write her here:

charlotte@charlotte-byrd.com

Check out her books here:

www.charlotte-byrd.com

Connect with her here:

www.facebook.com/charlottebyrdbooks

Instagram: @charlottebyrdbooks

Twitter: @ByrdAuthor

Facebook Group: Charlotte Byrd's Reader Club

Newsletter